C000150267

THE OF TAKING CHANCES

A Young Adult Contemporary Romance Anthology

FOREWORD BY
Cookie O'Gorman

EDITED BY
Kelsie Stelting

SHORT STORIES BY
Kelsie Stelting · Seven Steps · Kat Colmer
Michele Mathews · Yesenia Vargas
Kayla Tirrell · Melanie Hooyenga
Sally Henson · Deborah Balogun

FOREWORD

Cookie O'Gorman

Confession time: I've never written a foreword.

Just so you know, I can say that I've *read* (and enjoyed) several forewords. Each one is different, of course, but something they all have in common is that they give the reader a taste of what's to come. An introductory appetizer, if you will. A literary bloomin' onion before the main course.

When Kelsie approached me about writing the foreword for this young adult romance anthology, I was surprised and more-than-a-little flattered. This incredible lineup of ladies, writing a bunch of sweet, heartfelt YA romance stories? Oh yes please, sign me up! There was no way I could pass up the awesome opportunity. Plus, I love YA romance, talking about it, writing it, reading it. It's all good. Sounds like a perfect fit, right?

But the fear was there. The fear that suddenly appears whenever you decide to do something you've never done before, it was present and accounted for. In a rare show of bravery for my introverted/awkward/all-around-socially-inept self, I said "yes," took the plunge, and pressed send before I could talk myself out of it.

And that, my friends, is what this book is all about.

Taking chances, going for it, pulling on your big girl panties and doing the thing that frightens you most. That is something I truly admire about the YA genre and readership. Young adults are some of the bravest, most open-minded people around, and that is reflected in the characters in YA romance stories. I mean, where would we be if Eleanor never sat next to Park on the bus? And what if sweet Gilbert never told Anne how much he loved her—and accepted her even after he was rejected the first time? It's not that they're fearless. If you've read any YA, you know that a lot of the protagonists (girls and guys) are riddled with doubts and fears. They are vulnerable like everyone else. But what they do so well is something we adults often struggle with.

They overcome their fears.

Whether it's confessing to your secret crush or deciding to let go and trust a former enemy, whether it's falling in love for the first time, giving someone a second chance, or telling your best friend that you've loved him/her all along...YA shows us all how to be brave.

It also shows us how to love, how to laugh, and how to swoon along the way.

The stories in this anthology feature some fantastic YA romance tropes: enemies-to-lovers, second chance, secret admirer, best-friends-to-lovers, and many more. I must admit; that last one is my personal favorite, sigh. Who doesn't love seeing two best friends who've harbored feelings for each other finally get it together and find their happily-ever-after? I know I do.

And one of the best things about this anthology? You get to see romance from the perspective of each of these amazing YA romance authors. I won't lie. Growing up, I didn't read much. It took me forever to get into reading, and once I did, it took me even longer to find my favorite authors.

It's a risk, you see. Taking a chance on an author, reading a story from someone completely new to you, it's something I believe I can appreciate because I got a late start (the reading bug didn't really bite until I was out of high school). If I'd only read the awful required school reading, I'd never have gotten into YA romance and what a tragedy that would be!

I might've never found Rainbow Rowell, who is amazing

and wrote the most real and heartfelt YA romance I have ever read. I might've never read Meg Cabot, Katie McGarry, Abbi Glines, Kelly Oram, Jenny Han, Huntley Fitzpatrick, Kasie West. The list could go on and on. These are now some of my favorite authors, and I seem to add to this list every year! In fact, I go out of my way to add to it because I know there are incredible authors out there just waiting to be found.

In 2016, when I released my debut novel *Adorkable*, I knew one of the hardest parts was going to be finding readers. Were they even out there? Did anyone love sweet YA romance as much as I did? Would they even give my book a chance?

Luckily, they were out there, and they did give it a chance. I am thankful every day for every single reader, and I am so proud to be a part of the YA romance community! Young adult—and young adult romance in particular—has the power to lift people up. It can brighten your day, make you laugh out loud, allow you to experience first love again. Basically, it makes you feel all the feels. And it lets you know that it's okay to feel it all. This is why I think readers, young and not-so-young, relate to YA. It's all about feeling, and what bigger risk is there than putting your heart out there for all the world to see?

Like I said at the start, this is my first time writing a foreword. It was a completely new experience. Though I've written a few YA romance novels, it was a risk—and I'm so glad I took it. If you've stayed with me this long, I just want to say: Thank you so much, and I hope it wasn't too boring lol! If you skipped straight to the stories, I don't blame you one bit. The following pages are sure to be infinitely more entertaining, and if you're like me, you probably couldn't wait to dig into the awesome young adult romances that await you.

So without further ado, I hope you take a chance. Read the stories in this anthology and find a few new favorite authors while you're at it. Most of all, I hope this foreword and these stories remind you of all the reasons there are to love YA romance! There are so very many!

Happy reading,
Cookie O'Gorman

Table of Contents

FANGIRL

Deborah Balogun

CHAPTER ONE

HEATHER SIGHED. "I HATE SUMMER."

"No one can hate summer," I argued. "It's the best time of the year. You just hate working in the summer."

She tilted her head at me. "Yes Sadie, I hate working in the summer, and you wanna know why? Because I'd rather be someplace else, like I don't know, maybe, Ibiza, snapchatting with a very hot foreign guy!" Heather yelled out, all in one breath.

She ran off to the break room and shut the door behind her with a hard slam.

I jolted in my skin. Geez, someone was feeling the heat wave. I shook my head and sat down on the stool she'd gotten up from.

Although, I did understand her frustration. Well, sort of.

Even my wild imagination didn't travel as far as the Mediterranean coast, but I could picture myself on the beach right now. Outside the café window, the blue ocean waves beat at the shore. I couldn't wait to get off work so I could take a dip in the cool water.

Sweat dripped down both sides of my face, and I mopped my brow with the back of my hand, but I still felt icky as my clothes stuck to my skin.

I glanced up at the ancient air-conditioner at the corner of the ceiling. With all the loud buzzing it made, you'd think it was world-class, but it did absolutely nothing to cool down the café. If anything, it added to the exasperating heat by spreading all that hot air around.

Today had to be the hottest day of the summer. It already felt like a thousand degrees, and if the weather forecast was right, it was going to get hotter—something I couldn't even begin to comprehend.

Resignedly, I rested my chin against my hands and gazed out at the beachfront. My vantage point did nothing to conceal the great view and all the fun people were having. It was so unfair. Everyone out there was so jolly while I was here, baking like a Thanksgiving turkey.

What I'd give to run out to the beach right now.

I even had a bikini under my clothes––always prepared, like every L.A. girl should be.

Save for Heather and me, the café was deserted, and there was no way any customers would come by today. Who'd be crazy enough to get a coffee in this blistering heat?

The bell jingled above the front door, catching my attention. I frowned slightly at the guy walking in, but immediately straightened myself.

He went over to a table in the corner and sat down, and the only reasonable explanation I could think of was that he was either a lost tourist or just some dude looking for free Wi-Fi. If it was the latter, he'd be sorely disappointed.

Grabbing my notepad and pen, I went around the counter and made my way over to him.

"Good afternoon, welcome to Gray's Café," I said, putting on a half-hearted smile. "Would you like to order anything?"

He glanced down at the menu. "Yeah, um, I'll have the...full-cream macchiato," he finally said.

"Alrighty." I wrote down his order. "One

full-cream macchiato coming right up. Is there any-thing el--"

The remaining part of that sentence hung in the back of my throat as I looked up from my notepad and stared at the guy's face, really seeing him for the first time.

His forehead creased a little. "Are you okay?"

I blinked a few times. "I—I, um," was all I could manage.

"Do you want to say something?"

I nodded like an idiot, my mouth failing to pro-duce any logical words. But then, how could I when I was majorly freaking out inside?

By some miracle, I managed to pull myself to-gether for a whole five seconds, quickly blurting out, "Would you like anything else?"

He shook his head in response, and I ran like a bolt of lightning, only coming to a stop in the break room.

Oh my god! Oh my god! I can't believe I just saw him!

I literally had to pinch myself to believe it was all real. *He's actually here!*

I spotted Heather leaning against the wall across the room, eyes glued to her phone. I sped over to her, needing to share this news with someone or I would actually burst with excitement.

Unable to contain myself, I squealed, and she glanced up, eyeing me curiously.

"You'll never guess who I just saw!"

Heather looked less than interested. "Who?"

"Jesse Maldonado!" I said each word deliberately, and even as I did, I still couldn't believe it.

Her eyes went as wide as saucers. "No way!"

"Yes way!"

She frowned. "You mean *the* Jesse Maldonado, right?"

"Obviously!" I rolled my eyes at her. "Is there any other?"

We both screamed at the same time, bouncing up and down like the fangirls we were.

"Wait, but where did you see him?" Heather asked.

"That's the best part. He's here! In the café!"

Heather's eyes widened further—if that was even possible. "He's here?"

Before I could even blink, she rushed past me and out of the break room. I caught up with her, thankfully, and stopped her before she could go over to him.

"He can't know that anyone else knows he's here!"

"But I want to take a selfie with him," she whined.

"Are you insane?" I whispered loudly. "If you ask him for a selfie, he'll get uncomfortable, and if he gets uncomfortable, he'll leave, and if he leaves, he'll never come back. Is that what you want?" I asked in one exhaustive breath.

She eyed me like I was crazy, which was absolutely ridiculous. Heat-affected, sure. Crazy, no.

I looked over at Jesse Maldonado and let out a wistful sigh. Even with his back turned to us, I could tell his body was a work of art handcrafted by the gods.

Not only was he the most talented singer who ever walked the face of the earth, he was perfect in every other way. Great smooth, black hair, sea-green eyes that made you feel like you were staring right into an ocean, and his smile...oh my god, his smile was just... There was no word to describe the effect he had on lowly humans who had the rare privilege of gazing upon him in person.

I only started to notice that I was slowly melting in a puddle of my own drool when Heather distracted me with that loud tapping noise her fingers made whenever they hit her phone's screen.

Not that her obsession with posting about everything in sight was anything new, but the mischievous smile plastered on her face told me that once again she was up to no good.

"What are you doing?" I asked slowly, watching her reaction as her head remained buried in her phone.

"Tweeting."

"About?"

Heather looked up at me, her eyes becoming slits. "News flash: I can do whatever I want, Sadie. You're not the boss of me."

Technically, I was the boss of her since I was the weekend manager, but I doubted making her aware of that fact would help the situation.

I blew out a breath. "Heather, if you send out a tweet about Jesse being here, in less than five minutes the café will be flooded with people, not to mention the press would be all over this place."

"So? What's wrong with that?" Heather shrugged. "It'd be great for business."

My brow arched. "Since when do you care about what was 'great for business'? I thought you said you hated working here?"

"I'm allowed to change my mind."

"Oh, how fickle of you," I muttered, and she stuck her tongue out at me as she walked away.

"Excuse me?"

I gasped at the sound of Jesse Maldonado's

voice. With his head now turned in my direction, I straightened my stance and raced over to him, struggling to keep my composure.

"Yes?" My voice came out more high-pitched than I'd intended.

"When will my coffee be ready?"

Crap! I'd forgotten about his order!

"Uh...in just a few minutes."

I hurried to make the coffee, and once it was ready, I rushed back over and settled it right in front of him. "Sorry for the delay. Enjoy."

He offered me that heart-stopping smile of his. "Thanks."

I sighed longingly. I could have died happy right then.

Suddenly, Jesse gazed up at me with an expectant look on his face.

I smiled back at him and couldn't stop. My face had a habit of freezing when I was nervous. Like that wasn't weird enough, I started to fidget uncontrollably with the ends of my apron as the awkward staring contest continued, until I couldn't take it anymore and landed into the seat opposite him.

Releasing a long breath, I summoned up all the courage within me and looked Jesse Maldonado directly in his cute eyeballs.

"You're Jesse Maldonado!" I blurted out. "I-I can't believe you're here right now—and in front of me. I'm such a huge fan! I love all your songs, I know all the lyrics by heart. I'm just so excited to finally meet you!"

Man, it felt really good to let that all out!

He stared back at me blankly, and I realized I must have made him uncomfortable.

Great going, Sadie!

"I'm so sorry," I apologized, biting my bottom lip. "I really didn't want to bother you, but I just couldn't help it."

He opened his mouth.

"Please don't hate me," I added quickly.

"I'm not Jesse."

I frowned, majorly taken aback. "What do you mean? Of course you are."

He shook his head. "No, seriously, I'm not."

"I don't understand. You're Jesse Maldonado. I know you're him!"

He shook his head again before taking a sip of his coffee and setting it back down.

Totally confused at this point, I narrowed my eyes on him. Nope, he was Jesse all right. I would bet a million dollars--if I actually had a million dollars-- that he was Jesse Maldonado.

Why was he lying, though? Then it dawned on me.

"You don't have to worry about the press," I assured him, leaning in. "I didn't tell anyone you're here, and I don't plan to."

He stared at me squarely. "I'm not worried about the press, because I'm not Jesse Maldonado."

"Why do you keep saying that?" I was getting a tad frustrated now.

"'Cause it's the truth!" he insisted. "My name's Jason."

It was physically impossible. He had the same hair, same eyes and his smile was all Jesse Maldonado.

"You're not convinced, are you?"

"Nope."

I could sense a slight hesitation before he spoke again. "There is a reason why Jesse Maldonado and I look...a little alike."

I arched a brow. "A little? If I didn't know any better, I'd think you were––" I gasped. "Are you twins?" I saw the look on his face, confirming my guess. "Holy mother of macaroons, you are twins!"

Jason burst out laughing. "Did you just say 'holy mother of macaroons'?"

"How come he's never mentioned you though? From what I know, Jesse's an only child."

He hesitated again. "That's because he doesn't know about me."

"What?"

"It's a long story."

I gestured at the empty café. "Trust me, I've got a lot of time to spare."

Jason glanced down briefly and then up at me. "You're not going to let this go, are you?"

I shook my head unrelentingly.

"Fine, you win"—he glanced at my nametag and smiled—"Sadie."

Holding my breath, I waited eagerly for him to begin.

"Jesse and I didn't grow up together. We were separated at birth, and I was given up for adoption to amazing parents." He paused, looking out the window. "They died a couple of months ago in a car accident."

My lips parted. "I'm so sorry about that."

"Yeah." Jason gave me a tight smile, but insurmountable sadness dimmed his eyes. After a brief silence, he continued, "A few months before they died, my mom told me everything. She said she'd found my biological parents and that I had an identical twin."

He chuckled lightly. "I didn't even know he was a famous teen pop singer until I saw him on a billboard on my way from the airport. And I also didn't know that I'd be accosted by his fans." He playfully tilted his head at me.

I scoffed. "You make it sound like I mauled you to the ground! And you can't tell me I'm the only one who's mistaken you for him. You're literally identical!"

Jason laughed. "Yeah, I'm starting to think that's not a good thing."

I noticed something just then, and I couldn't believe I hadn't seen it earlier. "You know, now that I think about it, you do have a bit of an accent. One thing's for sure, you're not from around here, Jesse. I mean, Jason." I groaned. "I'm so confused!"

"You're right, I'm not. I'm from Canada."

Heather came over to us. I was honestly surprised she hadn't rushed over here sooner.

She stared at Jason for the longest time, glancing between her phone screen and him. Jason shot me a confused look, but I was just as oblivious as he was as to what could possibly be going on in that head of hers.

"Sadie, it's not him," Heather finally announced.

"I already know that."

She shrugged nonchalantly, and then pulled out a seat from another table, placed it next to mine, and sat down. Even as she did, she kept staring at Jason with curious eyes.

"You got everything but the hair," she said to

him. "It's way off. The real Jesse's at an album signing as we speak."

Jason frowned. "What's wrong with my hair?"

I rolled my eyes at Heather, and then turned to Jason. "Don't pay any attention to her. So, do your biological parents live here in L.A.?"

He nodded, leaning forward. "That's actually all I really know about them. I wasn't able to find out anything else."

"And Jesse?" I asked hopefully.

Jason shook his head. "I'm sure if I was able to contact him, though, he probably wouldn't believe me." He scoffed. "I doubt I'm the first person to claim to be his long-lost twin."

I had to agree with him there. Some people would say or do anything just to get close to a celebrity. I probably wouldn't have believed Jason's story if I hadn't actually mistaken him for Jesse Maldonado myself.

Heather jumped out of her seat. "Wait! You're Jesse Maldonado's twin?"

You're kinda late to the party, I wanted to say. How had she not figured that out by now?

"OMG!" she yelled, hurriedly tapping away at her phone again. "I so need to tweet about this!"

"No!" I grabbed her phone and held it out

of her reach. "My gosh, do you have to tweet about everything?"

She rolled her eyes. "Duh."

"Well, consider this the first time you don't," I said. "Look, no one else knows about this. Not even Jesse." I turned to Jason as the proverbial light bulb switched on atop of my head. "But tonight's going to change that."

Jason's brows furrowed. "What's happening tonight?"

My lips curved into a huge smile. "You, my new friend, are going to meet your brother for the first time. Face-to-face."

* * *

Brooke leaned back, observing her handiwork. Finally satisfied, she smiled. "All done!" she announced, placing the big fluffy brush on the dresser.

I gazed into the mirror, frowning when I barely recognized my reflection. My sister had gone way overboard with the makeup, as per usual, although to be fair, I hadn't done anything to stop her.

The minute I got home, Brooke had all but dragged me into our shared bedroom, insisting she do my makeup for the Jesse Maldonado concert tonight. Any other day, it would've been a total no-no, but today I didn't object.

In a way, I secretly hoped it would take away the twinge of guilt that had settled in my insides ever since I left the café. But now that I had to leave for the concert soon, I only felt worse because there really was no perfect way to break it to her.

She might have been eleven months older than me, but at times she acted like she was eleven years old, especially when things didn't go her way. Tonight would not be an exception.

Brooke looked at me then and smiled, probably at what she'd called the "work of art" on my face. Seemingly pleased, she skipped over to her bed and pulled out two tops among the pile of clothes strewn across it. "So, which one do you like better?"

The one on her right was neon pink, embellished with sequins. The other one, tie-dyed, had beautiful bold colors. Both were nice, but how could I tell Brooke she couldn't wear any of them to the concert? Well, at least this concert.

"Uh..."

"I'm really leaning towards this one though"—she raised the pink shirt a little higher—"'cause then I could put in neon highlights, and that would be so cool, right?"

I started to speak, but she continued, "On

second thought, this one would totally go with that lime-green purse—"

"You can't come with me to the concert," I rushed out in one breath, screwing my eyes shut.

There. I said it. I just had to rip the Band-Aid off.

It didn't make it hurt any less though.

Peeking through one eyelid, I saw her reaction, and just as I'd imagined, she was not taking this well.

She stood momentarily frozen, her mouth hanging to the floor. Her lower lip started to tremble, and she let out a loud groan.

"But why not?" she cried, throwing the clothes on the bed.

"I'm so sorry, Brooke. It's kinda complicated."

"Well, I suggest you *un*-complicate it!"

Okay, now she was angry.

I contemplated telling her the truth. I mean, Brooke would understand I needed the other ticket so Jason could finally meet Jesse. However, there was also a pretty good chance she wouldn't believe me when I told her Jesse Maldonado had an identical twin.

I stood up from the chair by the dresser and paced the room nervously. "Okay, so you're probably not going to believe me, but I met this guy--"

Brooke sprung over to me. "OMG! You have a boyfriend!"

"Huh?"

She pulled me into an unexpected hug, and I was left totally confused. When she released her hold of me, she said, "I thought this day would never come. No offense, but for a moment, I kinda thought you'd be alone forever."

I shot her a look, to which she smiled unapologetically and dragged me over to her bed. "I want to know all about him. Tell me everything. Don't leave anything out." She pointed warningly.

I really wasn't sure what to say to the expectant look on her face. But having her think I was going to the concert with my boyfriend didn't seem like a bad idea.

"Well, spill!"

"He's cute," I offered, unsure.

Brooke rolled her eyes. "Obviously. But I want to know more. Is he a surfer? Does he go to your school?" She then gasped dramatically, lowering her voice to a whisper, "Is he in college?"

"No, no, and I don't know," I said, answering her questions one after the other.

She made a dismissive sound. "Sounds boring."

"He isn't," I interjected quickly. "He's nice and

funny and so down to earth too. Oh, and his eyes are this beautiful aqua color like the ocean on a bright sunny day. His smile is just as amazing," I said, gazing at my open palms. "But aside from all that, he's really unlike anyone I've ever met before."

"Wow," Brooke said, "you must like him a lot."

I frowned. "Why do you say that?"

"Are you kidding? You were smiling the whole time you were talking about him. I would too, though. For some reason, he sounds a whole lot like Jesse Maldonado."

You have no idea.

"But you know, I'm just happy to see you happy," Brooke said, tucking a piece of curly brown hair behind her ear. "Ever since Mom left, I've never really seen you smile. It's good to see that again."

She placed her hand on top of mine and gave it a light squeeze, and I smiled at her.

"Just tell me if he ever hurts you, okay? I'll gladly break his face," she added the last part with a sardonic smile, which, coming from a certified black belt, was definitely something to worry about.

We laughed. She was a great older sis.

"So, what are you going to do all by yourself?" I asked, feeling guilty again.

"I don't know. There's a tub of ice cream in the

freezer with my name on it." She paused. "Seriously, I wrote my name on it. Don't touch it."

"But then you'll ruin your diet."

"Eh, I'll start again on the morrow," she said in a fake British accent and laughed. "Now go, or you'll be late."

"I feel bad," I admitted.

"Don't. I'll just binge on Netflix."

"I hear there's going to be a Channing Tatum marathon on TV."

Her eyes practically popped out of her head. "Holy guacamole!"

She rushed out of our room. If there was anything Brooke loved more than Jesse Maldonado's music, it was Channing Tatum movies.

Clasping my hands, I looked skyward and hoped that I'd gotten the times right, and there actually was going to be a Channing Tatum marathon on tonight.

***

When I got to the concert venue, Jason was already there. I saw him standing by a wall and waved at him to come over.

"Why didn't you get us a space in line?" I asked.

He looked unsure. "I wasn't really sure I could do that."

I frowned. "You've never been to a concert before?"

He shook his head.

"Well, it looks like we're going to be on this queue for a while. Just enough time to fill you on everything there is to know."

Jason gave me a lopsided smile, and my heart did a little flip flop. What was happening to me? Brooke words came to my mind, then but I shook it away just as quickly.

"No way!"

I spun at the sound of the voice. Two girls stepped in front of us, well, Jason to be specific. They were in identical Jesse Maldonado merch, from their hats down to their shoes!

"Has anyone told you, you look exactly like Jesse Maldonado?" The first girl said.

"Yeah, exactly like him," the second girl echoed.

I looked at Jason, and he had widened eyes that shouted "HELP!"

I laughed nervously. "Um, you see, he's uh—oh look, a flying duck!" I yelled, pointing toward the sky.

"Where?" they both asked at the same time.

With their attention diverted, I grabbed Jason's hand, and we skedaddled out of there until we were in line and out of sight.

Jason and I couldn't stop laughing at the looks on those girls' faces.

"That was close," Jason said.

I nodded. "Yeah. Then again, this is a Jesse concert. His fans are bound to recognize you." I pulled off my baseball cap and gave it to him. "Here, use this. It might not work, but it's worth a shot."

He winked at me. "Thanks."

I sighed. How was everything about him so cute?

By the time we got in, the arena was packed, and we had to hold hands to get through the huge crowd. As we shuffled down a row, the lights suddenly dimmed around us and the stage lit up. Stumbling through the dark, we managed to find our seats just in time.

As soon as Jesse came onstage, the whole crowd went into a frenzy, and I unabashedly chanted his name along with everyone else.

Jesse's vocals reverberated throughout the arena as he performed his opening song. Singing along, I danced to the music. I wanted to imprint this on my mind forever.

I was having such a great time that it wasn't until much later I noticed Jason standing practically motionless by my side. I stopped short, watching his gaze fixated on the stage.

There was something enthralling about the way

he observed his brother perform. He followed every move Jesse made as if he knew it before it happened. Seeing Jesse up there must have felt like he was seeing himself onstage too.

Loud screams emanated from everyone around me, pulling my attention away from Jason. The loud uproar continued as Jesse began singing his latest hit, "Cutie Pie." It was a personal favorite, he said, and I became immediately addicted as he sang.

At intervals, I glanced at Jason, wondering about the thoughts that could be whirling through his mind.

As if the night could get any better, as soon as the concert ended, we were being escorted backstage to meet Jesse Maldonado himself! I was still on a high after the mind-blowing concert.

"Did you hear Jesse's voice?" I gushed. "His music gives me life!"

"It was okay, I guess."

My head swiveled around at the monotone sound of Jason's voice. "'Okay'? Just *'okay'*?"

Jason shrugged. "I guess pop music isn't really my jam."

"So, what is your jam?"

"I don't know, really." He looked ahead thoughtfully. "I'm into a lot of folk and country music."

I never would have pictured him as a country music fan. It also kinda surprised me that although Jason and Jesse were identical twins they had different tastes.

I didn't have long to ponder on it, though, as we approached security.

They checked our passes, and I started getting really nervous.

I drew in a deep breath. *Keep it together, Sadie!*

Before walking through, I turned to Jason, and he looked worse than I did.

"Are you nervous?" I asked.

"No." The beads of perspiration on his forehead told me the opposite.

"It'll be fine. You can do this," I said, but it was more to myself than to him.

CHAPTER TWO

I REALLY WASN'T SURE WHAT TO EXPECT, BUT IT surprised me how chill everything was backstage. A few stagehands passed us by as they brought in equipment from the main stage. I took it all in, soaking in the atmosphere and all that it meant.

I couldn't believe I was breathing in the same air Jesse Maldonado had breathed! Through my peripheral, I spotted someone by the snack bar, and my heart lurched. Screaming internally, I ran over to him before I could stop myself.

"Hi, Jesse!"

He turned at the sound of my voice, and once he did, I almost fainted with sheer happiness.

"Hey." Jesse's lips lifted into a heart-stopping smile.

Seriously, my heart stopped!

I sighed wistfully. "Will you marry me?"

He laughed, and the sound was even better than all his songs combined.

"I can give you a hug," he offered.

The moment he wrapped his arms around me, I literally died. Oh. My. God. Jesse Maldonado was hugging me! How was this even real?

It felt like I was having an out-of-body experience—not that I'd ever had an out-of-body experience, but surely if I ever did, it would feel like this!

When he released his hold on me, I actually cried. If I wasn't worried that I'd smell like a hobo, I would never take a shower again. Ever. All I wanted was Jesse Maldonado's scent on me forever.

Somewhere through my daze, I remembered Jason and the reason why I came here.

Jesse's words cut through my thoughts. "Do you want me to sign something of yours or take a selfie?"

I shook my head, mostly to clear it. "Yes, but first, there's someone you have to meet."

I spotted Jason, surprised that he was standing

in a corner, his focus on the floor. I called out to get his attention and motioned for him to come over.

His hesitation showed in each step he took as he approached us. When he removed his hat, both brothers stood face-to-face for the very first time.

With bated breath, I watched their reactions as they stared at each other. Their stark resemblance was unbelievable. There was no doubt this moment was going to change their lives forever.

Jason spoke first. "Hi."

Jesse remained silent for the longest time, his expression unreadable. "Who the hell is this guy?" he turned to me, infuriated.

His words were far from what I expected. "He's your twin brother... Can't you see the resemblance?"

Jason moved forward. "I know this is a kind of a shock. It surprised me when I found out too. I grew up my whole life thinking I was an only child. I still haven't fully processed it."

Jesse stepped away from us, looking disgusted. "Is this some sort of a joke?"

Jason's brows creased. "No. Why would I joke about something like this?"

"I don't know, maybe to get money, fame. Isn't that what all you con artists are after?"

My jaw slackened at Jesse's insinuation. "He's telling you the truth."

He scoffed. "Oh yeah? What proof do you have?"

Jason shook his head. "I don't have any proof other than my word."

"And what good is that to me? Tell me." Jesse shrugged. "Any crazed fan could get a third-rate plastic surgeon to make him look exactly like me."

I couldn't believe Jesse Maldonado was being such a jerk! "You actually think he did this?"

"Wouldn't be the first time."

"I knew this was a bad idea," Jason muttered under his breath, a dejected look on his face. "Let's just go, Sadie."

"No. He has to know that you're telling the truth." I faced Jesse. "Jason came all the way from Canada to find you. Canada! Now, why would he go to all that trouble if he was making it all up?"

"You know who else is from Canada? *Big Tom*."

Before I even had time to ask who Big Tom was, Jesse hollered, and a super tall security guard stood next to us.

"Is there a problem, sir?"

"Yeah, actually there is." Jesse sent a cold stare at Jason and me. "Can you get these people out of here immediately?"

"What?" I gasped. "You're going to regret this."

He turned to the security guard. "You're my witness, Big Tom. That was a clear threat."

I rolled my eyes. "That wasn't a threat, Big Tom. I'm only telling you that by the time you realize the truth, it might be too late."

Big Tom threw us out of the arena, shoving us like we were common criminals. I actually wouldn't have minded committing the crime of sticking my fist to his face!

Outside in the open air, I fumed with rage. I would never have thought in a million years Jesse Maldonado could be such a huge jerk. I felt so responsible for everything that happened. Maybe if I hadn't convinced Jason to see him, he wouldn't have had to face all that.

"Jason, I'm so sorry," I apologized, feeling so guilty.

He avoided my eyes. "Can we just get out of here?"

CHAPTER THREE

WHENEVER I WANTED TO GET AWAY FROM THE world, I always went to the beach. Luckily, L.A. was filled with them. In the summer, there was always one party or another going on. However, I was able to find a quiet spot tonight, with only a few people nearby dancing around a bonfire.

The noise didn't distract from the peace and serenity I felt whenever I came here. There was something so healing about the warm sand beneath my feet and the smell of sweet, salty air. I could only hope that after everything, Jason would feel the same.

He hadn't said a word since we left the concert, but I could tell he was deep in thought. I was too—there were at least a million and one questions I wanted to ask him.

Waves crashed onto the shore, echoing softly.

"I've never been to a beach before," Jason said, breaking his silence. "It looks so beautiful."

"Wow, how far north do you live?"

Jason chuckled shortly. "Maybe a little too far."

For several long moments, we gazed at the ocean, basking in the beauty of it and its contrast to the starlit sky above.

Jason nudged me. "Thanks for helping me out today."

"I'm sorry it didn't work out."

"Me too." He glanced at his hands, and moments later, started laughing.

"What's so funny?"

"You knew everything there is to know about me in the first ten minutes after we met, but I don't know anything about you." He smiled. "Well, except that your name's Sadie, you work at Gray's Café, and you have the cutest laugh I've ever heard."

I laughed. "You think my laugh's cute?"

"I do now."

Heat warmed my cheeks, and I looked away,

glancing down at the sand. "What else do you wanna know?"

"Everything," he stated simply. "It only seems fair."

I twisted my lips as I thought about it. "In the fall I'll be a senior in high school. I have an older sister, Brooke, and we live with our dad. That's all there is really."

"What about your mom?"

I sucked in a harsh breath. "She abandoned us when I was about ten. She wanted to become an actress, and according to her, we just didn't fit in her plan." I paused. "She didn't want the extra baggage."

"That must've been tough," Jason said quietly.

I nodded. "My dad was a wreck for years, but he bounced back. We all did. We had to. And now we've just learned to live without her."

"It's the hardest thing, being without your parents," Jason said, looking thoughtful. "I would give anything to have one more moment with mine."

He sighed. "When I found out I was adopted, I didn't know what to think. I was so confused. I felt betrayed, like my whole life was a lie, you know. I said some really hurtful things to my parents. Things I wish I could take back. But I never got the opportunity to apologize to them before they passed away. I regret it every single day."

I couldn't even begin to imagine the pain Jason was going through, but I did know what it felt like to lose someone you loved and how you'd do just about anything to get them back.

In that moment, I felt closer to him than I had to probably anyone outside my family. There was a connection that I just couldn't describe, and it went deeper than the short time we'd known each other.

It made me feel a little weird, but I tried not to dwell on it too long. I grabbed his hand without fully thinking it through. We both stared at our entwined fingers. This was so soon.

"Let's go in the water," I said, pulling him up with me, and we raced to the ocean.

I stopped when the water reached my ankles and watched the full moon, completely in awe by the way it cast an ethereal glow across the water, making it shine even in the darkness.

"It's so beautiful, isn't it?" I sighed, absolutely content.

"Yes," Jason replied. "It really is."

I glanced at him, our eyes locked, his holding me firmly in place. Just like the ocean, Jason's sea-green eyes crashed into me. Or maybe it was something else.

I was too afraid to ask. Too afraid of the intensity I saw in them. Too afraid they matched the intensity in mine. How could I feel this way about someone I just met?

We were only inches apart now. All I could hear was the wild thundering of my heart against my chest and the waves lapping at my feet. I tried not to breathe because I didn't want anything to ruin this moment.

Jason started to say something, but a loud eruption of laughter came from some people nearby. He shifted his stare to the source of the noise, and I seized the opportunity to splash water on his face.

He looked mildly surprised, and then his lips curved. "Is that how it's gonna be?"

I ran before he could catch up with me but ended up getting splashed anyway. In less than twenty minutes, I was soaking wet, but I had to admit that it was the most fun I'd had in a long time.

CHAPTER FOUR

WE WERE ON THE WAY TO MY HOUSE WHEN I FELT my phone buzz in my pocket. I took it out and saw a notification that had my jaw dropping to the floor.

"What's wrong?" Jason asked.

"It's Heather. She just couldn't keep her big mouth shut." I showed him the blog post on Heather's gossip site discussing in detail everything Jason had told us in the café and then some.

Jason just shrugged it off. "It doesn't matter."

"Of course it does," I argued, surprised at his lackluster reaction. "Now that everyone knows who you are, they'll keep hounding you with questions. Questions you're probably not ready to answer yet."

"If they're anything like you, I'm sure I'll be

fine," he said with a wink, and I rolled my eyes at him, hoping for his sake that his words would prove true.

We got to my front door, and there was a brief, awkward silence that ensued--like the kind you have when you're on a first date.

Is he going to kiss me? Should I make the first move?

Except this wasn't a date, and instead, other questions whirled through my mind, like: *Is this good-bye? Am I ever going to see him again after tonight?*

"So..." I started, nervously tucking a lock of hair behind my ear. "How long will you be staying in L.A.?"

"I don't know." Jason let out a sigh, slipping his hands into his pockets. "I haven't really thought about that yet."

"Well, do you have a place to stay?"

"The beach seemed really nice."

My eyebrows shot up. "The beach?"

He rubbed the back of his neck, looking sheepish. "Yeah, I kind of used all my savings on the plane ticket."

"But you can't stay on the beach!" I thought for a moment. "How about you stay with us?"

"Seriously?"

"Yeah. I'd have to ask my dad first, but I'm sure he'll be fine with it."

"I don't know, Sadie," Jason said.

"Just crash here tonight," I told him. "You can leave tomorrow if you want."

He started to shake his head, but I didn't give him the time to say no. "It's decided. Just give me a few minutes," I said and rushed inside.

Dad was on the couch in the living room, watching a football game. He looked up when I walked in. "Hey, sweetie. How was the concert?"

"It was great," I sang, sitting next him and turning on the puppy dog eyes.

"Oh god," Dad groaned.

"What?"

"You've got that I-need-something-Daddy face on."

"No, I don't," I denied vehemently.

Dad arched a brow. "It was the same look you gave me when you were five and we went to that farm and suddenly you wanted a pony."

"But you never got me a pony."

"Exactly."

I rolled my eyes. "Fine, you caught me. I need something, Daddy."

"Ha!"

"But it's not a pony, and you're gonna say yes."

He shot me a look that told me not to be too confident.

Regardless, I went on to tell him about Jason and everything that had happened today, ending with, "And now he needs a place to stay."

"Sadie!" Dad looked more surprised than disappointed, which made me a little relieved.

"Look, I know I only met him today, but I promise he's a nice person. And aren't you the one always telling us to help people? This is 'helping people,' Dad."

He looked skyward, and after letting out an exhausted sigh, glanced at the front door. "Is he out there now?"

I nodded, pleading with my eyes for him to say yes.

"Alright, he can stay. But just for the night."

"Thank you, Daddy," I said and ran out to tell Jason.

CHAPTER FIVE

AFTER THE SOMEWHAT AWKWARD INTRODUC-tions between Dad and Jason, I took him to our guest bedroom and settled him in.

I sat on the bed, swinging my legs.

Jason sat next to me.

"Do you need anything?"

He smiled. "No, I'm good."

"Well, if you do end up needing anything, I'm right across the hall."

I'd barely finished my sentence when Dad yelled, "Go to bed, Sadie!"

I pressed my eyes shut, willing the ground to swallow me whole. My dad was so embarrassing!

"I'd better go." I stifled a yawn as I rose. "Goodnight."

"Goodnight, Sadie."

When I got to my room, I saw a note on Brooke's bed. She was staying over at her best friend's house. So, I couldn't even vent to her about all that had happened. With a sigh, I heaved onto my bed, underestimating how exhausted I was. I only remembered shutting my eyes, when the darkness fell.

* * *

A loud scream pierced through the air, and I bolted upright from the bed. Wide awake, I pushed the covers away and ran outside my room to find out what was going on.

There was no suspicious activity in the hallway, so it looked safe enough to walk through—that was until I reached the living room and saw Brooke standing in the doorway.

"What's going on?"

Brooke kept looking straight ahead, not blinking once. Confused, I waved my hand in front of her face before I could even get a reaction.

She jabbed her finger toward the living room, and I followed her eyes, seeing who she was staring at.

Jesse Maldonado, standing in front of the TV, right between our mismatched couches.

"Jesse?" I asked, unsure if it was really him.

"Sadie, right?"

"Yeah," I said, moving forward. "What are you doing here?"

He was about to say something when Jason approached down the hallway. "Sadie, can I borrow some..." Jason's voice faded when he caught sight of Jesse. "Why are you here?"

"I wanted to talk."

Jason folded his arms across his chest. "Oh, so now you want to talk?"

Brooke gasped suddenly, looking between both brothers. "There--there's two of them!"

That was all she got out before she fainted.

Thankfully, I was able to catch her in time.

Both guys rushed toward us, asking if she was okay.

Struggling to hold her up, I waved them off with a jerk of my head. "She's totally fine. Just a typical fangirl reaction. Nothing to worry about," I said, dragging an unconscious Brooke out of the living room, making a mental note to let her know when she came to that her new diet was not working at all.

I managed to haul her onto her bed, which, by the way, was a workout in itself.

"Brooke? Brooke, wake up!" I slapped her cheek, and her eyes immediately shot open. "Welcome back."

She sat upright, looking confused as she glanced at her surroundings. "Jesse Maldonado was here...and there was two of him...and...and..."

I patted her on the head. "Don't think too much."

She yanked me by the collar with surprising strength for a person who'd been unconscious less than a minute ago. "Where is he?" she asked through gritted teeth.

"He's in the living room," I blurted with widened eyes.

I barely had enough time to recover before she scurried out of the room.

I went after her. "What are you doing? You can't go in there!" I yelled in a whisper. "This is the first time they're actually sitting down and talking."

She stopped, frowning. "Who's 'they'?"

"Jesse and his twin brother, Jason."

Brooke's mouth hung to the floor. "Jesse Maldonado has a twin brother?"

I nodded quickly.

"You knew!" she fumed. "Well, this is just great. First you lie about there being a Channing Tatum marathon on yesterday, and now you don't tell me something as important as this?"

"I'm sorry," I said sincerely. "And for the record I really did think there was going to be a Channing Tatum marathon on yesterday."

Her eyes shot daggers. "Don't even talk to me."

She crouched down and wiggled along the wall until she got closer to the living room.

"Brooke, what are you up to?" I asked slowly.

"What does it look like, Einstein?"

Although this was technically eavesdropping, I had to admit that I was tad bit curious to hear what they were talking about. I rolled my eyes and kneeled next to her.

Jason and Jesse were sitting at opposite ends of the room, and by the stern expression on Jason's face, it seemed like he hadn't exchanged a word with his brother and didn't plan to anytime soon.

I could feel the tension between the two of them all the way from here, and I wished I could do something about it, but I knew they had to sort their issues out themselves--it was the only way.

"Why aren't they speaking to each other?" Brooke whispered loudly.

"I don't know, Jason's probably still upset. Jesse behaved like a total douche yesterday."

"Please, Sadie, all celebrities can be douches sometimes."

"Not to their own family," I countered.

Brooke gasped. "Oh my god, you have a crush on Jason!"

"No, I don't!" I denied, looking away.

"It's totally fine, Sadie, you can have him. But Jesse is all mine," Brooke said with an intensity that made me wonder if her obsession for Jesse Maldonado was even healthy at all.

"What are we looking at?" Dad's voice came from behind us.

"Shh!" Brooke and I turned at the same time.

He held his hands up. "Sorry."

"Jesse Maldonado's here," Brooke said.

Dad frowned slightly. "The singer?"

I nodded. "He's here to see Jason."

"Why?"

"Because he's his twin brother!" Brooke said, exasperated.

"Try to keep up, Dad!"

"Okay, okay, okay. Geez!" Dad said, and we turned back to blatantly eavesdrop on the people in question.

"You guys want breakfast?"

"We're kinda busy, Dad," Brooke said.

"Too bad. I just finished making a batch of *chocolate* pancakes. Guess I'll just have to eat them myself."

"I call dibs first!" I announced quickly.

"I was born first," Brooke countered.

"You're barely a year older than me," I reminded her.

"Who cares? There's a superstar in our living room!"

"She makes a good point," I said, smiling apologetically at Dad, who then let out a loud sigh before walking away.

I could barely catch anything from Jesse and Jason's conversation, and it was just as well when moments later they both stood up.

As Jason came toward the hallway, Brooke and I acted like we'd been discussing about changing the colors of the walls. Lame, I know.

Unexpectedly, Jesse followed and came toward me. "I just want to apologize for how I acted last night. I don't say it often, but I really am sorry. Are we cool?"

I smiled, really surprised by his apology. "We're cool."

Brooke pushed past me then, getting into Jesse's face. "I love you!" she squealed. "I would die for you."

"Uh, thanks?" Jesse rubbed the back of his neck,

looking all shades of uncomfortable. "I have to go now." His gaze shifted to Jason. "You'll consider my offer?"

"Yeah, I'll think about it," came his reply.

Brooke started to follow Jesse out the door, but I held her back, gripping the back of her shirt.

"Jesse! Jesse! I love you so much!"

Jesse hightailed it out of our house with athletic speed, which was a smart move because I wasn't sure how much longer I could hold onto Brooke. She was worse than a wild animal!

Once I was sure Jesse Maldonado was most likely halfway across town, I let Brooke go.

"Get a grip of yourself!" I told her, grabbing her by the shoulders.

She started taking several deep breaths.

"That's it. In and out. Nice and slow. Very good."

I left her with that and went by the guest room to see Jason. The door was slightly ajar, but I knocked anyway. He asked me to come in, and I saw him sitting on the bed with his backpack beside him.

He offered me a crooked smile. "Hey."

"Hey." I went to sit next to him. "So, what did Jesse say?"

He arched a brow. "I know you were listening in."

"I was not!" I immediately said, but when he

gave me another look, I conceded. "Okay, so maybe I was. But I didn't hear anything," I said truthfully, as if that somehow made it okay.

But when Jason laughed, I felt more at ease.

"Jesse apologized and said he wanted to get to know me," Jason said. "He even offered me a place to stay."

"Wow. What did you tell him?"

"I said I'd think about it." Jason shrugged. "I didn't know what else to say."

"Are you considering it though?"

He shook his head thoughtfully. "I don't know. It's a lot to take in for now."

I nodded. "I bet."

"I should go." He rose to his feet and slung his backpack over his shoulder. "You're a real sweet person, Sadie. No one's ever helped me out the way you have. I'll never forget it." He smiled. "Goodbye."

He walked out, and I sat there in the empty room, feeling this weird sinking sensation at the pit of my stomach. I didn't know why, but I just couldn't bear the thought of Jason leaving.

I hurried after him, and by the time I caught up, he was nearly out of the driveway.

"Is that it?" I asked loudly. "You're just going to

leave? I'll never see you again," I added that last part, sotto voce.

He turned to face me, bearing a slight frown. "I'm still going to be in L.A. At least for a while." He paused. "I can't go back to Canada right now. There's just too many memories there."

He walked back toward me, closing the distance between us. "I do want to see you again, Sadie," he said, looking deeply into my eyes.

"I'd like that." I smiled, biting my lower lip. "A lot."

"Really?"

"Yes, really." I laughed.

We shared a moment, just like last night on the beach, but today there were no distractions.

Jason lowered his head, and I could tell he was about to kiss me on the cheek, so I swerved, making sure he kissed me right where I wanted him to.

He froze, and I thought he was going to pull away, but then he relaxed into the kiss.

When we parted, I saw that his cheeks were a little red. He looked so cute when he blushed.

He rubbed the back of his neck nervously and looked toward the ground. "I was aiming for your cheek."

"I know. I made you miss," I admitted.

Jason offered me a lopsided grin, amused. "You did, huh?" He eyed me mischievously and pulled me close. "Sneaky."

I laughed, loving the feel of his arms around me.

"How about we try it again? You know, because I'll know this time and get my game right," he added quickly.

I feigned a serious look. "That seems fair."

He chuckled before capturing my lips in a sweet, soft kiss that tickled my insides and warmed my heart.

I wasn't sure what this meant for us or where we'd go from here. All I knew was that it felt so right. And to think I was just some crazy fangirl when we first met.

Now, I was his girl.

Thank you for reading "Fangirl" by Deborah Balogun! To connect with Deborah and learn more about her books and special offers, visit her on Facebook at www.facebook.com/dbalwrites.

FOREVER AND ALWAYS

A St. Mary's Academy Short Story

Seven Steps

CHAPTER ONE

Peter

IN RETROSPECT, IT WAS A BAD PLAN.

I, Peter Swift, would wait for Wendy Darling, my dream girl, to walk out of after-school fencing practice. When she arrived at her locker, I'd hold up my sign, asking her to choose me for the Winter Formal choosing ceremony. Xander and Xavier, my younger twin brothers, would each hand her a bouquet of roses while Barry Jackson sang the chorus of "Life Support" by Sam Smith, accompanied by Hunter Rosinski on the violin.

It'd taken a hundred bucks to bribe Hunter to play in a non-school sanctioned activity. We were friends, but Hunter was one of those *play by the rules* sort of guys. The kind that thought spontaneity was a dirty word. Luckily for me, his sense of self-preservation had a price.

Barry's voice had cost me five times what I'd paid Hunter. Apparently, Barry could sing on YouTube in front of millions of people for free, but I—his best friend since kindergarten—had to pay. He called it a "personal appearance" fee. Whatever. I didn't care.

Wendy was worth the risk.

She was worth everything.

Wendy Darling was the perfect girl. She was smart, funny, insanely beautiful, not to mention kind, patient, and crazy good with a sword. There was just one problem: to her, I didn't exist.

She'd never looked at me or said my name or even brushed by me in the hallway. We'd never shared a class—except lunch—and I'd never danced with her at a party. We weren't even close to being in the same social circle.

But those things didn't matter because Wendy Darling was meant to be mine, and after today, she was going to finally see me. That was all I wanted—for Wendy Darling to see me.

The hallways of St. Mary's Academy were silent, save for my ragged breathing and racing heart. I watched the red hand tick around the clock above Gym A's blue double doors. The gazillion and one after-school clubs were still in session and would be for another twenty seconds.

Nineteen seconds.

Eighteen seconds.

Seventeen.

Sixteen seconds until my life would change forever.

And it was all because of her.

I was glad it was because of her.

The bell rang, and my heart echoed its harsh clangs. My throat dried to desert levels, and my armpits and hands leaked sweat, making the white board I held slippery. I wiped my hands on my jeans, one at a time, and searched the crowd for the heart-shaped face and deep blue eyes I'd dreamed about for three years.

She wasn't yet among the students strolling out of their classrooms and into the hallway. No one seemed to be in a particular rush. Regular school was work, but afterschool programs were more about socializing and sports. People participated for the comradery and the love of something, not just for a grade.

A few people slowed down their already turtle-like pace to examine my sign or the flowers my brothers were holding. Walter Bradley threw a rolled-up paper ball at Hunter before laughing and jogging away. Barry had tucked the mic in his pocket, making him the most inconspicuous one in our little group. My gut was so twisted up I thought I'd puke right there in the hallway.

Don't puke, I begged my nervous stomach. *Please don't puke.*

After several insanely long minutes, two familiar faces strutted out of Gym A. Moira D'Angelo and Angela Washington. They were Wendy's best friends, not to mention the permanent arm candy of Wendy's gargantuan brothers John and Michael Darling.

Moira and Angela looked more like supermodels than students with their perfect makeup and fitted, trendy clothes. They even wore heels, which I thought was hot but completely impractical in a high school setting. I mean, they were just asking for broken ankles.

Their eyes swung to the flowers in the twins' hands, then to Barry's mostly hidden mic, Hunter's violin, and finally, my sign. Their perfect lips rose in derisive smiles. Then they giggled behind their hands and turned away.

Great. I was hoping to see Wendy before I saw my two least favorite members of her brute squad.

But Wendy wasn't with them. She was always with them. They were like Charlie's Angels, with Wendy being Farah Fawcett of course.

Where was she?

I passed my sign to Barry and jogged to reach the girls. A few feet behind them, I heard the tail end of a conversation involving the words "loser" and "in his dreams" before they turned.

"Hello ladies," I said, shoving my sweaty hands into my pockets.

Their brows knit together in an oddly similar fashion, as if shocked I would dare to speak to them in a public venue such as the hallway.

That didn't surprise me. After all, Moira and Angela were at the top of the social food chain, while I was more mid-level popular, thanks to my accomplishments on the track team.

Moira flicked her ink black hair over her shoulder in a way that I could only describe as intimidating. The way her nose curled, and her forehead wrinkled made me feel like dirt beneath her zebra-striped, Louboutin heels.

Angela was no better. One hand went to her hips, and her full, brick-red painted lips pursed, as if me standing there breathing her air was annoying her.

But this was about Wendy, so I cleared the thickness from my throat and stood my ground, forcing them to acknowledge me.

Finally, they did.

"Um, can we help you?" Moira asked.

Her makeup was flawless, but her attitude was a mess. What did Wendy see in these girls? Wendy was so kind. So down to earth. Nothing like these Kardashian wannabes.

"Yeah, I, uh," I cleared my throat, trying to sound casual. "I'm looking for Wendy. Have you seen her?"

Angela's light brown eyes scanned me, then she tilted her head to the side, staring at me as if I were a rain cloud on a good hair day.

"She's not here," Angela said shortly. "What's it to you?"

I took a deep breath, knowing that my next words would rock their worlds and, if their boyfriends got wind of it, possibly end my life.

"I'm going to ask her to choose me at the Winter Formal choosing ceremony."

Did I suddenly spout a red nose and clown

shoes? I must have, because Moira and Angela looked at each other with amused grins, then looked at me, and burst out laughing.

Ouch.

Moira scoffed. "You want to take Wendy to the Winter Formal? In your dreams, dork." Moira's eyes zeroed in onto me. "First of all, her brothers will break you, and your geeky friends, in half. Second, she's going with James Hawking. You know him, right? Tall, hot, king of lacrosse, allergic to nerds." She patted my head like I was a dog, and I bit back an unkind retort.

Angela made a shooing motion. "Run along, loser. Wendy's not into you."

The two girls laughed again and walked away, leaving me red-faced, angry, and embarrassed.

I was used to bullies, though they'd left me alone after junior high school. The boys, I could handle, but there was something about a girl's mocking that made me feel emasculated.

I squeezed my lips together and pushed back my mop of dark brown hair. My shoulders slumped, and my enthusiasm was beginning to slip away. Those girls punched a massive hole in my pride, and I was powerless to do anything about it.

I pivoted on my heel and walked back toward my friends.

Maybe Angela and Moira were right. What made me think a girl like Wendy would go out with me anyway? Maybe I was just a loser like those girls said? Maybe Wendy was more like those girls than I realized. But how could that be? She didn't make fun of everyone like Moira and Angela did. At least, not that I saw.

No, Wendy wasn't like those girls. She didn't look down on people or talk to them like they were ants ready to be stepped on. And later, when she saw me with my sign and flowers and heard the song that always reminded me of her, I was sure she'd recognize that I wasn't like those other jerky guys. She'd see that I was different. That I loved her.

"Peter."

I looked up and saw Bella French standing next to a locker. "Hey, Bella."

I'd known Bella for three years. We were friends. She was even briefly popular once. Not anymore though. Now she was a mid-lister, like me. Come to think about it, wasn't she in a cover band with her ex-jock boyfriend? Yeah, she may rank a little lower on the popularity pole now. But she was nice, and one of the fastest girls I'd ever seen run. Seriously, she should try out for the track team one day. She'd be unstoppable.

Her locker was open, and she had a pile of

winter clothes in her arms, ready to bundle up against the January chill.

"Looking for Wendy?" she asked, giving me a knowing smile and pulling on her gloves.

I nodded. Everyone who knew me knew I had a thing for Wendy Darling.

If only Wendy knew.

"I was going to ask her to choose me during the Winter Formal choosing ceremony, but, as it turns out, she's not here. She must've left after lunch or something."

"No, she's here. I just saw her."

My eyes went wide, and my back straightened. Maybe there was hope after all?

"She is?"

"Yup." She closed her locker and pulled a black hat over her dark brown curls. "She's in detention."

My heart screeched to a stop. Wendy's in detention? What could she possibly have done to merit going to detention?

Bella smirked. "She kicked James Hawking in a, let's say, very sensitive area."

I snorted, hard. James Hawking was a jerk who deserved worse than a shot in the giblets, but I'd take it. And the fact that it came from Wendy was encouraging. Looks like she wouldn't be choosing him after all.

I smiled gratefully. "You're a lifesaver, Bella."

She smiled back and slipped her arms into the sleeves of her brown and white pea coat. "Go get her, Peter."

Confidence restored, I ran back to the guys. Behind me, I heard Bella mutter, "This isn't my coat."

I didn't hang around for the rest of the story. I was too ready to continue with my plan.

I ran over to my friends and brothers. They were staring at me in awe, like I'd just come from climbing Mount Everest or something.

Xander looked from me to an empty space down the hall. "Did you just speak to Moira D'Angelo and Angela Washington?"

Hunter bounced on the balls of his feet. "What did they say?"

Barry added, "What did Angela smell like?"

"Guys, guys," Xavier chimed in. "The real question is, are they now single and looking to mingle?"

I shook my hand, as if swatting away their crazy questions. I succinctly answered them in the order they've asked them.

"Yes, not much, rose pedals, and no. But that's not the point. Wendy's in detention."

They looked at me in disbelief.

"What's she doing in detention?" Barry asked.

I grinned. "She practically neutered James Hawking."

I'd have to remember to look on social media tonight to see if anyone posted the video. Seeing James get his was an experience I did not want to miss.

Barry's glasses slipped down his nose, and he used his free hand to push them up.

The twins slapped each other five. "Awesome!"

"So, I guess this is it, then," Hunter said. "It's too bad. Barry and I spent like three hours practicing that song." He pulled at his navy-blue polo shirt and held up his hands defensively. "You're not going to want that hundred back, are you? I have a no refund policy."

I waved his comment away and rubbed my hands together. A plan was already taking shape in my mind.

It would be risky—dangerous even—but I'd already faced the two meanest girls on the planet today. How could things get any worse?

"Gentlemen, the time for action is nigh. We're going to bust Wendy out of detention. And I know exactly how to do it."

CHAPTER TWO

Peter

WE PEEKED AROUND THE CORNER OF THE HALL-
way, Barry above me, Hunter and the twins below, like
we were in a spy movie or something.

Directly in front of us, to the right, was the
main office and across from it, Principal Mann's office.
The chemistry lab was at the end of the hallway, on the
right.

Our target.

Xavier pulled back. "I don't know about this. What if we get in trouble? We could go to jail."

Xander craned his neck back to glare at Xavier. "Quit being a baby," Xander hissed. "Besides, we're too young for jail—they'd put us in juvie."

I heard Xavier swallow behind me. I swallowed too.

Yes, I'd been the ringmaster this whole time, but I still felt nervous. If we got caught, I'd be in detention for the rest of my life, *if* I was lucky. If I was not so lucky, I'd be expelled. Maybe even arrested. And not just me, but my brothers and friends too.

I looked above me, then below. I was willing to risk everything for Wendy, but I didn't want the others to suffer for it.

"Look." I stepped back along the wall and faced them. "This is dangerous. If we get caught, our lives will be over. If you want to back out, I won't hold it against you."

Xavier spoke up quickly. "I want to back out."

Then, Xander socked him in the gut, resulting in the sound of a fist hitting flesh and an "umph."

"Shut it," Xander growled. "If Peter goes down, we go down with him. It's called being a family, dipwad."

"It's called getting a rap sheet," Xavier argued, bent over with his hands on his belly.

Xander shook a finger in his face. "I promise that if you chicken out on me, I'll tell everyone about you and Adella behind the softball fields."

Xavier gasped. "She said I couldn't tell anyone."

"That sucks." Xander pulled his phone from his pocket. "What's her dad's phone number again? It's in here somewhere."

"Fine. Fine. I'm in."

"Me too," Barry said.

"And me," Hunter chimed in. "But if we get caught, I'm singing like a canary. Sorry, Peter."

I wasn't a softy, but this sort of strained, male comradery touched my heart. I nodded and grunted, because I was a guy and this was how we showed gratitude. To hide my face, I peeked back around the corner. The others resumed their spots with me on lookout.

To our left, Mr. Mann stepped out of his office and locked the door.

Excellent. With him gone, we could sneak past the main office and head towards the lab.

No problem.

Mr. Fish, the swim coach, jogged out of the main office. "Hey Joe. A word please?"

He caught Mr. Mann three steps from his locked door and started going on about a boys' swim team and someone named Michael.

"Crap," Hunter said. "How are we going to get past them?"

I was asking myself the same questions.

There was no way we could sneak past them. We had to find another way around. I couldn't have two plans fail in one day. Then I'd definitely be the loser Moira and Angela said I was.

"We can't wait here forever," I said. "We need a diversion."

"What kind of diversion?" Xavier asked.

Suddenly, I knew.

Xavier was a good kid, but he did tend to snitch a lot. Especially on Xander. Time to put his skills to good use.

"Xavier, tell them that there's a fight by the pool."

"But—"

"Do it."

Xavier sighed, then, a second later, he took off running, screaming his head off.

"Mr. Mann, two girls are fighting by the pool! They're ripping each other's hair out, and one of them is using flippers. Come quick!"

And then, without waiting, Xavier turned and shot off down the hallway toward the pool, Mr. Mann and Mr. Fish hot on his heels.

Nice job, Xavier. I'd have to give him kudos about the flipper thing—that was if I ever saw him again.

"He's an idiot," Xander said. "But he's a good idiot."

That was man-speak for: Xavier's bravery and loyalty would be held in our hearts forever.

"Yeah," I said.

When Mr. Mann and Mr. Fish were out of sight, we hurried past the offices, slid to a stop in front of the chemistry lab, pushed the door open, and ran inside.

Hunter leaned against the now closed door, holding onto his chest. His pale cheeks flushed red from the run. "Okay, we're here," he gasped out. "What do we do now?"

"I need a match," I said.

"A match?" Barry asked. "For what?"

"I need to start a fire."

Three sets of eyes gawked at me. This wasn't the first time I'd talked them into doing something daring. They should have been used to my antics by now.

Barry looked at me in horrified awe. "Your plan is to burn down the school for this chick?"

"No, I just need to set off the fire alarm."

Barry pushed up his glasses. "What are you setting off the fire alarm for?"

I threw my hands in the air. "Look, you'll see. Just find me a match."

Barry shook his head. "I've heard 'you'll see' before. The last time you said it, I ended up covered in poison ivy."

"In my defense, that was last summer, and if you'd worn sneakers like I said, not timberland boots, you wouldn't have fallen out of the tree. And"—I gestured to the room around me—"this is a chemistry lab. There's no poison ivy here, so you don't have to worry about it."

He snorted. "When it comes to your plans, I always have to worry about it."

I wrapped an arm around Barry's shoulders. "You love my plans. Now,"—I shoved him toward the supply cabinet—"come on. We have to find a match."

Barry muttered about "jail" and "YouTube," but he opened the supply cabinet and started digging for matches.

Xavier kept lookout by the door while Barry, Hunter, and I combed the room. A few minutes later, we came to the same conclusion: there were no matches in the entire lab.

I cursed under my breath.

Xander pulled at his light brown hair. "How

could there be not one match? It's a chemistry lab. Don't they do stuff with fire all the time?"

Hunter looked like he was going to be sick. "Maybe this is a bad idea. We should all just go home and watch TV or something."

I ignored Hunter's comment. I was running out of time, and his whining wasn't helping things.

Barry spoke up next. "We could pull the fire alarm."

I shook my head. "We'd have to break the glass first. Plus, it'll only sound the alarm. Then the detention kids will go out and come back in like two minutes. It's not enough time."

"Enough time for what?"

"For my big reveal."

Hunter crossed his arms over his chest. "Just text this girl. There's no need to go to prison over it."

"No, I won't 'just text' this girl,'" I replied. "First off, I don't have her number. Second off, texting is so impersonal. It needs to be face to face and not during school hours when she's distracted."

Xavier chuckled. "You're not going to talk him out of it, Hunter. He has a whole speech prepared. I heard him practicing it this morning."

I shrugged. "There may be a speech-like

structure of words involved, but most of it she already knows from the letters."

Ah, the letters. I had written Wendy a letter every week back in ninth grade. Then tenth grade. And again in eleventh grade. Every Monday morning, I'd slip one into the slats of her locker in a clean, white envelope.

I'd been patient, waiting for her to say something about them or to approach me. I signed each letter, so she had to know it was me who put them there. But it'd been three years, and she still hadn't looked in my direction. I was a patient guy, but three years should be more than enough time for a girl to make up her mind. Hence, my attempt to step up my game.

I scanned the room again. This time, something caught my eye. The silver of the Bunsen burner in an open cabinet door beckoned me, and I raced over to it, holding it high over my head like a prize fighter's trophy.

Hunter stared at it. "Dude, are you sure about this? Now we're talking about messing with the gas and—"

"Screw the matches. I need a flint."

I passed by an unhappy looking Hunter and handed Barry a red hose. He attached it to the gas line at the end of the row, and I attached my end to the valve at the bottom of the burner.

Barry wrung his hands. "We're going to get the chair for this."

But I was too far gone to listen to Barry and Hunter's complaints. I was so close. There was no stopping now.

I turned the barrel of the burner clockwise which closed the air inlet most of the way, then opened the gas valve. A faint hissing filled my ears.

Hunter held out a flint to me, but he didn't let go. "Are you sure?"

"I'm sure," I said.

Hunter's lips grew tight, then eased, and he released his grip. "You've never lead us wrong, Peter," he said. "I trust you."

"What about my poison ivy?" Barry demanded.

"Well, except the poison ivy thing," Hunter said.

"Guys, hurry up!" Xander called from the door.

Hunter released the flint, and I clicked it a few times over the top of the burner. A small flame sparked to life.

I picked up a nearby chemistry textbook and held the corner of the pages over the flame until they ignited. Then I pulled out a chair and positioned it in the center of the room.

"I'm sure," I whispered, more to myself then to anyone else. "I'm sure."

I held up the quickly burning book to the alarm and waited.

One second. Two seconds. Three.

Suddenly, the fire alarm sounded. A second after that, the sprinklers burst to life, spraying water all around the classroom and extinguishing both the flame in my hand and the flame on the Bunsen burner.

"Let's get out of here!" Xavier cried, swinging the door open.

Barry and Hunter were already sprinting to the hallway.

I jumped off the chair and slipped in a forming puddle.

Xavier pulled me up by my underarms. "Dude, let's go!" he screamed over the wailing fire alarm.

Once again steady on my feet, I followed Xavier out of the room.

"Guys, go out the back door!" I cried. "I'll find Wendy out front."

They nodded and sprinted one way down the hall, while I raced down the other.

Once I made it around the curve, I'd be okay. I'd find Wendy and tell her that I was in love with her. Then we'd live happily ever after.

I just had to make it to the front door.

I rounded the corner of the hallway and slammed into a hard chest. My foot slipped on the wet floor, and I went flying backwards. My head cracked against the floor, and I saw stars.

Then, I saw Mr. Mann's mocha cheeks flushed with anger, his jaw trembling. "Peter Swift. Where are you running off to?"

"I, uh, heard the fire alarm," I said. It wasn't a lie. I had heard the fire alarm. Heck, I was probably the first one to hear it.

"There are no afterschool programs at this end of the building. So, I ask you again, where are you off to so fast?"

Water ran down his face and soaked into his suit. It ran down my face too, puddling beneath my aching head.

"Mr. Mann, I—"

"Me and you are going to take a walk. Then you can tell me all about your recent whereabouts." He pulled me to my unsteady feet, then turned me around and escorted me down the hall, outside.

Where I wanted to go anyway.

A firetruck wailed, and a fireman raced past me.

Through the haze of my aching head, I started to realize exactly what I'd done. I'd triggered the sprinklers. Who knows how much damage I caused the school. Books, clothes, electronics—everything was probably ruined.

In retrospect, this was a very bad plan.

Mr. Mann pushed me ahead, making me stumble through the crowd of kids staring at the school. I felt sure they were waiting for flames to shoot out of the windows and the roof to blow off like in an action movie or something. They were going to be very disappointed when they found out it was just a lovesick dude with a Bunsen burner.

Then, by some miracle, I saw her. Wendy Darling. She was three feet from me, to my right.

She too was staring at the school, eyes wide, mouth slightly agape.

I'd done all of this for her, and now I didn't know if I'd ever see her again. Heck, I may never see the inside of St. Mary's Academy again. That meant no prom. No track team. No choosing ceremony. And most of all, no Wendy.

Some crazy hope infused me, and I decided to do the one thing I've wanted to do for three years.

"Wendy."

She turned her beautiful blue eyes to me, and, unable to stop myself, I took her hand. My words tumbled out of me like a waterfall. "I'm probably going to get expelled, but you're so beautiful, and I was wondering if maybe I can come over, or you can come to my house or wherever and we can talk, because I—"

Wendy's knee connected with my groin, knocking the wind out of me.

Our hands unclasped, and my stars returned.

"Pig!" She sneered. "Go find another girl to drool over!"

The pain was so bad I could barely think. I could barely breathe. All I could do was keel over and roll into a ball on the ground.

A single thought runs through my mind like a marquee.

This day was not turning out the way I planned.

CHAPTER THREE

Wendy

TO SOME, BEING GROUNDED FOR A MONTH WAS A prison sentence. But for me, it was the easiest time I'd ever do.

Well, maybe not the easiest.

I re-read page 113 of *The Blue Mermaid* by Tabitha Browning for the fifteenth time. I still didn't know what it said. The book was interesting, but I couldn't focus. My mind kept replaying James Hawking's face as I kneed him in the balls so hard his grandfather probably felt it. That instant when my knee connected with the seam of his jeans was the moment I took my life back. I reclaimed my body, and it was invigorating, freeing, and oh-so worth it.

James Hawking had made my life a living nightmare for far too long. He'd sneak up behind me and wrap his arms around my waist and whisper dirty things in my ear or get handsy when I didn't want him to.

At first, I thought it was just him being a guy. I told myself it'd be stupid to start a fuss over it. After all, he was the captain of the lacrosse team. What would my speaking out do to his position in the team? What would it do to the school? What would it do to my reputation?

When he grabbed my butt in the lunch line today, something broke inside me. In that moment, I didn't care about the school or the lacrosse team or even my reputation. I just wanted him to stop. I wanted him to never put his hands on me ever again. I wanted him to know the same violation and humiliation I'd felt for the last four months. So, I kneed him in the balls, and it was the single best decision I've ever made. James thought he could treat me any way he wanted, and I'd just have to take it. My knee had shown him, and that other boy, otherwise.

I put down my book and leaned against the headboard.

Thirty days without electronics or social media.

How would I know what was happening in the world? How much would I miss? Would anyone miss me? How would Moira and Angela react to my online absence? I loved them like sisters, but they were the kind of people whose self-worth depended on their social media following. They called it "staying relevant." I called it a digital addiction.

Would being disconnected on social media make Angela and Moira feel disconnected to me in the real world?

I didn't know, and not knowing scared the crap out of me. Yes, I wanted to stand up for myself, and, in some small way, for women everywhere, but if I'd known that it would come at the cost of my friends, I might have shown a little more restraint.

Maybe.

I clicked off the light switch, plunging the room into darkness. Above me, pearl moonlight cut four long lines into my ceiling. I watch the strips of light for a few minutes, then flipped onto my stomach.

I was bored, and right then, I felt totally alone. I couldn't talk to my friends, go online, or watch television. As the seconds crept by, my loneliness wrapped around my heart like a boa constrictor, squeezing tight and making my entire body ache. It was only eight o'clock, and it seemed like I'd been stuck in this room for years. I wasn't even tired enough to go to sleep.

I clicked on the light and wrapped my arms around myself. I needed something to occupy my mind. Something that I could sink into. Something that would make me feel a little less alone. Something like...

Suddenly, I knew exactly what I needed.

I yanked open the top drawer of my white night-stand and pulled out a stack of letters.

They were wrinkled, and the pen marks had started to fade on the older ones. Some of the edges were dog eared, and there were creases from where I'd folded them the wrong way. Still, the letters were the most precious things I owned.

In the pages of these letters, the writer proclaimed his love for me in a hundred different ways, but each time I read his words, I heard him say it a bit differently. Like a love song that still makes you cry, even though you've heard it a million times.

For three years, I'd slowly fallen in love with the man on the other side of these letters. He'd seduced me with words and pen marks and loose-leaf paper. I wondered if he knew I waited for my small deliveries every Monday morning. That I kept them next to my bed and read them over and over until I'd memorized every word.

I hoped he knew.

My favorite letter rested on the top of the pile, and I read it, muttering the familiar words to myself:

Dear Wendy,

I want you to know how proud of you I am. Your kindness and grace give me hope that there is still goodness in this world.

When Jeff Walowitz slipped in that milk puddle and you helped him up instead of laughing in his face like everyone else, it made my heart melt for you even more. Do you know how rare it is that a girl like you would even look at Jeff, let alone help him? He'll probably slip on milk every day for the rest of the schoolyear, just so you'll help him again. I don't know if he's said it to you, but you made his entire life. Just seeing you do stuff like that makes my entire life too. You inspire me to be a better person, just by being who you are.

With all the love in my heart.

P.S.

I held the letter against my chest and wondered if he could feel my heart race.

Who is this guy? Why wouldn't he show himself?

I sighed, folded the letters carefully, and put them back in the drawer.

Having a secret admirer was awesome, until you fell in love with them.

Then it sucked.

CHAPTER FOUR

Wendy

THE WEEKEND PASSED QUICKLY, THANKS TO A *Game of Thrones* marathon on HBO, and I arrived back at school ready for my new letter and some human contact.

I snatched my locker open and peered inside.

Odd.

There wasn't a white envelope.

But there was always a white envelope.

I felt around my locker, even though I could clearly see inside.

Nothing.

For three years, I'd always gotten a Monday letter. Now it wasn't here.

Had he lost interest? Had he moved away? Was he dead?

I frowned, took out a few books, and closed my locker. My heart raced with worry. Is he okay? Please, God, wherever he is, please let him be okay.

I squeezed my books to my chest and leaned against the cool metal.

"What's with the face?" John, my older brother, asked. His thick arm was wrapped around Moira's shoulder, while Michael, my younger brother, held hands with Angela.

I consciously wiped the frown from my face and blinked away the worry in my eyes.

"Nothing," I lied. It felt like someone cancelled Christmas morning.

"Wendy, come on." John narrowed his dark eyes at me. He was an expert at reading people and, right then, he was reading me. "What's the matter? Still thinking about that douche hole, James?"

John released Moira and hit Michael on the chest with the back of his hand. "Come on, we'll bring Wendy back one of his teeth."

Michael, who's always ready for a fight, brightened. "Alright!"

I raised my hand, stopping my brothers before they could run off and start a war. "Wait. I just... I usually get a letter on Mondays. There's no letter."

John, Moira, Michael, and Angela knew about the letters. They'd known since I started receiving them. We weren't ones to keep secrets from each other. Especially big ones like this.

"Ooh," Moira said. "Secret admirer drama."

I rolled my eyes at her.

John leaned against my locker, and Moira stepped into his arms. She pulled his ever-present gray cap down over his eyes and he smiled.

"Just remember," John said, tipping the cap back up, "if this douche ever contacts you for real, he has to go through the two Darling brothers first."

Michael, stockier then John but just as tall, pumped his fist. "Here, here."

I groaned. "Don't call him a douche. Besides, if he hasn't shown himself in three years, I doubt he'll do it now."

Michael ran his fingers through his dark, curly hair. Angela batted his hands away and started restyling it into a perfect bed head look.

"How do you know it's a he?" Michael asked. He pulled Angela's fingers from fussing with his hair and kissed the back of her hand. That was his way of telling her to knock off whatever she was doing. "Maybe he's a she. Ever think of that?"

That was Michael's favorite theory about my secret admirer. I, obviously, didn't agree with it. The way the author expressed himself was so masculine. Simple sentences and thoughts. Not floral and pretty, the way a girl would write.

"Shut up. It's not a girl."

Angela pulled her hands from Michael's grip and clapped them excitedly. A sure sign she'd just thought of something.

"What if we could find out for sure?" Her eyes widened with glee.

We all turn to her.

"How?" I asked.

"We just need a student roster. If you've been getting the letters for three years, then this guy—"

"Or girl," Michael chimed in.

Angela continued like she hasn't heard him, "—must be a junior. And the fact that they talk about stuff you've done means that they have classes with you, right?"

I nodded.

"So, we get the roster for the junior class and start digging." Her face lit up with her new plan, and she clapped her hands at hummingbird speed.

Angela loved investigative work. One time she thought Michael was cheating on her, and she followed him for a solid week before she realized he was working extra shifts at Dad's car dealership to buy her a present. When he gave her the diamond earrings, she managed to look surprised, even though she'd seen him purchase them at the jewelry store.

I frowned. "But we don't know anything about him—except maybe his initials."

"Initials?" Moira asked.

"Yeah. He writes a P.S. at the bottom of his letters. I'm not sure if P.S. is 'post script' or his name, but it's a start."

Michael squinted at me, "Why don't you just get a fingerprint kit or something?" He turned to Angela. "Isn't your dad a detective, babe?"

Angela nodded. "Yes, babe, but we don't have to get all CSI yet. If this P.S. guy—"

"Or girl," Michael chimed in.

Angela hit him with the back of her hand. "If he's not in the system, we're out of luck. We can't track him through fingerprints unless he has a criminal record."

"He better not have a criminal record," John muttered. He jerked his chin at me. "If he's a felon, I'll have to break his fingers."

I groaned.

"Look," Angela said, "I have a contact in the office. I can get the student roster by lunch."

A confident grin slid onto her face. It made me grin too.

"Get ready," she said. "We're about to out your secret admirer."

CHAPTER FIVE

Wendy

AT LUNCH, ANGELA SCROLLED THROUGH AN EX-cel spreadsheet on her pink, rhinestone phone.

I was pretty sure our "research" was against the rules, but my desire to discover P.S.'s identity overshadowed the urge to stay out of detention.

Angel passed around the phone so the five of us could all see it. "Here's a list of all of the kids in school, sorted by grade and last name,"

John squeezed his arm around her waist and rested his chin on her shoulder. "Babe, how'd you get this?"

"I told you. I have contacts in the office."

"This is cool," John said, clearly impressed with his girlfriend's snooping abilities. "I feel like I'm in a cop show or something."

"You're silly." Angela shook her head and smiled. "Anyway, there are only three boys in the junior class with the initials P.S."

"Who?" I asked. I wished she would just get to the point.

She held up three fingers and counted off the names. "Previt Singh, Paul Smalls, and Peter Swift."

I hurriedly wrote down each of the names. Now we were getting somewhere.

Moira scrunched her eyebrows. "I've never heard of any of those guys."

"Previt Singh is in the chess club," John said. "He tutored me in math last month."

Moira's eyes went wide. "A junior tutored you in math?"

He lifted his hands in a defensive position. "He's smart, and I suck at math."

"Does he seem like the type to write letters?" I asked.

John shook his head. "Not really. He was really into religion. You know, he wore that head wrap. Plus, he's not in our lunch period."

"Fine," Angela said. "We'll scratch Previt off the list."

I drew a line through his name. "What about Paul Smalls? Does anyone know him?"

"He's in art with me, I think," Moira said, tilting her head in contemplation. "Yeah, he's tall, and he paints, I think." She shrugged. "I guess he could write this stuff."

"A definite maybe." I put a check next to Paul. "What about Peter?"

"Track team," John said. "He won some meets last year. His picture is in the trophy case next to the gym."

"Yeah," Michael said. "He's a jock, but not like a jock jock. It could be him, I guess."

I put a check next to Peter's name. "Okay. So, two possible. Now we just have to find them."

I frowned. I'd never heard of any of these guys until now, but I mostly hung out with Michael, Moira, John, and Angela. Maybe I should look into expanding my circle of friends.

"I have their class schedules." Angela pulled three sheets of paper from her bookbag and handed them to me just as the bell rang. "Previt has English with Mrs. Mackey, but he's out of the race, so we can trash that. Paul has French with Mr. Coggs, and Peter has government with Mr. Goldblum."

"What do they even look like?" I asked.

My question was answered when I took a closer look at the paper. Beneath each schedule was a school ID card. I stared at Previt, Paul and Peter.

They were all handsome in their own way, but there was something about Peter's brown eyes. They sparkled with mischief. His brown hair was longish and swept to the side, and his ears were a little too big for his face. He smiled in his picture, unlike the other two. It was a wide, happy smile.

I smiled back.

"Wendy!" Angela called.

I looked up from gazing at Peter. They were already halfway to the double doors.

"Hurry up!" Angela said. "We can get to Mr. Mackey's class before the bell if we're fast enough."

I nodded, took one last look at Peter's smile, stuffed the papers into my jeans pocket, and rushed out of the cafeteria.

CHAPTER SIX

Peter

I SHOULD'VE BEEN EXPELLED.

I'd caused thousands of dollars worth of water damage to the school, not to mention I'd aggravated Mr. Mann. But, my dad was on the schoolboard and worked as the school's attorney.

I got a week's suspension instead. That meant no phone, no friends, and no PlayStation. Just me and TV for a week straight.

Perfect.

I turned on MTV and glanced at my notebook.

This was the first time in three years I hadn't been able to deliver a letter to Wendy.

Had she noticed? Did she care? I didn't know. I could only hope she had. My big proposal was supposed to be the start of us, but all I got was a kick in the pants. Literally. Every time I thought about it, it physically hurt.

I wrote my letter anyway, flipped on the television, and watched a few hours of MTV. A Teen Wolf marathon was playing.

What was it like to be extraordinary? To have powers? To have strength?

If I had all the power in the world, would Wendy notice me? Was being extraordinary enough for a girl like her?

CHAPTER SEVEN

Wendy

WE HADN'T BEEN ABLE TO LOCATE PETER SWIFT YET, but we were able to locate his twin brothers. They both had tall, athletic frames, and they both wore the same blue sweatshirt and dark jeans. It was like they wanted people to confuse them.

I stood in front of the boys, with Angela and Moira at my back. John and Michael had lost interest in our mission and had gone to start the car.

"You're Peter's brothers?" I asked.

They nodded in sync.

The one to the right put his hand on his chest.

"I'm Xander." He pointed to his brother. "This is Xavier."

I smiled at them and took a step closer.

"Nice to meet you, Xander and Xavier. Now, can you tell me where your brother is?"

"He's suspended," Xander, the one to the right, said.

"For how long?" I asked.

"For the rest of the week."

Xander's voice was deep. Strong. He was definitely the spokesman of the two. The other one, Xavier, looked at me with a mixture of guilt and awe.

Angela stepped next to me, hands on hips, eyes narrowed. "Why'd he get suspended?"

The brothers looked at each other, then back at her.

"I can't say."

Moira spoke up from behind me. "Does this have something to do with the lame sign he was holding up?" he asked.

"Sign?" I asked. "What sign?"

The brother's faces turned red, and they took a step back.

"I saw him on Friday with a sign that said, 'Wendy, please choose me'. And these two losers had roses. I told him that you weren't interested."

My chest tightened.

Peter was going to ask me to choose him at the choosing ceremony and Moira just blew him off. How could she do that? Since when did she start making decisions for me?

I let out a breath. There was no time to think about Moira's presumptuousness now. I had to find Peter, and finally get the truth about the letters.

I narrowed my eyes at Xavier and watched his face turn beet red. "Peter's spoken to you about me?"

He bit the inside of his cheek, refusing to look at me, and I knew I was on to something.

"Spill," I said. "Did Peter write me letters?"

His eyes shot to his brother, but I put my hand on Xavier's shoulder, drawing his attention back to me. "You're going to tell me everything I want to know."

"What's in it for us?" Xander asked. I looked at him, and he cleared his throat. "I'm not above ratting out my brother, but I come at a price. What's in it for us?"

"What do you want?"

"Alana Swimworthy." The words roll off his tongue like he'd been waiting for someone to ask him.

I frowned and turned to Angela and Moira.

"A freshman," Moira said. "Ariel Swimworthy's

sister. Michael and I went to their party a few weeks ago."

She gave me a look that said to get on with it.

I turned back to Xander. "I can promise one date with Alana. Just one."

"One's all I need," Xander said. "What do you want to know?"

I placed my other hand on Xander's shoulder, and the twins and I formed a triangle of intrigue. "Everything."

CHAPTER EIGHT

Peter

IT WAS ONLY MONDAY, BUT BEING AT HOME ALONE all day already sucked.

It was one thing to be sick and sleeping all day, but another entirely to be perfectly healthy and only have a television to connect to the outside world. I'd forgotten how much I checked my phone throughout the day. Sometimes, my fingers twitched and moved as if scrolling through something. Did that mean I was addicted? Maybe.

I paced the living room. It was too cold to go outside. That meant I was trapped like a rat. Nothing was on television, and I didn't feel like reading or catching up on homework. I was two seconds away from searching my brother's room for an electronic device when there was a knock on my front door. Finally. Another human being.

I jogged over to the door and snatched it open.

My heart stopped.

My mouth dropped open.

My heart leapt into my throat.

I could only stare in amazement.

There she was.

In my doorway.

Wendy Darling.

Was this real? Was I dreaming? Was she actually here?

I scanned her entire body, from her wavy brown hair to her blue eyes and puffy jacket, all the way down to her black boots. God, she was beautiful.

"Aren't you going to invite me in, Peter?" she asked.

I sucked in a breath and closed my gaping mouth. I'd been gawking at her for a full minute. She must've thought I was some sort of psycho or something.

"Yeah, of course. Sorry. Come in."

I pulled the door open, then wiped my suddenly sweaty hands on my jogging pants and cupped them in front of my mouth to check my breath. I'd brushed my teeth today. Thank God!

She walked down the short hallway and into the large living room. Her eyes took in the spiral staircase, the high windows, the black leather couches, and expensive rugs. Then, she turned to me.

"You weren't in school today," she said.

I blinked several times, still not able to believe Wendy Darling was really in my house. "Yeah, I, uh, I got expelled."

"Why?" she asked, taking a step closer. Her eyes were open and expectant.

I put one hand in my pocket and threw the other in the air.

"It, uh, it was a stupid prank. I—I set the chem lab on fire."

A brief look of disappointment crossed her face, then she smiled at me. "Oh. Well, I can see that you're busy." She looked around the living room again, then her eyes returned to me. "I just came to collect my letter."

My stomach twisted until I thought I was going to barf. I swallowed hard to keep my lunch down.

"Le-le-letters?" I croaked.

"Yes. You've been writing me letters every Monday, haven't you?"

My eyes opened so wide they ached. I thought I was ready to reveal myself to Wendy but, right now, I just wanted to go hide under a rock. "I, uh—"

"Well, have you or haven't you?"

What would she say if I told her I was her secret letter writer? What would she say if I said I wasn't? Would either answer make me less nervous than I was right at this very second? This seemed so much easier when I was planning it out, but now that she was in front of me, my heart felt like it was jumping between my throat and my gut.

"I, uh..."

There was that look again. Disappointment. She put her hands into her coat pockets and sighed. "I see. I guess you're not him. He's brave. Articulate. If he was here, he'd tell me how much he loved me." She examined me, waiting for something. Then, she took a step back. "I shouldn't have come. I'd better go."

I stood frozen as the girl of my dreams walked away.

The girl I'd spilled my guts to every Monday morning.

The girl who'd rooted herself deep in my soul without saying a word.

She opened the door and was gone.

Gone.

I swallowed and pushed my fingers through my hair.

What was I doing?

Why was I standing here?

I couldn't let her get away. If I did, I'd be a coward, and she didn't deserve that. She deserved someone extraordinary.

My brain finally woke from its stupor and screamed at me, "Move, you idiot!"

I dashed into my room, grabbed the letter from my desk, stuffed my feet into my boots, pulled on my coat, and ran out of my apartment to see Wendy stepping into the elevator.

"Wendy!" I called, running down the hallway. "Wendy, wait!"

I made it to the elevator in about three seconds and stuck my hand between the doors just as they were shutting. (I knew running track would come in handy one day).

The elevator dinged, and the doors opened, revealing a wide-eyed Wendy.

My Wendy.

I stepped inside and stood next to her.

"Here." I presented her with a white envelope. Her Monday letter.

She eyed me, then plucked the envelope from my hands.

The doors closed, and the elevator started down to the lobby.

"I write you a letter every Monday." There. It was out. I said it.

Heart, meet sleeve.

Her brows pressed together, and her mouth turned down. It was the same expression she'd had in my apartment. She was waiting for me to say something. But what?

"Why letters?" she asked.

I stared into Wendy's beautiful eyes, and all of my fear left. This was the moment I'd been waiting for. The moment when I could tell her the words I'd been dreaming about.

"Because I love you." My heart pounded in my chest like a fist. My stomach was so tight that I nearly doubled over.

What would she say? What would she do?

She let out a breath, and her cheeks turned pink. "I love you, too."

She held my letter in front of her lips, and from the light in her eyes, I could see she was hiding a smile.

My entire body felt weightless. Like I was floating in a sea of ecstasy. The girl I loved just told me she loved me too. This had to be what heaven felt like. Intoxicating. Warm. Beautiful.

She was beautiful.

"Can I read it now?" she asked

I nodded too fast. "Yeah. Of course. I mean, it's yours."

Her eyes went to the elevator panel. "We'll be downstairs soon." She looked up at me with that expectant expression.

I bit my inner cheek. I was really coming to like that expression.

"My brothers and their girlfriends are waiting for me. I feel like I need more time." A small huff of air left her lips. "With you."

Before I realized what I was doing, I pressed the emergency stop button. The lights dimmed, and the elevator jerked to a stop.

"Oh my God, what did you do?" she asked.

Enclosed spaces freaked me out a little. Well, a lot. But I had to play this cool. I sat cross legged on the floor. "Giving you more time to read."

She smiled then and tipped up her chin. I could see the happiness in her eyes. In that moment, I knew what my life's mission was. I was born to make her happy.

"Are you always so...unpredictable?" she asked.

"Sometimes." I smiled up at her. "When it comes to you."

She sat down, facing me.

I held out my hand. "May I?"

She nodded and placed the envelope in my palm. "You may."

And then I read her my letter. I hoped my words could be a mirror reflecting all of her best parts.

When I was done, she smiled at me. How could my entire life be complete with just one of her smiles?

"So, you *are* my secret admirer."

I nodded. "Is that okay?"

"No. I don't think so. I think the secret should be out."

"Like, I can just admire you?"

"Maybe a little more than that. Come here."

I leaned forward.

She did too.

Our lips met, and I swore the entire world turned upside down. Everything that was important was now meaningless. The only thing that mattered was this. Us.

I suddenly remembered I had something to ask her, and I pulled away, even though I didn't want to. "Before I can't think anymore, I have to ask you a question."

"Yes, Peter?"

"Wendy Darling, will you choose me at the Winter Formal choosing ceremony?"

"Will I still get flowers and songs?"

I looked at her in horror. "You knew about that?"

She nodded, still smiling. "Your brothers ratted you out."

"I'm going to kill them."

"Later, babe. Much later."

Our lips met again, and everything fell away.

It was just me and her.

The girl with the most beautiful soul in the world.

And the boy who was born to show her just how beautiful she was.

Thank you for reading "Forever and Always: A St. Mary's Academy Short Story" by Seven Steps! To connect with Seven and learn more about her books and special offers, visit www.sevenstepsauthor.com.

THE FRIEND RULES

Melanie Hooyenga

CHAPTER ONE

A FLASH OF YELLOW CUTS THROUGH THE TREES ahead of me. Topher whoops and hollers like a banshee as he hops his bike over roots and sideswipes branches. The rest of us ride in silence, staying focused on the trail. Out here in the middle of the forest, it's easy to let the clear air calm my mind until I forget about everything except the blood pumping through my body. At least it would be if it weren't for Topher.

Mica laughs from behind me. "He's going to break something."

"Wouldn't be the first time," I reply.

Kurt calls from behind Mica, "Ten bucks says it's a tire."

A smile spreads over my face despite my heavy breathing. Kurt has an uncanny ability to predict what's coming, but that doesn't mean I won't bet against him. "I call helmet."

Mica laughs. "You're horrible."

"Not too late to get in," Kurt says.

"Blood," Mica says.

I laughed. "That's a given." Another shout comes from farther ahead, and I stand to pedal harder. As much as we joke about Topher crashing, I don't actually want to see him get hurt.

The trail narrows into a series of switchbacks leading to our usual pit stop—the creek at the center of the forest. The leaves tickle my arms as I burst through the trees, the trail barely wide enough for me and my bike. Mica and Kurt are close behind me, breathing heavily. We always take turns leading, and I get a rush knowing that even though I'm a girl, I make them work to keep up.

Kurt shouts between breaths. "Any... sign... of him?"

"Not yet," I call over my shoulder.

"He's probably swimming in the creek," Mica says.

"He better have clothes on." I shake my head at the memory of him skinny dipping in the creek last week. "One Topher peep show is enough." He'd beat us to the creek, and in crazy Topher logic, his bare backside was our reward. Kurt threatened to take off with Topher's clothes so he'd have to ride back naked, and only gave them back after I practically dragged him into the creek. My cheeks flush at the memory. I've been one of the guys for so long they've forgotten I'm a girl, but lately, something has changed.

A high-pitched shout echoes through the trees, snapping me back to reality. "Was that—"

"That was him," Mica says, his voice tight.

We power down the trail, our tires so close we risk crashing into each other, and skid to a stop alongside the creek. Topher's bike is halfway in the bushes, but he's gone.

"Toph?" Mica calls.

A groan carries from beyond the trail.

Kurt stands near me. I reach for his arm to anchor myself, and we jump apart like we've been shocked. We've wrestled and tackled and pushed and shoved more times than I can count, but that—that electricity thing that just zipped through me, and based on his reaction, did to him as well—is new. But I can't worry about that now.

Mica edges past Topher's bike and crouches with his hands on his knees, studying something in the bushes. After several heart-stopping moments, he stands, smiling. "Jackpot."

"A trifecta?" Kurt asks.

"Blood, tire, helmet."

"Are you gonna just stare at me?" Topher whines from the bushes.

The three of us lock eyes, and without a word, move to Topher's side and pick him up. Blood's running down his arm and leg, and dirt's smeared across his face beneath his cracked helmet.

"Hey!" He tries to squirm out of our grasp, but Kurt and Mica's arms are ridiculously strong—and mine aren't too shabby either.

We step around the bikes, and with one swing, toss him into the creek. Water splashes my legs, and before I can register what's happening, I'm flying through the air, Kurt's arms locked around my waist. He twists before we hit the shallow water so instead of landing directly on the smooth rocks that cover the bottom, I land with an "oof."

On him.

The cool water is a shock after riding, and I'm hyper-aware of the way the length of our bodies are pressed together, the way our limbs fit together like a puzzle. One of my long braids dangles in the water between us so I grab it and smack him in the chest.

He laughs, untangling his arm from my waist, and a tiny part of me yearns for him to put it back.

Friend Rule #1: No lusting after your friends.

Swallowing the unfamiliar emotions, I dunk his head under the water. I scramble over the wet rocks and am almost to dry land when his strong hand grips my ankle.

"Not so fast." His voice is light, teasing, and my stomach does a weird flippy thing that unnerves me.

I pretend to struggle, but am quietly thrilled as he yanks me back to him. Instead of dunking me like I expect, he pulls me into a headlock and lightly smacks the top of my helmet. The boys started doing that years ago when they realized noogies weren't as effective with a helmet in the way. His wet shirt is pressed against my face, and while I'm enjoying the feel of his muscular arms, it's time for retaliation. I dig my fingers into his side, and he squirms away, laughing.

"That's cheating!" His dark eyes dance in the light filtering through the trees, like he's ready for more. But more what? Horsing around? Or something else?

I splash water in his face. I need him to stop looking at me like that, just for a second, so I can slow this sudden rush of I-don't-know-what that I'm feeling. This is Kurt. He's one of my best friends. We're like brother and sister—or at least close cousins—and he'd be horrified if he knew what I was thinking.

His gaze drops to my knee, and the smile slips from his face. "Did I do that?"

Blood trickles over my kneecap, running into the clear water swirling around us. I don't remember hitting it, but my mind was on other things.

He moves closer and scoops water over my knee. The blood washes away, revealing a tiny scrape. His fingers trail lightly over my knee, sending chills up my leg.

"Bully," I tease, hoping he doesn't notice that I can't breathe.

"Sorry." His voice is almost a whisper.

Topher's standing in water up to his knees. The blood and mud have been washed away, and he's smirking at us. "You two about done over there?"

"You owe us each ten bucks," Kurt says.

Topher kicks water at us. "That's not how this works!"

Mica laughs at us from the shore, the only one of us who's still dry. His arms are crossed over his chest, and when our eyes meet, a curious expression dances on his face. I shake my head and squeeze water from my braids. Whatever questions he's got are no match for my own.

We climb out of the creek, and while Mica helps Topher fix his tire, Kurt gives me a serious look. "I really am sorry."

I smile up at him. At five foot nine, I'm no slouch, but he's a full head taller than me. Water drips from his dark hair beneath his helmet, running in rivulets down his face. I hold out my arms, turning them over. "Do you know how many scars I have from you boys?"

His gaze runs over my arms, then my legs, and stalls before returning to my eyes. It seems like he wants to say something, and for a moment, I wonder if maybe this isn't one-sided. Then his cocky grin is back, and he wraps my braid around his finger and tugs. "You love it, and you know it."

The jumble of his words and the fact that he's still touching me does a number on my pulse. I yank my braid from his hand, but our hands graze, making my stomach backflip. My eyes close, and I take a deep breath.

This is Kurt.

One of my best friends.

He's off limits.

When I open them, he's watching me, an unreadable expression on his face. "You okay?"

Instead of answering him, I head toward Mica and Topher. "You boys about done?"

Topher looks up from his tire pump. "I'm not paying you."

"Aww, Toph," Kurt nudges Topher's bike with his toe. "It's only ten bucks."

Mica clears his throat. "Each."

Topher picks up his bike and sets it on the ground. "On one condition." He looks at each of us. "I still get to lead."

"Nope," we all say.

Mica grabs his bike and swings a leg over the crossbar. "Last one back's a rotten egg!"

A different excitement races through me—one I'm more familiar with. Adrenaline pushes me onto my bike, and in seconds, I'm pedaling hard up the trail behind Mica. Kurt and Topher are right behind me. We've been riding these trails for years, and there isn't a switchback we don't know, so racing is like a blood sport with rules—no intentionally hurting anyone, that sort of thing—and bragging rights for the winner.

The trees thicken, closing in on the trail, but right after the next turn, it widens just enough that I should be able to squeeze past Mica.

Which he knows.

We make the turn, and he sticks to the middle of the path, his strong legs powering him over roots and rocks and underbrush. But my legs are strong too. I stand to pedal harder, my grip firm, all my focus on the foot of space to his left. He knows what I'm attempting, and with a burst of speed, I rocket past him.

"Nice," he says behind me.

"It's not over yet," Kurt shouts.

Twigs snap behind me, and seconds later, Kurt's by my side. "Not so fast, Alex."

Hearing my name come out of his mouth almost makes me lose my balance. Almost. "Can't keep up?" I glance at him out of the corner of my eye. Like me, he's standing on his pedals, and as much as I'd like to think I can beat him, he's almost twice my weight and all muscle.

He laughs, then he blows by me, leaving me with a breathtaking view of his backside.

Maybe being second isn't all bad.

We wind through the forest, the stillness calming me in a way nothing else can—even as we battle for first. These woods, these boys, are my everything, and I'm terrified that it's going to change. Friends date all the time, but it's the after part that scares me.

Because there's always an after.

Maybe the stars will align and he'll like me back, but when it falls apart, it won't be just us that's over. It'll mean the end of this, the four of us, and no amount of belly flips and racing hearts is worth that.

Mica whips past me, followed by Topher, and their shouts carry back to me.

"Oh, no you don't!" I shake my head free of everything but the trail ahead, and for the next half hour we race up and down the hills like it's the only thing that matters.

We tumble into the parking lot in a photo finish—Kurt, me, Mica, then Topher—and sit on the bumper of my car, guzzling water. Nothing compares to the all-body exhaustion after a hard ride, especially on a day as perfect as today. Fluffy clouds dot the blue sky, and a light breeze cools the sweat on my skin.

Another thing I like about hanging with guys? They don't feel the need to fill every waking moment talking. They're content to just sit here and—

"I think I might need stiches," Topher announces.

I lean forward. "You sure, Toph?"

He lifts his leg, showing us a gash on his shin, and waits for us to weigh in.

Mica and I shrug—we've all had cuts like

that—and Kurt lifts his own leg, which is still healing from a crash a few weeks ago. "Chicks dig scars."

I quickly look away and gulp more water to stop my cheeks from flaming. It's almost like he WANTS me to look at his legs. Not that I'm complaining...

Topher juts his chin at Mica. "Will you come with me?" For all his bluster, Topher is still an insecure little kid deep down. His uncertainty balances the non-stop energy rippling through him ninety percent of the day, and it's what endears him to me.

Mica finishes toweling himself off and hoists his bike onto the rack on his SUV. "Let's go."

I linger on the bumper as they say goodbye and drive off, and Kurt doesn't seem to be in a hurry either. He bumps his knee against mine, his gaze on my cut. "You don't need stitches, do you?" The corner of his mouth curls up, and I bend over, pretending to inspect my knee—anything to avoid looking into his eyes. The scratch is barely visible, the blood long gone.

"It's pretty bad," I say, holding in a laugh. "Might need to be amputated."

This time his shoulder bumps mine, and I wish I could freeze this moment to replay over and over again later. The sun shining on us, the feel of his arm against mine like this is the only place in the world he wants to be. His fingers brush my knee and I hold my breath.

"That'll make it hard to ride." His hand drops to his side, and his eyes meet mine. "I'm really sorry."

My voice comes out a whisper. "You should be."

Something in his eyes makes everything inside me go haywire. My heart races, I can't catch my breath, and a fresh layer of sweat breaks out all over me. I catch my lower lip between my teeth, and his gaze dips to my mouth, just for a moment.

His mouth opens, then closes, like he changed his mind about whatever he was about to say. Every ounce of me wants him to feel what I'm feeling. Is he aware of this pull between us? Is that why he's looking at me like he's trying to figure me out? Or is this all in my head and we're just Kurt and Alex, part of the Fabulous Foursome who never think of each other like that?

Friend Rule #2: Friends before crushes. Even if your friend is the one crushing you.

It takes all my strength, but I stand, putting space between us. He clears his throat and runs a hand through his hair, and even that makes him look good.

Man, I am totally screwed.

"I should probably get going," I say.

He stands. "Yeah."

There's another beat where we're just watching each other, and I'm dying to know what he's thinking.

But neither of us says anything. We grab our bikes and strap them to our separate vehicles. I take my time securing the frame, not ready to leave but not sure what else to do or say. He seems to be moving slower, too, or maybe it's all in my head.

When there's nothing left to do but say goodbye, I lift my hand to wave. "See you Monday."

He frowns. "You're not riding tomorrow?"

I point at my knee. "Amputation, remember?" He smiles, and my stomach flutters. Okay, no more jokes. "I'm working."

He nods, and then he's moving toward me. A thousand thoughts bounce through my head, all of them ending with us kissing, but he grabs my braid and flicks the end against my nose. "See you Monday."

CHAPTER TWO

THE NEXT DAY AT WORK, KURT IS ALL I CAN THINK about. Mica and I work Sundays together at the Bike and Hike Shop, and since the weekends are our busiest time, we've barely had a chance to talk. Not that I'm sure if I want to talk to him about this. The minute I say the words out loud, that I like Kurt as more than a friend, I risk ruining our perfect little group.

Customers come and go in a blur, and I go through the motions, my distraction obvious to the regulars.

It's late afternoon when the crowds finally die down. Mica grabs an apple from his backpack and holds it out to me, offering a bite. I shake my head and let out a long sigh.

"What's wrong with you?" Mica asks.

"It's nothing."

"You've locked yourself out of the register three times, you forgot Butch Cleary's name, and you've been dropping things all day." He takes a bite of the apple and raises his brows at me, daring me to contradict him. "Something's up."

Blanking on Butch's name was the low point of my day. He runs a riding clinic not far from here and comes in every weekend. I've known him for years, yet today I had to rely on calling him Buddy—something Butch frowned at and Mica clearly didn't miss. I grab my water bottle from beneath the counter and take a long drink, stalling.

"Alex." Mica's voice is firm yet soft. "You know you can't hide things from me."

The corner of my mouth lifts in a smile, then fades. "I can't do anything about it, so there's no point telling you."

"Is this about a guy?"

My head snaps up.

He smiles. "Ah, now we're getting somewhere." He takes another bite and chews slowly. "Anyone I know?" The look he gives me says he already knows it's Kurt, but how can he? I've been so careful.

"Why would you think that?"

"Does this have anything to do with the little creek-side wrestling match yesterday?"

And like that, my cheeks flush. I press my hands to them, but that just draws more attention to the sudden spike in my body temperature.

Mica watches me as he finishes his apple. "You don't deny it. Interesting."

I drop my hands and shove them in the pockets of my cargo pants. "Not interesting. Ridiculous." *Impossible*, I add to myself.

The bell on the front door rings as a customer enters. He heads straight for the water bottles, and Mica returns his gaze to me. "Maybe not."

My heart pounds.

I take a deep breath and pick at a scratch on the counter.

Count to three in my head.

Take another breath and try to sound casual. "Why do you say that?"

A smile softens his face, and I know my cover's blown. But he doesn't rub it in. Mica's too sweet for that. "Nothing he's said. Just me paying attention."

A dozen questions leap to the tip of my tongue, none of which I'll ask. My friendship with Kurt is sacred, and a couple fluttery butterflies aren't worth risking what we have for what would surely end in disaster.

"So do you like him?" he asks.

I bite my lip, unsure how to answer, when the customer approaches the counter. I let Mica handle him and am lost in thoughts of Kurt when a giggly voice interrupts my daydream.

"Hey!" My friend Kaylee's standing on the other side of the counter.

"You're way too dolled up for a Sunday afternoon," I say.

She smiles, taking my remark as a compliment. Her brown hair reaches halfway down her back—like mine—but unlike mine, it's curled and tousled and looks like she stepped off the set of a photo shoot. Makeup highlights her already flawless skin and her fitted t-shirt shows off her curves in ways I never dare to.

In the two years I've worked here, this is the first time she's come to visit. Kaylee's not afraid to sweat, but her preferred method of exercise involves yoga mats and stretchy bands. Not bikes and dirt and nature.

I twist a braid around my finger. "What's up?"

She leans against the counter so her cleavage is on display and glances at Mica, who's still helping the customer. "Not much. I was wondering..." she trails off, and I groan inwardly, not wanting to play her game.

We've been friends since elementary school,

and we're so different now that sometimes I wonder if we'd still be friends without our history. Where I'm straightforward and to the point, she likes to draw things out and make the other person guess what she's trying to say.

The customer grabs his bag and heads for the door.

From the corner of my eye, I see Mica smirk at me. "I'm gonna check the display." That's our code for "good luck with this one." We typically use it for obnoxious customers, but in this case, it works.

"You do that," I mumble.

Kaylee leans back so her cleavage isn't lunging for my throat. Her eyes follow Mica as he moves around the store, checking the non-existent display. "You riding next weekend?"

I raise an eyebrow, the expression on my face saying, "When do I not ride on the weekends?"

"Maybe I can join you?"

Mica stretches to grab a bike rack off a high shelf, his insane calves flexing with the effort. Kaylee licks her bottom lip, and I roll my eyes. She's less subtle than most girls, and not really Mica's type, but it could be fun.

"Sure. Meet us at Crestpoint Saturday at ten."

Her finger trails back and forth over the glass

counter. Mica's totally cleaning that later. "Can you... I mean, is it cool if I ride with you? I don't have a rack for my car."

I smile. She actually seems nervous, and match-making is my thing. "My house at nine-thirty."

Her face lights up as Mica returns to the counter. He glances between us like he doesn't want to know what we're talking about, and Kaylee lets out a breath. "Well, I better get going. You two have fun." She waves goodbye, and her hand trails over Mica's shoulder. "See you Saturday."

His eyebrows practically shoot off his head, and I hold in a laugh. When she's gone, he whirls on me. "What did you do?"

I shrug, but can't help the grin that's plastered to my face. "You'll see."

CHAPTER THREE

KAYLEE SURPRISES ME BY BEING A FEW MINUTES early, and we pull into the Crestpoint parking lot before the guys. She's been fidgety since we got in the car, and now she can barely stand still. Once I have our bikes on the ground, I put my hand on my hips and tilt my head at her. "What's going on?"

Her gaze flicks from me to the head of the trail. "I... do you..." She shifts from one foot to the other. "How hard is this trail?"

I give her a soft smile. It's been years since I've seen this side of her. The human, maybe-I'm-not-perfect-at-everything side. "There's a mix of levels here. I'll make sure we stay off the blacks."

Her shoulders relax, and she lets out a breath. "Thanks."

Kurt arrives moments later, and whatever uncertainty Kaylee was feeling flips off like a switch. Her smile brightens, her boobs push out, and all traces of nerves disappear.

Just as mine amp up.

"Hey, Kurt," she says, practically purring. She moves toward his bike and runs a finger over the crossbar. "Our bikes are the same color."

Never mind that black is one of the most common bike colors out there.

"Hi, Kaylee." He raises an eyebrow at me as if to say, "Is she serious?" then unstraps his bike and maneuvers around her to set it on the ground.

Inside, I thrill at the private moment, even if it is at her expense.

"Where are the other guys?" she asks, and I swear she flutters her lashes at him.

But she's here for Mica, isn't she?

Fortunately, Kurt doesn't seem to notice.

I glance at my wrist, even though I don't wear a watch. "Topher's never on time. And Mica usually rides with him." I expect her to react when I say Mica's name, but her gaze hasn't left Kurt.

Or more specifically, his legs.

A spark of jealousy flares through me. What is she doing? Not that I have any claim to Kurt, but...but... she made me think she was interested in Mica.

After several minutes of awkward conversation, Topher parks next to Kurt and hops out of his Jeep. "Hey, newbie!" He waves at Kaylee, oblivious to my current torment. He bows deeply like she's a queen, then straightens and gives her a genuine smile. "Awesome you came out."

Mica eyes me as he gets out of the car. I told him Kaylee invited herself to join us but left out the part about her being interested in him. But based on the way she's hovering around Kurt and hasn't even glanced at Mica, I think I was played.

She rests a hand on Kurt's bicep so he can't help but look at her. "Alex promised you'd go easy on me today."

I said nothing of the sort, and now I'm tempted to trick her onto a black so he'll see how ridiculous she is. I'm not typically a spiteful person, but a little revenge for lying seems appropriate. Kurt catches my eye over Kaylee's head, and I mouth, "Sorry." But there's more than just irritation in his expression. He looks confused.

"We'll skip the blacks," Topher says.

Kaylee gives him a grateful smile.

"You ladies ready?" Mica asks, giving me another questioning look.

"Yeah," I say while shaking my head. I've always said that a bad day riding is better than a day not riding, but something tells me I'm going to have to eat my words.

We mount our bikes and pedal slowly to the start of the trail, with Topher leading and Kurt in front of Kaylee. She looks like she's at an all-you-can-eat buffet with her favorite foods on display in front of her.

The boys quickly get ahead of us, and I use this chance to confront her. "What are you doing?"

"What do you mean?"

"I thought you liked Mica?"

Her lips purse like she's choosing between ice cream flavors, not my best friends. "He's cute, but Kurt." She fans herself. "Have mercy."

Yeah, no kidding.

Her eyebrow quirks. "Do you like him or something?"

Friend Rule #3: Friends don't fight over the same guy.

But how good of a friend is she if she lied about who she likes?

"Me? No!" I answer too quickly, and her eyebrow

stays halfway up her forehead. "You seemed into Mica at the store so I was just surprised."

She shrugs. "What can I say? I appreciate men of all forms." She nods ahead at Kurt, who keeps glancing back at us. "Some more than others."

A sinking feeling grips my stomach and makes it hard to pedal. If I thought I had a chance with Kurt, it's over now. Boys don't resist Kaylee once she sets her sights on them.

Even though I silently plead with Topher to take us on a black, he stays true to his word and sticks to blues. Kaylee does better than I expected, and when we take a break near the creek, my irritation is starting to fade.

Until she goes right up to Kurt and says something too low for me to hear.

I stay with my bike instead of joining the rest of them near the creek and take a long drink of water.

Kaylee lifts her elbow, and Kurt dips his head the way I've imagined him lowering his head to mine. But in my daydreams he doesn't smile at the perky brunette who can have anyone she wants, like he is now. He touches a scrape on her elbow, she giggles, and my chest tightens.

I can't watch this.

Crouching next to my bike, I'm pretending to check my chain when leaves crunch near me.

"Chain loose?" Mica asks.

My fingers poke and prod the greasy chain. Mica's the one person who knows bikes better than I do, so there's no fooling him. I wipe my hands on my shorts and look up at him. "Something like that."

"Can I ask a question?"

How am I such an idiot? Good question. "Sure."

"Why did you let her come if she's into Kurt?"

My eyes roll before I can stop them. "I didn't bring her for Kurt."

His head tilts, then his lips part as understanding hits him. He presses a hand to his chest. "Me?"

I shrug. "She couldn't stop staring at you at the shop the other day, so I figured..."

We both turn as Kaylee doubles over laughing, presumably at something Kurt said. But based on the puzzled look he gives us over her head, he's not in on the joke. Topher's nearby, also laughing, but he lifts his hands at us like he's not sure what's so funny.

"I'm going to kill her," I mumble to myself, but Mica hears.

"If it helps, he doesn't seem into her."

"How can he not be?" I wave a hand in their direction. "Have you seen her?"

He elbows me in the side. "Have you seen you? Besides, it's not all about looks. She's grating, self-centered, and doesn't actually listen when people talk. Not good qualities in my book."

"You, sir, have a way with words."

He gives me a serious look. "Maybe you should talk to him."

"Maybe you can talk to him for me."

"What, are we in middle school?"

I sigh. "I'd rather take a header into the creek."

"It worked last week." He smirks, and I smack his arm.

"I'll think about it."

We join the others by the creek. Mica takes one for the team and asks Kaylee to see her elbow.

I dip my hand in the cool water and run my fingers over the smooth rocks at the bottom. Black grime from my chain sticks to them, and I yank my hand back, not wanting to leave any trace of pollution here.

"You okay?" Kurt's voice startles me, and I *do* almost take a header into the creek. He's squatting next to me, his bare leg inches from mine.

"I'm just feeling a little off today."

"Me too," he says, and I turn to face him. His dark eyes lock onto mine, and my heart beats so loudly he can probably hear it over Kaylee's giggling. "Can I ask you something?"

I smile. "What is it with you boys and your questions?" He lifts an eyebrow, and I nod. "Ask away."

He plucks a rock from the creek bed and bounces it in his hand, not looking at me. "Did you..." Bounce. Bounce, bounce. "Did you think I'd be into her?" He nods in Kaylee's direction.

"No, definitely not."

"Then why..."

"I thought she liked Mica. She made it seem that way when she invited herself." I pick up my greasy rock and roll it in my hand while I take a deep breath. "So you're not?"

"No, definitely not." His use of my words loosens the tension in my gut.

"Why not?" Now we're both bouncing our rocks.

After what feels like forever, he says, "You really don't know?"

My heart screams what I want, but life doesn't work out that way. My parents are a prime example of that. Which is why I focus on helping my friends find love—not myself. But something about the way Kurt is looking at me says maybe I've been wrong to try to hide my feelings.

He drops his rock with a splash, then reaches

for my braid and twists it around his hand. But instead of tugging or hitting me with it like he normally does, he holds on like he's afraid I'll slip away. His hand brushes my neck, sending a million butterflies loose in my stomach. My eyes drift shut, and when I open them, his face is exposed, raw. Vulnerable.

Like we're seeing each other for the first time.

"Are you guys about ready?" Kaylee's voice obliterates the butterflies.

I toss my rock near a tree and push to my feet, forcing Kurt to let go of my braid. Even though I couldn't feel his touch, I miss it as soon as it's gone. Kaylee's watching us with her hip pushed out, arms crossed, and an expression that's definitely not flirtatious.

"You guys go ahead," Kurt says. "Alex's chain needs a little TLC."

A flood of emotions whoosh through me so fast all I hear is the roar of my pulse in my head. He must have been watching me while Kaylee was hitting on him.

Me.

Kaylee's lips tighten into a scowl, but Topher and Mica exchange smiles.

"Yeah it does." Topher laughs, and Mica shoves his shoulder.

"We'll find you on the trail," Mica says.

I don't dare look at Kurt until they're swallowed by the forest and I feel a tug on my braid. He's looking at my hair in his hand.

"I've always liked these," he says, a wistful smile playing on his lips.

My nerve endings are on fire, but I somehow manage to laugh. "Is that why you're always hitting me with them?" My voice is light, teasing.

On reflex, I touch my braid—the one he's twirling between his fingers—and our hands touch. But instead of moving away, his fingers twist with mine.

Everything stops. My breathing, the birds in the trees high above, even the water near our feet. Time stands still as his other hand grazes my arm. His touch is feather-light over my collarbone, and when his fingers slide into the hair at the base of my neck my knees go weak.

"They're a nice excuse," he says.

I'm ninety-nine percent certain I know where this is going, but I need to make sure. "For what?"

"To touch you." His voice is soft, drawing my body toward him.

My free hand drifts to his bicep—the same arm Kaylee tried to claim earlier—and the intensity in his gaze nearly sets me on fire. Then he's dipping his head toward mine.

Our lips touch first, a gentle brush asking permission, then we move closer until our bodies press together. As if thinking the same thing, we untangle our hands, each reaching for the other as the kiss deepens.

My fingers trail over his shoulder, up his neck, and into his hair, while his free hand wraps around my waist, holding me firmly against him.

In the moments I dared to dream this might happen, this is how I imagined it—in the middle of the woods with the sun shining down on us through the trees.

His lips move from my mouth to my neck, and I sigh against him. "Why haven't we done this before?" I ask.

"Believe me, I've wanted to."

I pull back to look him in the eyes, my heart full. All the fear I had over losing him as a friend vanishes as I realize how much more we can have. How being friends first doesn't mean it can never happen—it means it'll be that much better when it does.

As his lips capture mine, one final thought dances through my mind: falling for your best friend totally rules.

Thank you for reading "The Friend Rules" by Melanie Hooyenga! To connect with Melanie and learn more about her books and special offers, visit www.melaniehoo.com.

MORE THAN
A LIST

Yesenia Vargas

CHAPTER ONE

I SAT ON THE LIVING ROOM COUCH, STARING AT my phone and wishing I was the one going to the Demi Lovato concert tonight.

A girl from my math class had posted about it on Instagram, saying she and her group of friends were already in Atlanta gearing up for the night of a lifetime.

I kept on scrolling through my Instagram feed, trying to get the concert out of my mind. My dad was heading out of town today anyway. He'd never let me go at the last minute, and the first thing he'd ask was who I was going with. I had a handful of friends at school, but we'd grown apart the last few months, and I knew they were busy with graduation anyway.

I came to another post and stopped scrolling. It

was from one of my friends, Kelly. We hadn't talked in a while, but I usually knew what was going on with her because she posted several times a day.

This one featured her with a silly exasperated expression on her face. I could tell she was shopping somewhere. Kelly's mom was behind her with a cart full of supplies for her dorm, and it looked like she was about to put something else in there. I could make out a metallic desk lamp, and bed sheets. Kelly was going away to college in August, but apparently, her mom was already freaking out about it and buying everything in sight.

I grinned to myself before reading the caption.

UGHHH. My mom won't stop buying stuff for my dorm. I'm pretty sure it won't even all fit in there! SEND HELPPPP #momsofinstagram #isitsummeryet

The smile slowly faded from my face and morphed into pain. The post was funny—that was Kelly. But the post hit too close to home.

I turned off my phone and threw it toward the opposite end of the couch before bringing my knees up to my chest and wrapping my arms around them.

I took a deep breath, trying to calm down. I was tired of crying. I didn't want to go back to breaking down every time I thought of my mom. It had been six months, but time had frozen with her death. I knew I had to move on at some point, even though life felt all kinds of wrong without her in it.

I bit my lip, hard, and blinked away the tears as I practiced deep breathing. Then I grabbed my phone, stuck it in my back pocket, and headed upstairs. Sometimes all it took was a movie on TV or an unguarded comment from one of my teachers, but something always reminded me of her being gone.

I slowly opened the door to her studio. It was the smallest room in the house, but she had loved spending time in here working on her art. Local schools and libraries commissioned her a few times a year to create something for their buildings, usually murals. Whatever it was, mom dreamed up all her pieces in here first.

I made my way over to the window and opened the blinds, letting the sun's rays cover the room with their morning light. The room seemed to come alive again. I walked over to my mom's desk and sat down.

Everything was still there. Whiteboards and calendars hung on the wall, and sketchpads with pastels and colored pencils covered her desk. A couple of easels propping up blank canvases were posted around the room, just the way she had left them. My dad had wanted to empty the room out not long after the funeral, but I had asked him to leave it a while longer. And here it still was, six months later.

I brushed my fingers on the wooden desk. I missed my mom more than ever. The doctors had found the cancer when I was in eighth grade. After a while, the doctor told us she was getting better, that it was going away. That she had beat it. But last year, it'd come back with a vengeance and taken her away in a matter of weeks. A few more months, and she would have been here to see me graduate tomorrow.

But life didn't work that way. At least not for us.

I exhaled and paged through some of her sketchpads, tears brimming my eyes and making everything blurry. I set those aside and touched all the tiny things left on the surface of her desk. Paperclips. Pencils of different kinds. Erasers. A used-up checkbook. Her favorite pencil sharpener. So many pieces of her were still here.

I spun around in her desk chair, my hand still on the desk as if I were holding onto it. The empty moving boxes my dad had carted in here after the funeral sat unwanted in the corner.

A knock sounded at the door, and he walked in. My dad was in his usual suit and tie, and there was a carry-on bag behind him. His eyes lit up as he gave me a soft smile, but I noticed the way they dimmed when he glanced around the room. "Hey, pumpkin. I'm heading out. Are you sure you'll be okay?"

I looked up at him. "Yeah, of course. I was just thinking I could start sorting through some of Mom's things while I wait for Aunt Sheryl to pick me up."

He nodded and gave me that look. The same one he always gave me when my mom came up. It said he was sad about losing his wife but was completely devastated that his daughter had lost her mother.

"Okay, then," he said. "I'll be back tomorrow just in time for your graduation. Then we'll have dinner at your favorite place."

"That sounds great, Dad. I can't wait."

He sighed and put his hand on my head, then my shoulder. "How are you eighteen already? It seems like just yesterday your mom and I were walking you into pre-K. Remember you said your name was Wiley? You couldn't say Riley."

I laughed. "Dad, you promised you wouldn't do or say anything embarrassing tomorrow."

"Did I?" he said with a little gleam in his eye.

I stood up and squeezed him. He hugged me back and kissed me on the forehead. "Call me if you need me. But I'm sure you'll be fine."

"I will," I said and then teased, "I mean, I *am* legally an adult now. You don't have to worry about me."

"I always do." He kissed me on the head one more time. "Promise you'll save me leftovers? You know that shrimp fried rice is my favorite."

"Definitely."

My Aunt Sheryl and I always got Chinese take-out when we hung out, and my dad loved it. I always saved him some. It was our thing.

He gave me one more hug, and then he was gone, off on another business trip. I sat back down and opened the top drawer of my mom's desk. It had the usual office and art supplies. I grabbed three cardboard boxes and started sorting things into Keep, Donate, and Trash.

I was on her filing cabinet when I came across the envelope. It wasn't the usual flimsy white envelope. This one was thick and cream-colored—the fancy kind. And it had my name on the front, in my mom's handwriting. I'd recognize it anywhere.

I opened it without thinking, wondering if I'd find my birth certificate or passport or something like that. But what I found was a short letter.

The words inside were pretty much what she had said to me before she'd died.

My beautiful Riley,

I'm so sorry I had to leave you so soon. I wish I had more time to see you grow up, but you're strong. Remember that life won't give you anything you can't handle.

You're blooming into a young woman before my eyes, and it breaks my heart that I won't be there to see it. Oh, what I would give to watch you experience what's still ahead of you and be there for you when life is hard.

I wish I could have seen you as a lovely blushing bride on your wedding day or be the extra set of arms you need when you have a newborn. Your dad will have to do it for me.

Riley, know that I'll always be with you. No matter what, I'm proud of you, and we love you so much.

You've got this.

Mom

Her words became illegible through the fresh tears in my eyes. My mouth turned upward at the same time. I couldn't believe I'd have something like this from her to keep forever but I was also devastated I wouldn't get another letter from her again.

There was something else too. My fingers found a second sheet. I slid the letter behind it and scanned the page in front of me.

A list. I recognized it right away.

We had created a checklist during my freshman year while she had been in remission. It had been our way of celebrating her victory against breast cancer. The list contained everything we'd do together by the time I graduated high school, almost like a reverse bucket list. There were only a handful of items. We'd meant to add to it, but I guess we'd forgotten about it. At least I had. My mom hadn't. Her letter was dated not long before she'd passed away.

I blinked several times, my eyes full of tears again as I realized that she had wanted me to do all of this before I graduated. I sat down, biting my trembling lip as I thought of her writing this letter and enclosing the list for me.

I read through it again, remembering the fun we had writing down every item.

Mom had bent over the paper, shielding it from me as she wrote down the last one. She laughed and pushed the paper toward me. "You'll need to do this one without me."

Have my first kiss.

I had laughed so hard my stomach hurt.

"You can't go off to college without having had your first kiss," she'd said, still smiling, but her tone told me she was completely serious.

The sound of the doorbell jarred me back to reality. I walked downstairs, sure my dad had forgotten something and come back so I swung the front door open.

Only it wasn't my dad. Axel, my best friend and neighbor, stood in the doorway.

"Morning," he said, walking in. Then his eyes went to the letter still in my hand. "What's that?"

I shut the door behind him and ran my thumb over the letter in my hand. "Oh, it's...my mom's. I found it in her office."

"Oh. Okay. That's cool," He shoved his hands in his pockets and avoided my eyes. He knew this was still hard for me to talk about. So I usually didn't.

I folded up the list and looked at him. "So, what are you up to?"

Axel relaxed a little. "I was going to ask you the same thing. My mom and brothers are shopping the whole day, and I have nothing to do. You want to watch a movie or something later? Order takeout?" Then he paused. "But if you're busy, that's okay—"

"No, uh, actually," I started, taking a seat on the couch. I pulled the letter out again.

Axel sat down beside me.

I took a breath. "I was just looking at this. It's a list of things I was supposed to do before graduating.

My mom and I came up with it a while back, when she'd gotten better. I just found it again, but graduation's tomorrow. So much for doing it."

My voice came out a little wobbly at the end, and my throat tightened.

I wanted to say I wished I had found it sooner, but I didn't want to cry in front of him.

Axel held out his hand. "May I?"

I nodded and gave him the list. I immediately felt calmer. He read it for a minute. "This isn't that long. I bet we could do it."

I looked at him, a small smile forming on my face.

"I mean, not we, you, obviously, but I'll come with you. Keep you safe and whatnot..."

I involuntarily snorted, already feeling better. That was Axel, and why he'd become my closest friend this year. He was such a gentleman, the guy who helped you carry something heavy without having to ask him. Who would do anything to make your day a little brighter.

"What? I'm the better driver," he said with a laugh and then looked at the list again. "Road trip? Totally doable. Concert..."

He paused to think.

"The Demi concert is actually happening

tonight," I said. "But no way I can go. My dad would kill me if I just went, especially on my own."

Aunt Sheryl probably wouldn't think it was a good idea either.

"Oh yeah. Isn't it a few hours away?"

I nodded. "Like three."

Axel looked at the clock on our living room wall. "We could totally make it if you wanted."

I laughed. "No way."

"And this dye your hair thing. We could do that on the way. Pit stop."

"I cannot believe you," I said, but I was having fun listening to him.

"Now this first kiss thing," he said, and I felt my cheeks turn hot. "I don't have a lot to work with here, but I'm sure I can find you someone at that concert. Maybe the hair dye thing will help."

I grabbed a cushion and swung it at his head, but we were both laughing.

"Seriously, though," he said. "We've got nothing to do tonight and tomorrow. You said your dad's out of town? I'll tell my mom I'm staying with a friend tonight. She won't care."

"My aunt is supposed to be picking me up later so I can stay at her place."

Axel thought for a moment. "Tell her your dad

didn't go out of town after all. His trip got cancelled." He shrugged.

I stared at him and couldn't help but smile. "Axel, he would murder me if I snuck off. Like murder me. Forget graduating and going to college."

"He won't find out, Riley. Trust me. And we'll be back before he is." He raised his eyebrows repeatedly with a silly grin on his face.

He had me laughing again, but I thought about what he was proposing. "You know, he gets so busy he doesn't usually call except on his way back and it's usually me, not my aunt..."

"There you go," Axel said, raising his arms. "We can totally do this. Who says you can't do everything on this list by graduation?"

"Axel, we cannot miss graduation."

He stood up. "We won't miss graduation. We have plenty of time." He pointed to the list. "Your mom wanted you to have an adventure before heading off to college. We should do it."

I sighed and stood up. "Your car or mine?"

CHAPTER TWO

AN HOUR LATER, WE EACH HAD A SMALL DUFFEL bag ready. I bought the tickets online with most of my savings, Axel was analyzing the route on his GPS app, and I had called my aunt, lying to her and telling her my dad's trip had been cancelled after all.

It was way easier than I imagined, both the lying part and how quickly she believed me. It turned out something had come up for her anyway.

Now we were on the road, our stuff in the back and the radio on loud as we cruised down the freeway. Just outside of town, Axel pulled into a tiny gas station.

"Let's go ahead and fill her up," he said, hopping out of my Honda and pulling out his wallet. "You paid for the tickets. I got gas, hotel, and food."

I gave him a hug. "I'll go grab us some snacks."

A few minutes later, we were on our way again, this time with enough Doritos, Rice Krispies Treats, doughnuts, nachos, sour gummy worms, and Dr. Pepper to hold us over until after college. And just like I had imagined my first road trip back in ninth grade, there was lots of music and bad karaoke. I pulled out and we took our first selfie. Obviously, I couldn't share it, but we had to save the memories. I stared at the picture, the bittersweet moment hitting my chest like a hammer. This should have been my mom and me, but I was also grateful I had ended up here with Axel.

In between songs, I rolled down the window and stared out toward the horizon, letting my hair fly uncontrollably in the wind. The cool air felt incredible against my face and neck, and I let my head fall back as Axel drove us closer and closer to freedom.

A few minutes later, I rolled the window back up and turned to Axel.

"You look like Medusa or something," he said with a grin.

I tried to gain control of my hair but quickly gave up. "Want me to drive for a while?"

"Um, I'd like it if we actually made it to the concert tonight in one piece."

I scoffed. "I am a good driver,"

Now he scoffed. "Uh huh. Tell that to Mrs. Peters' mailbox. You killed it."

I crossed my arms and rolled my eyes. "That was almost a year ago. Besides, I replaced it."

Axel didn't look convinced, though.

"I'm hungry," I said. "For real food."

"Me too," he said. Twenty minutes later, we were pulling into a small town off the exit.

"There are some interesting places to eat here," I said, looking out the window. "Rosita's Diner. Ooh, that looks good. Let's go there."

Axel pulled in, and not too long after that, we were having the best burgers we'd ever tasted and chatting with Rosita herself. She was plump and sweet and reminded me of Mrs. Peters.

"You kids aren't from around here, are you?" she asked.

We shook our heads. "We're on our way to a concert. Road trip," I explained.

"We graduate tomorrow," Axel went on. "So we thought we'd have one last adventure."

I smiled at him.

"Well, that sounds lovely," she said. "Just make sure you take care of your girlfriend here. Concerts can get a little crazy, I hear."

Axel stammered, and I blushed again, but it was too late to correct her.

"Since you're here, try my apple pie. On the house. For making it to graduation. Congratulations to you both."

Then she was gone, and Axel and I were left staring at each other. Then we burst out laughing.

I caught my breath enough to finish my fries. "Remind me to thank you when all of this is over."

"I don't know about you, but this trip was worth it for coming here alone. Free apple pie," Axel said, pleased. "Promise me we'll come back someday."

"Deal," I asked, meeting his eyes.

He paid, and we walked out of Rosita's more stuffed full of good food than we've ever been in our lives.

"I'm not gonna lie." Axel yawned. He must have been as sleepy as me. "She cooks better than my mom."

Then he stopped, and I bumped into him.

"What is it?" I asked. "You're not gonna barf, are you? Because that would ruin this trip. And our friendship."

He just shook his head and pointed, turning around to see my reaction. A grin formed on his lips as he watched me read the sign.

"A hair salon? Named Kuts and Kolors? You

want me to get my hair done at a place that spells cuts and colors with a k?"

A satisfied gleam in his eye, he nodded.

The entire way to the salon, I was freaking out. What if they ruined my hair right before graduation—those pictures would last a lifetime.

* * *

At Kuts and Kolors, a girl named Kortney worked to wrap well over a dozen little pieces of my plain brown hair in aluminum foil. I stared in the mirror in front of me, not believing I was doing this.

But it was on the list. My mom had been ready to take me to get my hair dyed black when she was in remission, and I had totally chickened out.

I took a deep breath. No more of that. This was part of the adventure. And part of a new me. I wasn't sure how I felt about that last part. Maybe I'd know once I saw how my hair looked in a couple hours.

Axel leaned forward in his seat from the nearby waiting area. "Your hair reminds me of my mom's tamales. It's making me hungry again."

The hair stylist laughed and folded another strand into the foil. "Okay, I'm all done here. We'll let it sit for a few minutes, and then I'll be back."

There was one other lady in here, a much older lady with gray hair. Her hair style looked like it

158

belonged in the fifties. I wondered if mine would turn out anything like I had pictured in my head.

I turned back to Axel.

"I can't believe I'm doing this," I said. "I'm pretty sure my dad's gonna find out I was up to something when he sees me with red hair."

The old lady stood up and took off the poncho-looking thing covering her clothes. "You'd be surprised at what men fail to notice."

Axel and I laughed.

"That's true," I said, looking at her through the mirror.

"Five dollars your dad doesn't even notice," Axel said.

"Deal," I said with a smile.

We waited in silence for the chemicals to color my hair. Soon Axel's soft snores filled the salon, and I saw him drooped over in his chair.

The stylist whispered to me, "Want me to take these out while sleeping beauty naps over there?"

She washed, dried, and styled my hair, and Axel slept through it all. Then, the moment of truth. She turned me to face the mirror, and I gasped. The shade of dark crimson my hair had turned out to be was absolutely perfect.

"I can't get over this color on you," she said,

tousling a wave in my do. "It really brings out your sun-kissed skin tone."

I beamed. "Thanks."

We made our way to the front, and I paid up, effectively depleting the rest of my savings. I walked over to Axel, who was still snoring in his chair.

"Heavy sleeper," the hair stylist said with a small smile.

"Oh yeah," I said. I turned back to Axel and gently knocked him slightly on the head. "Wake up, sleepy head. It's time to go."

That woke him up. He rubbed the sleep from his eyes and looked around before he found me. "You done?"

I didn't have to answer that question because he stood up, his gaze fixed on me. Or rather, my hair.

"Whoa," he said. "You look...really great."

"Thanks." My ears grew hot under my locks. "We should get going."

His hand came up, and he brushed his fingers over my hair, a look on his face I'd never seen before.

A weird feeling rose in my chest as I looked at Axel. For the first time, I noticed the curve of his bottom lip and how his shirt hugged his wide shoulders perfectly. Meanwhile, my brain battled with a million different thoughts, but my body froze like a deer in headlights at his touch. A part of me wanted to step closer to Axel while another panicked, screaming that we were best friends.

He seemed to come back to reality as he put his hand down and finally looked at me.

"Sorry. It's just...really red. I mean, it's nice," he said kind of quieter than usual.

I smiled at him, not able to meet his eyes anymore, and turned towards the door. "Come on."

We got back on the road, riding in an awkward silence. Pretty soon, Axel twisted the volume knob and started singing. Then I did too, closing my eyes and letting the music take over. We both did. I'd never sung like this in front of him, though. Loud and heartfelt and with everything inside me.

Maybe it was the new hair. I couldn't stop staring at it.

An hour and a half later, the sun dipped low in the sky, and a sign on the road said we were closer than ever to our destination.

I looked at the GPS on his phone. "Just a few more minutes."

"I am getting so pumped for this thing," he said. "Even if it is Demi Lovato."

I laughed. "I'm excited too. Have you ever been to a concert before?"

He shook his head. "Nope. I mean, plenty of road trips because we visit my grandparents in Mexico every summer and sometimes at Christmas too. But no concerts."

We were both doing something completely new tonight then.

I opened up my second bag of gummy worms and grabbed a few for Axel. He leaned over and opened his mouth. I shoved them in.

"Thanks," he said, and all I could do was smile. A minute later, he said, "You should look for a Holiday Inn or something. We can drop off our bags there, and then we can go straight back to our room whenever the concert is over. We probably shouldn't be looking for somewhere to stay for the night at like two in the morning."

"Good point," I said, pulling out my phone and tapping away. "It looks like there's one not too far from the concert."

I set the GPS to the new location and went back to eating more candy and staring at the road.

"It's the next exit," I said, reading the sign.

A cloud of smoke rose from the hood just as I said it.

"Uh oh," Axel said, sitting up and checking his mirrors. "I'm pulling over."

I turned around. "You're clear."

He switched lanes, his foot already off the gas and on the brakes as he shifted onto the shoulder.

He looked at the dash, so I did too. "What is it?"

"The temperature is way up." He put the car in park and turned it off. "Wait here."

Eighteen wheelers whooshed by like thunder as he waited for traffic to clear so he could get out.

Oh, man. I sat back in my seat and blinked, wondering what we were supposed to do now. What if we came all this way just to break down and not make it to the concert?

Then we'd have to call my dad for sure to come get us. And I'd be in so much trouble.

Maybe this hadn't been such a smart idea after all.

Axel finally opened his door and ran around to the hood of the car. He lifted it, and that's when I saw that it was steam, not smoke, coming from the left part of the car.

I got out and joined him. "I think it needs more water," he said. "I guess I should have checked it before we left."

I looked at him. "We don't have water. All we have is Dr. Pepper."

He looked down at the car again. At least the

steam was starting to go away. "I don't think that's gonna work."

I bit my lip. "Maybe we can walk to a gas station?"

"That would take at least an hour. Probably more by the time we get back here."

"The concert starts in an hour," I said more to myself than anything.

We stood like that for a full minute, not sure what to do next.

"Maybe I should just call my dad," I said, looking up at Axel.

He looked serious, like he wanted to tell me no. "Maybe you're right. Sorry I couldn't get you to the concert, Riley."

I instinctively took his hand. "It's not your fault. Besides, we had a ton of fun already." Axel's hand squeezed mine, and my heart faltered for a second before I resumed my train of thought. "Not to mention this new hair."

He smiled, but the moment turned awkward when we realized we were still holding hands. I pulled mine back, and he did the same.

"I should call my dad, then." I pulled up my contacts, trying to focus on finding his number.

Just before I tapped his name, though, a black

truck joined us on the shoulder, parking just behind us. Axel and I glanced at each other for a second before he walked around to meet whoever was stepping out of the truck.

"Hello, there," the man called. He looked like a cowboy. He wore fitted light wash jeans and a long-sleeved plaid button-up. Not to mention his cowboy hat and boots. He looked around my dad's age. "You two got car trouble?"

"Yeah, uh, it actually needs water," Axel said as they walked around to the hood.

I followed them, not sure what I was supposed to be doing.

"Okay, let's take a look," the man said and turned to face us. "I'm Jack, by the way."

He shook Axel's hand.

"Axel. Nice to meet you," Axel replied. "Thanks for stopping."

Jack nodded.

"I'm Riley," I piped up.

"Pleasure, Riley," he said with a smile that lit up his eyes.

Jack went back checking under the hood, inspecting this and that. "Yep, it just needs a little water."

"Would it be too much to ask for a ride to the nearest gas station?" Axel tried.

Jack smiled and adjusted his hat. "I can do you one better." He walked back to his truck, and a minute later, he was back with a full gallon of water. "I always carry a couple of these just in case."

Axel's eyes lit up, and I'm sure I had the same expression on my face.

"Thank you so much," I said. Jack smiled as he poured the water in.

"Happy to help." He left with a wave and his empty gallon.

We hopped back into my car and Axel turned the ignition. We gave it a second to be sure, then Axel and I high-fived and whooped. My car was back to normal.

Axel pulled onto the shoulder, right behind Jack's truck.

"We're going to make it!" I said. "We're only a bit behind schedule."

Axel pshed at me. "We're right on schedule. Who's ever on time for a concert?" We smiled at each other and got back to staring at the road ahead of us, closer than ever to completing my list.

I thought of my mom looking down at us, happy to see me living life and making memories.

CHAPTER THREE

THE CONCERT WAS LOUD AND DARK, BUT WITH crazy-colored lights everywhere. And the people. There were so many people. Older people. Kids my age. Lots of kids my age.

A girl with short blonde hair shouted something at me.

"What?" I yelled back.

"I love your hair!"

"Thanks!" I shouted back with a smile.

Axel nudged my arm, grinning at me. He didn't need to say anything for me to hear his "I told you so."

Still smiling, I turned my gaze toward the stage. We didn't have the best seats, but we could see Demi well enough, and her voice was just as beautiful as on

TV. Axel and I had a special meeting spot in case we got separated (his idea), but if we stayed this close the entire time, we wouldn't need it.

We were closer than ever before. I could feel the warmth of his body near mine as we sang and screamed along with everyone else. With every person in the crowd singing the lyrics, it was like we were all in sync, brought together here and now by this talented singer.

Near the end of the concert, during my favorite song, Axel tapped my shoulder. I looked up at him, his face near mine. He came close to my ear.

"Another thing crossed off your checklist," he shouted.

I nodded and smiled, mouthing a sincere thank you. I knew I couldn't have done this without him. I never would have had the courage to get here alone and make my mom's checklist a reality.

Axel was already turned back to the stage. That same feeling in my chest rose again as I took him in.

Oh god. There was one more thing on that list, and I wasn't sure I would have the courage to do it even a second from now. Axel had been a friend since we were kids, and my closest friend in the past year, but that's not why I was about to do this. In the past several hours, he'd become even more to me.

I wrapped my hand in his, and he turned to me,

his expression surprised and unsure. He studied me for a second. He blinked, his mouth opening a little as he understood.

Then I stood on my tiptoes, reached up for him, and took his face in my hands, my eyes automatically closing. His hands landed on my waist and brought me closer as our mouths met. I sank into our kiss, Demi's music filling my ears, making this moment unforgettable.

What seemed like both an eon and a nanosecond later, we pulled away. Axel put his arm around me, his chin resting on my head. I put my arm around him too, and we went back to listening to Demi. I wondered if my heart could feel any fuller than right now.

In that moment, it felt like the concert would never end, but at the same time, it was over too soon. I realized I wanted to be on this trip forever, maybe forget about graduation.

We walked back to our room at the Holiday Inn.

I held Axel's hand as we made our way down the block. What had been awkward just a few hours ago now felt completely right, even if it meant I could hardly think straight. "That...was the best night of my life," I said.

"Mine too," Axel said, squeezing my hand.

I laughed. "You don't even like Demi," I said.

"I do now," he replied. "She's good. Plus, I was with you."

My stomach did a somersault as I smiled up at him.

We got back to the room and went right for our snacks, talking and reliving the past few hours. Things weren't awkward anymore. They felt just right.

When I couldn't keep my eyes open any longer, I grabbed my toothbrush and headed to the bathroom with a change of clothes. Something comfortable to sleep in.

Axel had the list in his hand when I walked back into the room. He had changed too. He grabbed a pen from the desk. "Want to do the honors?"

All of a sudden, it felt like this journey was about both of us. I realized I was more than fine sharing this with Axel.

I walked over, and we sat on the bed together. I took the pen and looked down at the list, reading over it one more time. This was it. I took a deep breath.

"First road trip. Check." I crossed each item off as I read. "First hair dye. Check. First concert. Check."

With each checkmark, the tears came a little closer to the surface, even though today had been the happiest I'd been in a long time.

Every new experience that I lived, I'd now have

to do without my mom, the one person who was supposed to be there for me. This was only the beginning of that.

I exhaled and pushed the sadness away. She *was* with me, and I wasn't alone. I had my dad.

I had Axel.

My cheeks felt a little hot as my eyes landed on the last item.

"I think you're forgetting one," Axel said with a tease. His voice broke the silence and brought me back to the present.

I smiled but crossed off the first kiss without looking up. I put the pen down. The list was done.

Deciding to do all of this without my mom hadn't been easy, but a weight lifted off my chest now that I was on the other side.

A moment later, Axel turned towards me and gently lifted my chin until our eyes met. His mouth was hardly an inch or two from mine when he said, "You know I've liked you since the sixth grade?" His voice was just above a whisper.

I almost gasped. "Why didn't you ever say anything?"

He blinked. "Did you feel the same way?" he asked.

I looked down for a second before shaking my head the slightest bit.

"I didn't want to lose you as a friend," Axel said.

Neither of us said anything for a moment or two, at least not out loud. Inside, I was screaming at myself, wondering why I'd never seen it before. But maybe he was right.

My breath hitched as he came in close but held off on contact. My gut told me he still wasn't sure about us. He wanted me to be sure about this.

His hand traveled up near my ear and cheek, and my eyes closed on their own. My skin buzzed with ecstasy when his forehead touched my own. I thought my heart might leap out of my chest from beating so hard and still he wasn't closing the gap between us.

So I did it without thinking. My arm closest to Axel moved to his neck, and I pulled him towards me. I found his mouth in an instant. My body finally relaxed as we sank into our kiss.

We pulled away slowly. I looked at the list again and brought it to my chest, tears pooling in my eyes. What was going on with me? This day couldn't have ended any better.

"You okay?" he asked quietly, taking my hand.

I nodded. "I just miss her. I wish we could have

done this stuff together like we planned. But getting to do it with you was also really cool."

He hugged me, and I let the tears fall. How was it possible to be this sad and this happy at the same time? It didn't make sense.

I lay down, the warmth of the bed calling to me. My hand reached for Axel until he was beside me. I turned my body toward him, my hand wrapping around his torso as he pulled me in close with his arm. My breathing slowed, and I let my eyelids turn the world dark. The sun would be up soon.

Before I was too far gone, Axel got up and lay the covers over me. His lips brushed my forehead, and then I drifted off into sleep.

CHAPTER FOUR

THE SOUND OF MY PHONE GOING OFF WOKE ME up the next morning. I sat up, remembering where I was and wondering who could be calling me.

My stomach sank as I saw my dad's caller ID on the screen. I looked around. Axel was fast asleep on the couch, a wool blanket over his body.

Should I answer? I pressed the green button. "Hello?"

Axel rolled over and opened his eyes, watching me.

"Riley, where have you been? I just talked to your Aunt Sheryl, and she told me what you told her yesterday. Why would you say that? And where are you?"

I cringed. He did not sound happy.

"Sorry, Dad. I'm okay. I promise."

"Where are you? I'm on my way home. I'll come pick you up."

He'd left his business trip early? Uh oh.

"I checked the credit card account. There's a charge for a hotel room? Where'd you go? And why wouldn't you just tell me, Riley? We raised you better than this."

Now he sounded disappointed, which was a thousand times worse than him being angry. Axel sat down next to me, but I didn't look at him.

"I'm sorry, Dad. I promise I'll be home soon. I'm okay."

"Don't do this to me again, Riley, you hear me?" he said, his voice calm for the first time the entire conversation.

I promised to be home by the time he was, and we hung up.

"Was that..." Axel started.

"My dad," I said, finally meeting his eyes. "He knows."

"Oh, man," Axel said. "Am I dead meat? Will my mom ever find my remains?"

For some reason, I couldn't bring myself to laugh, and he sounded like he wasn't quite joking either.

"It's okay. I'll explain everything. He has to understand. But we've got to go." I got up and grabbed my duffel bag, and Axel packed his stuff too.

We did a last scan around the room, and I pocketed the checklist before walking out.

"I'm hungry," I said as we left the hotel parking lot.

Axel pulled into a nearby drive-thru for a late breakfast.

"It was fun while it lasted," Axel offered once we were done eating and on the freeway.

I nodded and stared out the window. How was I going to explain this to my dad?

Yesterday, taking this risk hadn't sounded that bad. And we had fun, but more important than that, I had done everything on that list. Everything my mom wanted for me.

And our kiss. That meant a lot. In the past year, I'd grown to trust Axel more than anyone because he'd been there for me. He had been an exceptional friend, never crossing a line or expecting anything more than friendship from me. But last night, my feelings for him had changed, and that wouldn't have happened without this trip or anything else on that list.

I thought about all that and more as we drove

home, whooshing past the green pines and the warming sun, Axel's hand in mine.

*　*　*

By the time we pulled into my driveway, I was supposed to be getting ready for graduation. We had to leave in an hour for rehearsal.

I looked over at Axel and told him he could go straight home if he wanted. I wouldn't be mad. He didn't have to face my dad.

But he answered by getting out of the car. I did the same. We met at the hood.

Then he took my hand. "This was my idea. As scary as your dad is, I couldn't live with myself if I let you go in there by yourself."

I gave him a small smile as we walked inside together, hand in hand.

Dad was already waiting for us in the living room. He did a double-take once he saw Axel behind me. His eyebrows almost reached his receding hairline when he saw us holding hands.

"Riley, Axel, what's the meaning of this?" he asked, his face turning a shade of red I hadn't seen in a very long time.

"Good afternoon, Mr. Stephens," Axel said, not letting go of my hand.

"Dad, I'm sorry we worried you. I should have told—"

"Told me what, Riley? Where have you been the past 24 hours? Have you at least been...safe?" He looked away for the first time.

I wanted to curl up and die, and from Axel's expression, I guessed he felt the same.

"Dad, it wasn't like that, I promise. We went to a concert. Nothing happened," I said. "I mean—"

"You mean what?" he asked, his voice angry again.

"I mean, Axel has always been my friend, Dad," I said, trying to just get the words out. "And now he's more. But we didn't do anything...like that. I promise."

"We promise, sir. I'm sorry too. I guess this was my idea—"

Now my dad turned to him, a vein in his temple looking dangerously close to rupturing. "This was your idea?" he demanded. "Axel, I can't believe—"

"Dad!" I went over to him. This was going all wrong, and I still hadn't been able to tell him the most important part. He finally looked at me and started breathing normally. "Can we please talk, just you and me?"

I turned back to Axel, and he nodded. I looked at my dad again.

"Okay," he said. He turned to Axel. "But we're not done yet, young man."

"Yes, sir," he said, turning to leave.

The front door closed behind him, and Dad and I sat on the couch. I gave him a hug, and after a second, he hugged me back.

"Riley, do you know what started going through my mind? The worst. Why would you leave without telling me? Why would you lie?" he added quietly.

I grabbed the list out of my pocket and handed it to him. "Just read this."

He unfolded it slowly. The paper was already well worn just from the past day. He took a minute to read it, and I saw his chin quiver before he folded it back up and handed it back.

"Now do you understand?" I asked. "I know it was wrong for me to just go without asking you first. I'm sorry, Dad. I'll never do that to you again. But I had to do it. And Axel was with me the whole time. You know he'd never let anything happen to me."

He sat there, silent, for a long time.

It gave me time to observe the wrinkles he'd gotten the past couple years. On his forehead, around his eyes. His hands. All of a sudden, he looked a lot older, almost frail, and bile filled my stomach as the guilt descended on me.

He lay his hand on my cheek. "The older you get, the more you become like your mother," he said.

I smiled at him. "Really?"

My mom had been the risk-taker of the family, the loud one. The extrovert. I always thought I was more like him, serious and quiet.

"I know I'm not your mother, Riley, and it's not the same, but you know you can tell me anything, right? You can trust me."

I nodded. "I know, Dad. But I promise there's not much to tell. We went to a Demi Lovato concert, we stayed at a Holiday Inn, Axel slept on the couch, and all we did was..." I blushed as I held up the list. "And only because I do like him, Dad."

He nodded, exhaling. "I hate to say it, but I always did like that kid. He's the only boy your age I'd trust to take care of you."

I smiled and leaned on his shoulder.

He put his arm around me. "Your mom would be proud of you. And I know she'd be really happy that you got out and lived a little, even if it did almost give me a heart attack."

The tension evaporated as the sound of chuckles and laughter filled the living room.

A minute later, I said, "So, uh, am I grounded forever?"

"Oh yeah, at least a month, young lady," he said, standing up.

I stood up too. "Okay, that's fair, I guess. Even if it is my last summer before leaving for college."

"Nice try," he said. "You're still grounded. But first, we have a graduation to get to. And a nice dinner."

"Sounds like a plan," I said and headed upstairs.

"And Riley?" he called, and I turned back. "Ask Axel and his family if they'd like to join us. I'd like to get to know them better."

I smiled. "Sure thing, Dad."

I started back toward the stairs, then turned to look at him one more time to sear this memory in my heart forever.

He froze. "Wait. Riley Stephens, what did you do to your hair?"

CHAPTER FIVE

AXEL RODRIGUEZ WALKED ACROSS THE STAGE TO receive his diploma. An adorable baby picture of him popped up on the screen beside the stage, and everyone awwed. He was the chubbiest baby I had ever seen, and he had on his signature smile even as an infant.

Then it was my turn.

"Riley Stephens."

My whole life up until now had led up to this, and I couldn't believe how fast it was happening.

I took the rolled-up diploma in my hand, and applause filled the auditorium. I stared out at the crowd and bit my lip as everyone rose to their feet for me. A lot of people were staring at the huge screen to my right.

My dad had picked out my baby picture for tonight. He'd taken it. In it, my mom was holding me. I was about six months old and hugging her entire face. I blinked several times as I took her in, and suddenly, I felt like she was with me, right on stage.

I found Axel not too far away. And my dad. I smiled at them.

And then I was walking off the stage, and the next person's name was being called out.

As I made my way back to my seat, it hit me that I was headed for college in two months. Thinking about it made my stomach turn, but then I thought of my mom again. And Axel. My dad.

The next four years would be full of all kinds of new things, many more firsts than in the last day. But I wouldn't be alone. They would be with me.

Thank you for reading "More Than a List" by Yesenia Vargas! To connect with Yesenia and learn more about her books and special offers, visit www.yeseniavargas.com.

(NOT SO) PERFECT CHEMISTRY

Kayla Tirrell

CHAPTER ONE

"JESSI JONES AND MASON ALEXANDER."

A collective gasp went through the room as our science teacher called out our lab partner assignments.

No, no, no, no, no.

Mason and I were opposites of the worst kind. Oil and water. Black and white. Or, more appropriate for our current class, ammonia and bleach.

Not that we had always been so at odds. Was it only a couple of months ago that we were close friends?

I didn't expect Mrs. Jacobs to follow all the drama of our senior class, but a little awareness wouldn't hurt. I couldn't be lab partners with Mason. We would end up killing each other.

I looked back at my best friend, Mia. If I had any say, we'd be together for this project.

"I'm sorry," she mouthed to me, but I turned away.

I was too afraid the compassion in her eyes would bring me to tears. And that was so not happening in front of everyone. I would play the part—act like the tough girl everyone thought I was.

I leaned back in my seat and crossed my arms over my chest in what I hoped was defiant stance and not a pouty one.

Mrs. Jacobs continued to call out names, but my heart was pounding too loudly in my ears to hear any of the other pairings.

I stole a glance over at Mason. He sat in his chair with his feet propped up on the seat in front of him. Everything from his stupid blond hair (that was too long, by the way) to his lean, muscled arms (that he had coolly crossed over his chest), made me want to throw a pen at him. Or five.

He mirrored me almost exactly, down to the sneers playing across both of our faces.

"Okay class," Mrs. Jacobs said, saving Mason from the daggers I was staring in his direction. "Find your partner and get started. And remember, you and your partner will be together for the next nine weeks." She looked at me. "Try not to let your personal lives get in the way of your work."

Maybe Mrs. Jacobs wasn't as clueless as I thought. The woman just happened to be completely heartless.

I sighed as I got up from my seat and grabbed my backpack off the floor. I could only assume Mason would be staying put, expecting me to come to him.

Each high-top desk was covered with a black countertop that sat four people. That meant Mason and I would be sharing our station with one other couple. It looked like our tablemates were Angel and Melissa.

I didn't know either of them very well, but the latter was Mason's neighbor. And while I knew it wasn't fair to dislike someone you barely knew, Melissa always rubbed me the wrong way. Even before she became a huge online participant in *JesMageddon*.

The two girls gave us plenty of space but kept glancing over in our direction. That was going to get old fast.

The third time Melissa looked at me, I raised my eyebrows at her. I hadn't even had a chance to speak to Mason yet. Her face turned red before she looked away and pulled out the instructions for the lab.

"That wasn't very nice." I looked up to see Mason smirking at me.

I gave him the same look I'd just given Melissa. "Do you really want to lecture me about being nice?"

"I don't know. I think you can be quite the wildcat."

"Ew." I scrunched up my nose in disgust. "Was that supposed to be seductive?"

His smiled widened as he waggled his eyebrows. "Why? Do you want it to be?"

I narrowed my gaze, and, to my surprise, he winked. Mason freaking winked at me.

I slammed my hands on the table, causing more than one head to turn in our direction, including Mrs. Jacobs.

"Let's get a few things straight before we get started," I hissed. "You are not going to flirt with me. In fact, I'm okay with not talking at all. We can follow the lab directions in silence, get a passing grade, and rejoice when the nine weeks is over."

"Where's the fun in that?"

"This isn't supposed to be fun. It's work," I explained, my voice low and even.

"Technically, it's school."

"Please, Mason, can we just try to get through this without adding fodder to the gossip mill?"

His head cocked to the side. "I'm not sure that analogy makes any sense."

I growled. Unfortunately, Mason's chuckle confirmed he had heard it. Taking a few deeps breaths, I tried again.

"This"—I pointed my finger back and forth between us—"doesn't make any sense. There is no reason for the two of us to be lab partners, and I'm honestly still hoping this is some terrible nightmare and I'm going to wake up."

"It's not that bad." He leaned over the table, and his voice came out in a deep rumble I swore I could feel in my bones. "Maybe it'll force us to come to a truce."

"There is never going to be anything but hatred between us."

Mason looked upset for the briefest moment before his smile came back. "That wasn't always the case."

I didn't argue, and he didn't push any further.

We spent the next forty-five minutes going through that day's lab instructions. It was nothing more than identifying the different instruments we'd be using and going over the steps for the next day.

When the bell rang, I grabbed my stuff and ran up to Mrs. Jacob's desk. She had her glasses on and was grading some assignments from the week before.

"Please let me switch partners."

Mrs. Jacobs looked up, pulled the glasses from her face, and stared at me. "The partners are set, Miss Jones."

"But Mason and I...we don't play well together. Surely, even you can see why that's bad?"

"Even me?" she asked, a small crease forming between her eyes.

"What I mean is..." What did I mean? I wasn't sure. "Please, I'll do anything."

"You and Mr. Alexander are partners for the next several weeks. I think you need to figure out how to work together instead of looking for ways to get out of it."

Ugh! Teachers could be so frustrating. I stormed out of the classroom, my fists clenched.

Thankfully, Mia was waiting for me outside the door. "That's rough, Jessi."

"Tell me about it," I grumbled, continuing toward the parking lot.

Her perfect messy bun bounced as she fell into step with me.

"What did Mrs. Jacobs say?"

"That I'm stuck with Mr. Douche Canoe."

"Who knows? Maybe you guys will end up

having...chemistry." She giggled at her joke, and I gave her a playful shove.

"Don't ever say that again."

"Why not?" Mia shrugged her shoulders. "They say there's a thin line between love and hate. Maybe being lab partners is that line."

I snorted. "I'm pretty sure *JesMageddon* was that line, and I am firmly planted on my side."

"Are you sure there's no going back?"

I sighed. "I don't think so."

"Poor Jessi," she said with an exaggerated pout. She linked her arm with mine and started walking faster toward her car. "Then let's go get some ice cream. My treat."

I certainly wasn't going to argue.

CHAPTER TWO

DETERMINED NOT TO LET MASON WIN, I WOKE UP earlier the next morning and used the extra time to make myself look perfect. If I was going to be forced to sit next to my enemy every day, I was going to look good doing it. Show him what he was missing because of our fallout.

Even though it was mid-October, I was able to wear my favorite dress, a short fit-and-flare number. The humidity might be killer in Florida, but at least I could show off a little skin in the middle of autumn.

The first part of the day went by without a hitch. My Tuesday classes were no-brainers, and no one mentioned anything about what happened in Chemistry the day before. When I sat down for lunch, I checked all my social media feeds. They were also surprisingly clear of drama.

I let out a sigh of relief and started eating my school lunch.

A couple of minutes later, Mia flopped down in the seat beside me. She pulled out a bag of chips from her backpack. Her lunch usually consisted of that and a can of soda.

Around a bite of food, Mia said, "I'm still not sure how you can eat that mystery meat."

"It's probably closer to real food than the orange powder they coat your chips with," I retorted. "And besides, the chicken sandwich isn't so bad."

"It's debatable."

I opened my mouth, giving her a view of the food she was protesting.

Mia covered her eyes. "You, Jessi Jones, are one disgusting woman."

"I don't know about that," said a familiar voice from behind me.

I turned to see Mason standing with a lunch tray in his hands. I felt tempted to spit my food on it, just to see his reaction. Instead, I quickly swallowed my bite and asked him what he was doing at our table.

"I just thought, since we're lab partners and all, it might be a good idea to figure out how we're going to approach the lab today." His face was frustratingly blank, and gorgeous as always, as he took a seat next to me.

"First of all, I'd rather eat glass than talk to you during lunch." I felt my blood pressure rising. "Second of all, there's nothing to prepare for. We read the instructions yesterday. And third—"

"Hey Mia," Mason interrupted my tirade.

The coy smile on her face made me feel oddly betrayed. "Mason."

"You look positively stunning today."

Mia blushed, and I sat up a little straighter in my seat. The thing was, Mia did look stunning. She always looked amazing, and usually, I wasn't jealous of her. Especially not because of Mason's attention.

Today was different though. I had spent way too long perfecting my eyeliner. My hair was smooth and straight—no small task in the muggy weather.

I cleared my throat, causing both Mason and Mia to face me. They both wore looks of pure satisfaction.

"You look nice too, Jessi," Mason said.

"That's not why I coughed." I grabbed my milk carton and took a sip. "I was choking."

"Uh huh." Mason nodded his head slowly.

I lifted my brows in defense. "It's true. Probably from that little display between the two of you."

Mia laughed and stood up. "I gotta go use the restroom. I'll see you in English."

"I'll go with you." I started to get up.

"I think I can handle it all by my lonesome, Jessi. Seriously, I'll see you in a few."

Traitor.

I plastered a plastic smile on my face and turned in my chair to face Mason again. His smile looked genuine as he looked back at me. He lifted his sandwich to his mouth and took a bite, never taking his eyes off me.

I closed my eyes and let out a long breath. "Mason, what do you want from me?"

He shrugged. "I just want to spend some time together. Is that so weird?"

I looked at Mason. "Yes, it is weird. Mostly because we haven't spoken in two months. Mrs. Jacobs pairs us together, and all of a sudden you want to be besties?"

"Maybe I want to make amends." He almost looked apologetic.

"Maybe it's too late." I checked to see if anyone was watching us. They wouldn't hear what we were saying—the cafeteria was too loud for that. That didn't mean some of the nosier students wouldn't pick up on our body language.

I swore Melissa had been looking in our

direction, but I couldn't be sure. I didn't want her to catch me staring, so I brought my gaze back to the boy sitting beside me.

It really was unfair how good looking he was. Why was it that the cutest guys always had the worst personalities? Mason Alexander was a walking cliché.

Neither of us spoke, while I continued watching the clock on the wall. It was the old-fashioned kind that had an hour and minute hands, and I knew they were somehow mocking me. The longer I stared, the more stubborn the minute hand became. At one point, it almost looked like it ticked in the wrong direction.

When the bell signaled the end of lunch, I hurried to get up with my tray in hand. Mason walked beside me, carrying his own.

I slammed my tray down in the small window of the kitchen, earning a frown from the lunch lady on the other side.

Turning to face my archenemy, I whisper-yelled, "Are you trying to stir crap up again?"

It had taken months for the drama to die down. Our falling out had been a social media nightmare, our dirty laundry littered all over Twitter, Snapchat, and Facebook. We even had our own hashtag. #JesMageddon

It wasn't the most creative thing I'd ever seen, but once one person used it, everyone in our high school followed along. Tweets of the fights we had in the cafeteria, screenshots of comments we made back and forth. And one stupid text message that somehow became public.

What was it about a feud that had everyone rallying on one side or another?

Mason's smile was sad as he set his tray down. His shoulders sagged ever so slightly. Not that I cared. "I'll see you in Chemistry, Jess."

With that, he turned and walked away.

CHAPTER THREE

I BARELY MADE IT TO CLASS IN TIME, SO I DIDN'T get a chance to talk to Mia again. The fact that she sat on the opposite side of the room only added to my frustration.

I glared at her from my spot, but she didn't look in my direction during the entire class. As soon as the bell rang, I stormed over to where she sat at her desk. "You really are the worst, you know that?"

She closed her notebook and looked up with an unrepentant grin. "But you love me."

"Something like that," I grumbled. "Why did you leave me alone with Mason at lunch? Why aren't you backing me up? He's sitting with us at lunch, and you're acting like it's normal—"

"It used to be," Mia interrupted.

"Yeah," I answered slowly, "but not anymore."

Mia took her sweet time packing her bag. She stood up from her desk and looked me directly in my eyes. "Sometimes people make mistakes. Did you ever stop to think that this thing between you and Mason is one giant misunderstanding?"

I lifted my brows. "That lasted for two months?"

"You can be intimidating when you want to be. And you said a lot of hurtful things directed at Mason. Just remember, there are always two sides to every story."

"Whatever." I left without looking back and made my way toward the science wing.

Of course, every story had two sides, but he was the one who called me pathetic when I finally expressed my feelings via text message. Rejection would have hurt, but not nearly as much as the rumor mill that had followed. I kicked myself every day for sending something that could have a screenshot taken and be shared with everyone in the school. I should have told him face to face.

When I walked into Chemistry, Mason was sitting at our desk. It was covered with vials of different liquids for that day's lab, an assortment of glass beakers, and a small paper bag that looked completely out of place. It had a small bow attached to the top. As I got closer, I saw my name written on the front of it.

"What's that?" I asked, stealing a quick glance at Angel and Melissa.

They both had their heads down, and yet somehow, I knew they would be paying attention to *everything* that was happening.

Mason tilted his head slightly to the side, his expression innocent. "I guess you'll just have to open it to find out."

"Is it a bomb?"

He laughed, a deep, easy sound.

I told my stupid heart to cool its jets. There was no reason to get excited by Mason Alexander.

He didn't say anything, but continued watching me expectantly, a smile stuck on his face. I opened the bag just get it over with. When I did, my breath caught in my chest. It was a cupcake from my favorite bakery.

I looked up at Mason in confusion. "What's this?"

"It's a cupcake."

"I know it's a cupcake," I said flatly, earning a smile. "I want to know why you gave it to me."

He shrugged his shoulders. "Consider it a peace offering."

I lifted the treat to my mouth. The lemon scent

hit my nose just as the frosting touched my lips. My eyes closed in blissful anticipation. I was just about to take a bite when I thought better of it and stuck it out to Mason.

"You first."

His hands went to his chest in a dramatic fashion. "I'm honored you want to share with me. Is it altruism or a secret plot to swap spit with me?"

"Gross." I crinkled my nose. "It's more of a self-preservation tactic. I figure if there's laxative mixed in, I won't be the only one running to the bathroom."

A smirk played across his face. "As lovely of a visual as that is, I promise I didn't put poop powder in your cupcake. It came straight from Patty's Cakes, and she wouldn't take a bribe."

I found my lips curling into a small smile, much against my wishes. It had been so long since I'd talked to Mason. I had forgotten how fun it was to tease each other instead of ripping one another to shreds.

Falling into that way of thinking came far too easily. Between the teasing tone of his voice and the cupcake, it was like we were friends again.

Why did he have to go and mess everything up like this? He was the one who told me I was pathetic, that he wanted nothing to do with me. And now, he was stirring up feelings I thought were long gone.

I covertly took one last whiff of the sugary goodness in my hands, then got up and threw it in the garbage can across the room. Anyone in class would see. If Angel and Melissa wanted to report to the student body that Mason and I were flirting, my little show of defiance would set everyone straight.

I wasn't going down that path again.

Mason refused to look at me as I sat back down.

I told myself I didn't care, that it was what he would do in my shoes. I told myself I wasn't the jerk in this situation. But, for some reason, the silence between Mason and me as we worked on our lab project had me questioning the last couple of months.

We measured different liquids, then combined them to see what the results were. For a lab, it was pretty tame, and I was thankful for the ease of the work considering the friction between my partner and me.

We finished with plenty of time, and I brought our papers to Mrs. Jacob's desk. I stuck them out, but she didn't grab them. Instead, she took a quick glance at my lab station, then looked back at me. "Are things going any better today, Miss Jones?"

I forced a smile, willing her to take the paper from my hand and be done with it. "Totally."

The smile she returned was much more genuine. "Well, I'm glad neither of you is letting your personal lives get in the way of your assignments." She finally took the papers. "Go ahead and clean up your workstation. If you finish that, you can start reading chapter six."

Mason and I cleaned up as our classmates did the same. Everything looked good except for one loose piece of paper on Mason's side.

I tipped my chin at it. "You going to throw that away?"

The bell rang.

"Actually, it's for you. Put red cabbage juice on it when you get home."

"What the..." I started to ask, but my voice trailed off. He was already out the door and out of sight.

I turned to see Mia standing near the classroom door, obviously waiting for me.

"You ready to go?" she asked as I walked over.

"Yeah, but we need to make one quick stop on the way home."

CHAPTER FOUR

"WHAT IS THAT SMELL?" MY MOTHER ASKED, WALK-
ing into the kitchen. She was home from work early.

That was unfortunate. I had hoped to finish my
mystery project before she got home.

"Cabbage," I answered as if having a pot of
boiling cabbage on the stovetop was an everyday
occurrence.

My mom was right about one thing though—it
didn't smell great.

"Yes, honey, I know what cabbage looks like.
What I want to know is why you are boiling it. You ar-
en't trying to make dinner, are you?"

I snorted. "No, I was just trying to make cabbage juice."

She leaned against the kitchen counter and crossed her arms. "Why?"

"Because apparently, I need to put it on that." I pointed to the blank piece of paper on the counter next to her.

She picked it up and looked at it. "Oh, like invisible ink."

"I guess." I was only slightly aggravated that she knew more about the mystery paper than I did. Okay, maybe more than slightly.

My mom's brows crinkled together. "Jessi, why didn't you buy canned cabbage or cabbage juice? It would have been a lot faster. And easier."

Probably because I didn't know those things existed, I thought, but simply shrugged in response.

"Is it part of an assignment?"

"You could say that," I mumbled, stirring the pot.

I was pleased to see the water was a deeper color than it had been even minutes earlier. I ladled some out into a bowl to cool.

"What does it say?" The smile on my mom's face was bright.

"If I knew, I wouldn't have to boil cabbage, now would I?" I was teasing, and thankfully my mom knew that.

She laughed. "I guess not. You'll have to let me know later, because right now I'm heading upstairs for a bath."

"Sounds good." I was glad she wouldn't be standing over my shoulder when I uncovered the secret message Mason left for me.

After everything, I couldn't be sure what it would say. It could be anything from *I hope you die* to *Next time there will be laxatives.*

I grabbed the pastry brush from the drawer and began painting cabbage juice over the paper. I would never have guessed what it really said.

CHAPTER FIVE

WHEN SOMEONE BREAKS YOUR HEART, THERE ARE certain measures you can take to keep yourself from doing something stupid.

Delete their number. Unfollow them on social media. And never, ever, under any circumstances, meet them somewhere to talk.

Unfortunately, I hadn't deleted Mason's number. I hadn't unfollowed him, and I was on my way to meet Mason at the local park like he'd asked me to in the note.

The park was more than a playground. It also had several walking trails surrounding the large, grassy expanse—trails Mason and I had walked many times over the last couple years.

I found him at the trailhead where we used to meet, and without greeting each other, or saying anything, we started walking, both of us careful not to get too close.

"Jessi," Mason's voice broke the silence after several minutes of walking side by side.

Holding the still damp paper in my hands, I asked, "What do you want from me?"

"I don't know how things got so out of control between us."

"Oh, I don't know, maybe when you called me pathetic?"

"I didn't—"

"Or when you told everyone I drool in my sleep?"

"Only because you told people I fart when I get nervous!"

"Yeah"—I sped up to match his angry strides—"but I said that after you told everyone I was still afraid of the dark."

"And I said that because you told Mr. Anders I plagiarized my paper on Madame Bovary."

Now our paces had quickened so much we were practically speed walking.

"Well, you did," I said.

"You didn't have to tattle on me like some twelve-year-old girl."

I froze on the sidewalk.

I still remembered going to our English teacher's office after school. To this day, telling on Mason wasn't something I felt proud of. It was right after Mason had told me how pathetic I was for thinking we might try going out. I was hurt, and I had lashed out. He'd gotten in trouble and had to rewrite his paper. His parents had grounded him. That had been the beginning of the end.

Mason realized I'd stopped and turned back to me. With a curious look, he stepped closer.

"You're right." I closed my eyes. "I shouldn't have said anything to Mr. Anders, but I was so upset by what you said the night before."

Mason didn't reply, and I opened my eyes to see him standing less than a foot from me, his brows furrowed. "What do you mean, what I said?"

I shook my head and looked down at my feet. "Please don't make me say it, Mason. It was bad enough reading it."

Suddenly, his hand came under my chin, tipping my face up to look at him. His eyes were full of confusion as he searched my expression. "I have no idea what you're talking about."

My vision became blurry with the tears forming in my eyes. Not necessarily from sadness, but a mixture of frustration and longing for what used to be.

I refused to let them fall and blinked quickly before lifting my gaze to meet his. "I'm talking about when I put my freaking heart on the line. I'm talking about when I asked if you ever considered being more than friends, and you called me pathetic."

He stepped back, his brows scrunched together. Running one hand through his hair, he paced back and forth a few times. I watched him silently, wondering what was going through his mind.

When he didn't talk, I called his name.

"These last couple of months I've been trying to figure out what happened. How it all started. I kept going back to the English paper." He stopped and looked at me. "You thought I rejected you?"

I nodded my head. "Because you did."

"That's the thing though. I didn't. I wouldn't. I had just been telling Melissa..." His words trailed off as his eyes widened. "I'm such an idiot. I told her about my feelings for you right before our fight."

I bit my bottom lip. I so badly wanted to believe the tale he was weaving. If he'd been talking about wanting to be with me, why did he say those awful things?

Probably for the same reason I said some of the things I had. We were hurt. We were embarrassed.

"Jessi." He walked toward me and took my hands in his.

I was self-conscious about the way they shook but didn't pull them away.

"I don't know what to say. I don't know how we recover from this."

When I didn't answer, he spoke again. "Can we recover from this?"

I wanted to say yes. Every part of me wanted to say that one word.

"I don't know," I answered.

And then I walked away, leaving Mason alone at the park.

CHAPTER SIX

I DROVE MYSELF TO SCHOOL THE NEXT DAY, HAVing ignored all of Mia's texts the night before. I was being a crappy friend right now, and eventually, I'd have to address it. I just couldn't think clearly after everything that had happened with Mason.

The more I thought about it, the more I believed him.

I read through that particular exchange with fresh eyes, and when I did, I could see how much those texts didn't sound like Mason. How hadn't I seen it then? Why didn't I talk to him instead of letting things escalate the way they had?

I couldn't stop thinking about how things went

wrong. But more than that, I couldn't stop thinking about his question.

Could we recover?

I couldn't decide if I was looking forward to or dreading the moment when I walked in and saw Mason in Chemistry. So, when I entered the science class and saw only Angel and Melissa, I felt more confused than ever.

I glanced around the room. Melissa was watching me, her chin lifted, a smug smile on her face.

When my eyes met Mia's, she lifted her hands and mouthed, "What the heck?"

"I'm sorry," I lip-spoke back. I knew it was crappy of me to avoid her all day, but I was still trying to sort out my own feelings.

"Later," she replied, still silent, before turning back toward the front.

"If you girls are done," Mrs. Jacobs said, giving us a pointed look from the front of the room, "I'd like to get started with today's assignment."

Giggles broke out around the class, but I ignored them and raised my hand.

"Yes, Miss Jones?"

"Mason isn't here today."

"How astute of you to notice."

More laughter. Great, apparently my teacher thought herself quite the comedian.

"Join Melissa and Angel's group today," she finally added before beginning her rounds around the class.

The three of us worked in awkward silence. I thought about what Mason had said the night before. Had Melissa sabotaged our relationship?

I didn't call her out and stayed focused on our assignment.

At the end of class, Mia came directly to my desk. "I've been texting you like crazy, woman. What gives?"

I loaded my backpack and flung it over one shoulder. "I'm sorry. It was a weird night."

We started walking toward the parking lot.

"What happened?" she asked.

"Mason happened."

Mia stopped. "Oh, no. Please tell me you two haven't started fighting again. It felt so good to have the three of us sitting together at lunch yesterday."

I raised my brows.

"What? I make no apologies. You know I think the two of you would be perfect for each other if you could pull your heads out of your—"

"He said it wasn't him," I interrupted.

"What wasn't him?" she asked slowly.

"The text. Mason said he didn't send it. It might have been Melissa. I think I believe him."

"Jessi, this is huge." Her voice was full of enthusiasm I didn't feel. "Do you know what this means?"

"Yeah. It means we hurt each other a lot, over a misunderstanding."

"Does he like you?"

"What?"

This time her voice was loud as she annunciated each syllable. "Does. He. Like. You?"

I nodded my head. "I think so."

"Then go figure it out."

"I wouldn't know where to begin," I answered honestly.

A huge smile played across my best friend's face. She lifted one of her hands and pointed. I hadn't been paying attention, but when I followed the direction of her finger, I saw Mason standing next to my car, carrying a bouquet of red roses.

I looked back at Mia, terrified. "What do I do?" I whispered.

"I think you go say hi." She reached out, grabbed one of my hands, and squeezed. "Good luck."

I walked toward Mason, my eyes not leaving his the entire time. Covering the distance between us felt like it took an eternity, though I knew it was only seconds.

"Hi," I said once I was close enough.

"Hi," he echoed with a smile. Mason held up the flowers. "Jessi, I know we hurt each other. We both said some things we wish we could take back, but doesn't that happen in every relationship?"

I shook my head. "Not like that."

He let out a sad laugh. "Maybe we're overachievers, and we got it all out of the way. I mean, we've basically revealed every secret we know about each other. What more can we do?"

"You could give me hope, only to break my heart again."

Mason set the flowers on the hood of my car. He reached out, put his arms around me, and pulled me close. Bringing his lips to my ear, he whispered, "I would never."

I lifted my face to see him. "You can't say that."

"You're right, but I can promise never to let it get out of hand like this. I won't let it. I love you too much, Jessi Jones."

My breath caught. "What did you say?"

Mason chuckled. "Don't act like that surprises you."

But it did surprise me. We'd been fighting for months. How could you love someone you hated?

Mia's words about the thin line between love and hate came back to me. Maybe she was right. Maybe it was possible Mason and I were meant for each other—that we were two people in love who happened to get a little lost.

"I love you too, Mason." The words felt strange on my tongue, but I knew they were true the moment I said them.

"Then why are we just standing here?" Mason asked, leaning down so that our faces were close. Our noses were almost touching, and I felt his breath against my lips. "I think this is the part where we kiss."

His lips met mine as we kissed for the first time. I poured every emotion I was feeling into that kiss, hoping Mason would know exactly what it meant to me. All the while, I could tell he was doing the same.

The best part was, the emotions we were sharing felt a lot like love, and not at all like hate.

Thank you for reading "(Not So) Perfect Chemistry" by Kayla Tirrell! To connect with Kayla and learn more about her books and special offers, visit tirrellblewrites.com.

SPARK

Sally Henson

CHAPTER ONE

Regan

LANE AND I CROSS MY LAWN TO THE DRIVEWAY. I shouldn't bring this up again, but I can't seem to help myself. "I've got a gut feeling this party's a bad idea. Just because you're a senior doesn't mean you have to go."

He glances at me and chuckles. "Aw, give it a rest, Mom."

"Shut up." I smack the bill of his EIU hat so it covers his eyes.

"Hey," his voice turns serious. "Don't mess with my baby."

He veers toward the driver's side door, taking off his cap and rolls the bill before slipping it back on, making sure it's got the country-boy look to it.

I snicker.

"Sometimes things aren't what you think, Regan. It'll be fine." He climbs into his side of the pickup.

I get in my side and look over at him. Today's the day he said goodbye to our podunk high school. "I'm so jealous of you right now."

He glances over at me with a smirk.

I flinch my hand toward his hat. "I'm going to grab that cap off your head and stomp on it."

"You better not lay a finger on this hat. It's my prize possession."

He looks better without a cap on, but whatever. I roll my eyes and look out the passenger window. The soft light from the sun, well into its downward trajectory, casts long shadows to the east. Maybe tonight won't be so bad.

We drive over the small hill in the rock quarry

and see the cars. The bonfire graduation party's happening along the banks of the pond.

Lane mumbles. "They're jumping off the cliffs?"

"That water's too cold." I shiver just thinking about it. "We should wait for it to warm up more before we go swimming again."

Lane snorts. "No kidding."

We turn down the gravel road opposite the cliffs, and Lane parks in the grass with the tailgate facing the water so we'll have a place to sit. He tosses his cap on the dash and combs his fingers through his hair.

Lane didn't spend a lot of time hanging out with his classmates, so I'm surprised he wanted to come to this party tonight. It's been our gang—Lane, Tobi, Cameron, Haylee, and me—for two years now.

Lane and me, well, we've been best friends since forever.

CHAPTER TWO

Regan

CRACKLING ROCK SIGNALS ANOTHER VEHICLE AR-riving. It's becoming a steady occurrence, and soon I'll be even more overwhelmed with bodies. I grumble to myself. Where's Tobi? Why haven't Cam and Haylee shown up yet? Lane and I've been here for what seems like hours.

When Lane had asked me earlier if I wanted to hang out with him and Nick by the water, I declined. Honestly, I thought I'd be fine coming here, but watching him laughing with them is making me wish I'd stayed home. But for now, my butt is glued to this tailgate, waiting for my other friends to show. I check over my shoulder to the gravel road that runs through the rock quarry for any sign of them.

Smoke from the fire drifts my way, causing me to cough and wave it from my face. A puff of wind wisps it away, and I take a deep breath of fresh air, scanning the water's edge for Lane. Daylight barely hangs on with a remnant of orange and red light from the setting sun behind Lane and the guys he's talking to.

Guilt seeps into my body. Lane's my best friend, and being here tonight is part of my graduation present to him.

Quit being such a jerk about this, Regan.

My eyes flicker down to the shirt I'm wearing. Ugh. I either look like a disco peacock or a giant fishing lure. It's too snug for my taste, but Lane said it was fine.

I shake my head. Tobi thinks she's my stylist. I wish she'd stick to styling herself.

Heat from the growing fire warms my face. The burning embers and chunks of wood wrapped in ribbons of fire remind me of wiener-roasts with my family and Lane's when we were kids and life was easy.

My feet dangle from the tailgate, lifting my mood, sparking the carefree child in me. Soon the sunset will turn into twilight, and everyone will become a shadow that grows braver. A party like this is always full of people teetering on the edge—the edge of everything.

A truck rips and roars down the gravel road, through the grassy field. I don't have to look to know who it is. Cameron. Finally. He stops along the shoreline and revs the engine. Lane's group moves out of the way, closer to the fire.

Giggles bubble up in my chest as I watch a few crazy people run through the cars, howling, and jump in the water. My tension is washing away now that my friends are here.

Lane looks up from his conversation to Cam's truck, laughing at Cam's audaciousness before latching on to my sight. We shake our heads in unison and share the moment. He makes a move toward me, but someone pulls him back.

Through a gap between Nick and another guy's shoulders, I see a trail of long blonde hair sway beside Lane. She seems a little too close to him, but I can't tell who it is. Maybe I should go over there.

I reach for a couple of water bottles from the cooler to take with me. When I look back up, Tobi plants her bum on the tailgate next to me. She checks out the shirt she assigned me for the night. "That shirt looks"—she touches her fingertips to her lips and kisses them—"on you."

"So you're Italian now?" I roll my eyes and hand her a water bottle. "Did he drive like that all the way out here?"

She twists the cap off the bottle. "No, actually. Only when we pulled in."

I snort. "That's a surprise. Where's Haylee?"

"Cam's showing her how to operate the light bars or something."

"I'm glad you're—" A movement across the fire catches my eye, stealing my words.

Tobi asks, "Why do you look like you just took a shot of vinegar?"

Normally, a comment like that would make me laugh, but there's nothing funny about this train wreck happening before my eyes. "Who is that?"

Tobi takes a swig of water and stares in the same direction as me. "Who?"

I can't tear my eyes away from what's going on. "The blonde who's about to fall out of her bikini top, invading Lane's space."

"Oh! Wow. That is"—she pauses—"blatant. Uh, that looks like Brea Adams. Nick's sister. She's a couple years older than Lane, I think."

I growl in disgust. "It's gross."

Tobi laughs. "Agreed." She leans into me. "You don't need to do anything like that to get Lane's attention."

My eyes are glued on Lane and Brea. "What?"

Tobi giggles. "Oh, nothing."

A slow burn grows in my chest. Brea tickles Lane's bicep with her talon fingernails, chatting up Lane, Nick, and some guy with a fancy haircut. I've never seen him before. The guy swivels to look at Tobi and me. His dark eyes match his hair. Nick whispers something in his ear as Brea leans to catch a glimpse of us. She flashes a devilish grin before focusing her attention back on Lane.

His eyes are transfixed to the hot-pink camo bikini top.

CHAPTER THREE

Lane

"HEY, I'VE GOT TO CHECK ON SOMETHING." I NOD toward my truck where Regan and Tobi are sitting on the tailgate. "I'll catch you guys later."

Nick and his cousin Bobby glance over their shoulders and then to each other before huge grins break across their faces.

Nick chuckles. "Yeah, I bet."

"Those girls are the prettiest things I've seen since I got to this lousy state," Bobby drawls out in his annoying southern accent.

"Huh," Brea squeaks out, moving closer to me. If that's even possible. "They're not that pretty."

Bobby bows to Brea, placing his hand over his heart. "Except for you, cousin."

Brea giggles. She's so fake, and I'm trying real hard to be a gentleman. I take a step toward my truck, and Brea hooks her arm around mine. Her fingernails trace down my arm.

I open my mouth to ask her to stop, but it feels so good. I tell her I like her nails. I'm such an idiot.

"Lane, man," Nick's voice grabs my attention. "You know you're gonna have to give them up when you leave."

Bobby leans back. "You're seeing both of them? And they don't have a problem with that?"

Brea huffs, but everyone ignores her.

I snort. "We're just really good friends, Nick. You've been hounding me about it for years."

"What am I supposed to think? You tell everyone they're off limits, you hang out with them all the time, and Regan *never* acts interested in anyone but you."

I shrug and look to the fire.

Bobby lowers his chin, cocking his head to the side. "Seriously? You're not dating either of them?"

Nick and Bobby look back over their shoulders

again at the girls. Nick whispers something, triggering a smirk from his cousin.

"You won't mind if I go talk to your friends, then?" Bobby asks.

Brea nods eagerly. "Oh, you should, Bobby. You, too, Nick."

If Tobi didn't have a boyfriend, I'd probably tell them no way. Regan doesn't go out, so I'm absolutely positive these guys will strike out.

Nick nudges Bobby's shoulder. "Regan's definitely your type."

I scoff. This pretty boy? "What type is that?"

"Smart, on the verge of nerdy. Quiet." Bobby moans. "And blue eyes. Blue eyes are my kryptonite."

My lip curls with disgust at the thought of this guy getting behind Regan's shield. Not that she would allow it.

"She doesn't date," I deadpan. This guy's going to crash and burn, and I'm going to enjoy watching it.

A wolfish smile covers his face. "I'm not going to date her."

Nick and Bobby turn toward Regan and Tobi.

Brea giggles, drawing my attention back to her.

A couple baseball teammates come to chat, and In between sentences I keep checking on my friends. Relief loosens my shoulders when the girls hop off the tailgate and walk the opposite direction before Nick and Bobby even get to them.

I laugh to myself. I'm totally satisfied the girls didn't give them the time of day.

CHAPTER FOUR

Regan

TOBI'S COUSIN SHOWED UP AND CALLED HER OVER to his car, leaving me by myself again. She told me I need to let loose and talk to a guy tonight. I don't see the point. I'm not going to date anyone.

Our conversation plays back as I wind through the cars to my perch. I'm not blowing my plan of getting out of this town for some boy. There's no way I'm going to end up like my cousin, falling in love and getting pregnant before I get to college.

As soon as I sit down on the tailgate, I notice

the guy with the fancy haircut is sauntering this direction. Everything about him stands out. From his thick rimmed glasses to his khaki pants and perfectly rumpled button-down shirt—he doesn't fit in with the rest of the hicks here. Which isn't a bad thing, but still, I grip the edge of the tailgate and try to be invisible while I spy on Lane and what's-her-name.

"Hey," A soft southern voice pulls my attention away from the disastrous duo.

My muscles stiffen. I do my best to give him a small, polite smile, but my eyes quickly dart through the crowd, searching for Tobi or Haylee or Cameron—someone who has the attentiveness to intervene.

The guy with the southern voice stops inches away. "I'm Rhett. Nick and Brea's cousin."

His name catches me off-guard, and I nearly laugh out loud "As in Gone With the Wind?" I ask, glancing at his face. It's tanned and smooth and looks not so much like a teenaged boy.

He shifts his feet. "Or do you prefer Ashley?"

I draw my brows together. "Neither." Who says this stuff? I kind of like his accent and soft voice, but I can tell by what Tobi would call his pickup line that he must be a jerk.

"Whew." Southern Boy wipes the back of his hand across his brow. "I hate that movie."

I chuckle involuntarily, amused and confused with this guy. *He's a jerk, Regan.* Jerks talk like this, don't they?

Movement near Lane catches my eye. Brea acts as if she's cold and nestles in between Lane and the fire, triggering a twist of my stomach. Ugh! Maybe if she's cold, she ought to get some clothes on.

Lane still doesn't see me, but he sure sees Brea. Who am I to advise Lane on the value of virtue? I'm only his best friend who's been going to church with him our whole lives. The one whose opinion he respects. Or used to—he's clearly ignoring me now.

Southern Boy moves to lean against the taillight of the truck and clears his throat. "My name's actually, Beauregard."

I laugh out loud this time. Okay. He's a funny jerk.

His face brightens, causing a strange energy inside me.

"You're laughing at my name?" Beauregard tilts his head wearing a new sad puppy dog face.

"I'm sorry." I chuckle. "I can't help it."

If that's the kind of girl Lane's into now...well, fine. Laughing at this guy's a whole lot better than watching Lane wreck his dignity.

"Hmm." Beauregard studies me, sending

another quiver of energy fizzing through me, and I dart my eyes away from his. "Seriously, though, my friends call me Hook."

I giggle. Maybe he's not a jerk.

"For real this time." His dark brown eyes are like lasers on me.

Something about the way he's looking at me makes my insides jittery. I fold one arm against my stomach. Maybe I'm getting sick. "Is Hook short for something?"

He rests his hand on the bed of the truck and leans toward me. "My momma calls me Booker. In junior high, the kids at school started calling me Hooker. It somehow ended up as Hook."

I'm feeling light and free to laugh at how truly funny this guy is. He continues making me giggle at almost everything he says.

He calls to Nick who's standing by the fire, not far from Lane.

When Nick looks over his shoulder, Booker motions him over, and I catch Lane eyeing me.

Lane shakes his head, giving me a look of disapproval.

My eyes shift to the ground, and I swallow down a lump of guilt. It sets heavy in my stomach.

Why should I feel guilty, though? I'm not the one letting some girl flaunt her half-naked body at me.

I lift my head and reciprocate Lane's glare.

CHAPTER FIVE

Regan

NICK PASSES THE FIRE ON HIS WAY OVER TO Booker. I can see him from my peripheral vision, but my eyes stay focused on Lane's as we duke it out in a silent battle of wills.

Booker's voice sounds like a melody when he says to Nick, "Tell this pretty girl what my name is."

Heat spreads across my cheeks, and I tilt my head toward the ground to hide my embarrassment.

"Bobby," Nick says.

I look up to Nick and then to Bobby. "What?" I

laugh out, unable to stop the laughter rolling through me. This guy is nothing I expected.

Bobby or Hook or whoever this guy is, thanks Nick, and Nick returns to his place by the fire.

Southern Boy's dark locks fall down on his forehead in a wavy clump as he leans toward me, probably making sure I'm still breathing from laughing so hard.

This smile on my face isn't going anywhere soon. "Do you lie all the time, Bobby?"

"No, ma'am. I'm not much of a liar. But I could tell you didn't want to talk to me, so I had to do something to soften you up."

I press my lips together and tug a few strands of my mane against my cheek.

He runs his fingers through his fallen wavy tuft, pushing it back in place. "So you're Regan? Like the president?"

I look down at my hands fidgeting in my lap. "Yeah."

Lane told him my name? Is he trying to set me up? That's not like him. He didn't act like it when he glared at me earlier, shaking his head.

Bobby bows his head. "It's not as unique as Bobby, but it's still a nice name."

I laugh again. My eyes scroll up from his red Chuck's to his soft brown irises. "Are you always this funny, Hook?" After listening to him and taking a really good look at him, he's got a nerdy, gentlemanlike vibe to him—similar to Lane.

"May I?" He motions to the spot next to me.

I scoot over to make more room on the tailgate of Lane's truck.

Hook sits too close and leans his lips near my ear. "I'm kind of a nerd." He watches my expression. "And in case you haven't heard, scientists don't have a sense of humor."

I swallow my excitement, turning my gaze away from him to wander through the crowd in hopes of distracting myself. Cam and another guy are sitting in his truck with the cab light on.

Hook's fingers graze my hand, and even though it makes me flinch, he rests his pinky finger on top of mine.

I chance a sideways glance, contemplating what this means. I just met this guy. His gentle grin tells me he's harmless, but I slide my pinky from under his, calculating a more sage option—parallel pinkies.

I don't think I've stopped smiling since he started joking with me. "It's obvious you're not from around here."

He chuckles, and the sound inspires the formation of the word "sexy" in my thoughts. Heat quickly rises up my neck. This guy has a knack for embarrassing me.

"Nah," he says, "I'm from Alabama. Not far from Mobile." He nods to Nick and Brea. "My family drove up for Nick's graduation."

My sight zeroes in on Nick and Brea at the mention of their names. I wish I hadn't. The taste of jealousy is bitter on my tongue. It's obvious why guys want to look at her. She's pretty all over. At least she's not hanging on Lane at the moment.

I do a quick scan of the area for him and breathe easier when I can't find him. Maybe he's escaped.

CHAPTER SIX

Lane

BREA'S DROPPING HINTS SHE'D LIKE ME TO WARM her up. There's no way I'm warming her up, no matter what shape or form of heat she's thinking. While Nick and Joey are swapping "remember when" stories from baseball and school, I'm keeping my eyes on Bobby. There's something about this guy cozying up to Regan that has me on edge.

"Lane, dude, you listening?" Nick moves his head in my line of sight, blocking the happy couple I was glaring at. "Remember that double play against T-Town freshman year?"

I nod as if I'm paying attention.

Brea tugs on my shirt and clears her throat in a girly tone.

I look down at her. It's an automatic reaction, but I'd rather keep my eyes on Regan.

"I forgot I have a jacket in my car." Brea looks down at her fingers pinching the edge of my T-shirt. "You want to help me find it?"

If she likes younger guys, then... "Maybe Joey here can help you." I step back from her. "I gotta—" my eyes find Regan before telling the guys, "Uh, I'll be back."

I escape into the dark with my pounding heart, wandering aimlessly in hopes Brea doesn't follow me. Thoughts of Bobby making the moves on Regan is turning me inside out.

What's Regan think she's doing? I scrub my hand down my face with a heavy breath. Why am I so mad?

I end up at Cam's truck. Haylee's sitting on the edge of the bed with her legs dangling over the edge. Cam and a couple of his basketball buddies are talking beside her. I consider leaving, but I need his help.

I call out, "Cam."

Cam turns toward me. "Yeah?"

I'm close enough he can see me wave him over.

Haylee swings her legs over the bed of the truck and climbs down. "Hey, Lane."

The guys take off.

Haylee's lips twist to one side. "Everything okay?"

I nod even though it's not okay. Regan and that guy are definitely not okay.

Cam joins us at the backend of the truck

"Hey, uh,"—Haylee takes a step backwards, pointing behind her with her thumb—"I'm going to find Tobi and Regan."

Between the awkward silence and the ice coming off me, I don't blame her for taking off. After Haylee's gone, I unload.

"Have you seen Regan with Nick's cousin?" I rest my forearms on the closed tailgate and bend over, feeling out of breath for some reason.

"Ah, Nick's cousin. Yeah. I saw her." He doesn't sound thrilled about it either.

"She's not supposed to be doing that. She's not supposed to like guys." I lift my hands in the air.

Cam chuckles. "What?"

How can he joke at a time like this? "She has a no dating rule."

"She's not dating the guy, yet." Cam rests his arm on the corner of the truck rail. "Where's he from?"

"Mississippi or Alabama or something. Did you see how he—he's—she's—" I rub the back of my neck and pace in a circle. "She likes him."

Cam steps closer to me. "You're her best-friend, shouldn't you be happy for her?"

I turn, stretching my hand toward him, trying to get him to see reason. "She's breaking her rules."

He chuckles. "You know how I feel about the rules."

"I know, I know." I clasp my fingers and rest them behind my head, trying to calm the caged animal scratching at my insides.

Cam met me before graduation to let me know he's over rule number three, no dating within our group of friends, and that he wants to ask Regan out. I talked him out of it and then this guy shows up and Regan's all over him.

"He's from out of state. Nothing's going to happen." He pats me on the back.

"He's into her. Can you go check on her? Maybe get rid of him?" I plead for his help.

He blows out a long breath. "I'll go over there. But you're fooling yourself if you think this guy's the only one who wants her attention. If you don't make your move before the end of summer, someone else will."

CHAPTER SEVEN

Regan

WHEN I WANTED ONE OF MY FRIENDS TO COME help me out of this situation with Hook earlier, no one was around. Now that I'm having fun, Cam decides to make sure I'm okay? He probably came over here with the sole purpose to irritate me, as usual.

Cam strolls away, whistling, but I want to sock him. Instead, I take my seat beside Hook. "Sorry about that. Cam's—"

"Hey, I don't want to cause problems." Hook slides off the tailgate. "When Lane said you two weren't a thing, I assumed you weren't seeing anyone else."

"Oh." I look down to the ground. Lane and I aren't a thing, but I'm surprised he encouraged Hook. "Well...I don't date."

Hook turns back to me with one brow arched high. "You don't date?" He leans against the tailgate, inching closer to me. "Why?"

My stomach does this little quiver thing when I hear his soft drawl. I focus on my fingernails, pushing the cuticles back. He's going to think I'm crazy.

I keep my head down and answer, "It probably sounds—"

"Regan?" An unfamiliar voice interrupts me.

When I look up and see Brea up close and personal, my whole body tenses—screaming to retreat.

Brea chomps her gum in my face. "That's your name isn't it?"

I nod, in shock she's addressing me. Ugh, she's even prettier up close.

"Have you seen Lane? He said he'd be right back, but he's not, so if you did, can you tell me where he went or where he is or something?" she rambles on.

Brea's just like...ugh. My muscles were just starting to loosen up after Cam's spectacle, and this chick drudges up Lane's ex. Brea is the blonde version of Johanna. *Please, Lane. Please don't do this again.*

Hook answers for me.

Brea looks down her nose at me and flashes a familiar "don't even mess with me" look. The same look every one of those girls who think they're better than everyone else throws at girls like me, trying to intimidate.

I match it with one of my own, and she leaves. I've had plenty of experience with "the look," but I'm not sure if I can deal with another Johanna.

CHAPTER EIGHT

Regan

HANGING WITH HOOK WAS FUN AND EASY UNTIL Brea showed up, bringing the nightmare memories of Lane's ex with her. Now it's awkward and wrong. And I can't push aside the fact that I saw Stacey Faniger leading her pack of fork-tongued gossips toward the bonfire. I've been bitten by those vipers more than once. She's the main reason I try to stay away from crowds.

Going to college in Florida, hours and hours from here, would be so great. I can't wait to get out of this town and away from the Faniger family fan club.

"Tell me more about Eckerd College. I want to know everything."

Hook and his talk about college takes my mind off the Fanigers and Lane and his ex in a matter of minutes. He looks handsome in the glow of this new Atlantis he's telling me about. Eckerd sounds like heaven on earth. Campus right on the beach, sun, surf, science...amazing. I must be dreaming.

"Regan?" Hook pauses.

"Yeah?" My mind is floating in my possible future.

We're both reclined back, resting the palms of our hands on the truck bed. His thumb grazes the top of my hand, causing my breath to catch in my throat.

The shadows hide his soft brown eyes. "Would you like to—"

"Hey, come on." Lane's snarly growl startles me, pulling me out of my bubble.

My body jumps. Epinephrine shoots through my veins, causing my heart to whirl. I look down at the space between Hook and me. Except, there's not much space. With Lane scaring me and being this close to Hook, I probably look like one of those bulging-eyed cartoon characters.

Hook slides his fingers over the top of my hand. Now my heart's never going to slow down.

I close my eyes and breathe out the words, "Lane. You scared me."

Lane glares at me. "Cameron wants us." He nearly spits the words at me.

I lean away from his acid-tainted breath, unsure of where this attitude is coming from. Lane chews on the inside of his cheek. What's he so annoyed at?

I scowl back at him. "What's wrong?"

He folds his arms in front of him, taking the stance as if he's digging in for the night. He tosses Hook a glare and then turns it back on me. "Are you coming?" It wasn't really a question.

I slide off the tailgate. "I guess." I shake my head, silently asking Lane what his problem is.

He grabs my hand, squeezing a little too hard, and leads me toward Cameron's truck. When I glance back to Hook, I'm positive my mouth is gaping open like a fool. I quickly turn back to see where Lane's hauling me so I don't trip and become more of a laughing stock.

"Quit dragging me," I push out the words under my breath.

He doesn't listen.

Lane finally stops when we're standing next to Cameron's truck near the water's edge. It's dark, except for the light shining on the water. At least the crowd is back at the bonfire.

CHAPTER NINE

Regan

I'M ABOUT TO JUMP LANE'S CASE WHEN HE HUFFS, "What are you doing hanging all over that guy?" His hushed voice is barely under control.

"What are you talking about?" My blood's about to boil.

"You've been throwing yourself at him all night." Lane doesn't get riled up easily, but now he's pushing words out through clenched teeth. He's been acting weird since graduation earlier today, but that's no excuse.

"I wasn't hanging on anyone." He's out of his head. Brea was hanging all over him.

He barks out a cynical laugh. "You were practically sitting on his lap before I pulled you off of him."

Oh, it's on. "I think you need to get your eyes checked. No, it's your brain. It's all fogged up from that fleshy little number hanging all over you."

Lane's nose scrunches, causing his face to look like a shriveled prune.

I push up on my toes and keep dishing it to him. Nose-to-nose. He's going to get the same clenched-teeth treatment as he gave me. "You know, that girl who was shoving her boobs in your face."

He scoffs. "I haven't seen anyone shoving their boobs in my face." His volume is quiet, but snarkiness practically drips off his voice. "Trust me, I'd notice if they were."

I stay on my toes. "Oh, I think everyone noticed."

"Don't be laying your guilt on me." Lane's smug words hang in the air while he shifts away from me as if this is over.

This isn't over. I step into his space and whisper as sweetly as I can. "Brea. You know, the girl who was about to fall out of her bikini top? The girl who was in your space, trying to get your hands all over her." I push his chest with my pointer finger. "*That* fleshy little number. So, you better get that giant log out of your eye before you try pulling the splinter out of mine."

He snorts and turns toward me. We're kind of hidden on the other side of Cameron's truck, but Cam's light bars cast enough light for me to see Lane's sneering face.

"Splinter? That's a joke. You need to worry about that guy I rescued you from. I don't know what line of crap he's been feeding you, but you're swallowing it hook, line, and sinker." He touches his finger to the end of my nose. "You were all over him. And you liked it."

My mouth flies open. Nothing comes out. His accusation drives through my chest and wraps around my heart like a boa constrictor. "I was not—I didn't—I can't believe you said that."

Lane inches closer. "He must have had some real southern charm." His voice drips with spoiled honey.

"We were talking about college." I lean forward, too. "Not that it's any of your business."

"College?" He tosses his head back. "Ha!"

I turn away and cross my arms over my chest, digging my fingernails into the flesh of my arms.

Lane moves closer, breathing down the back of my neck. "The way he was checkin' you out in that low-cut, tight fitting, sparkly shirt? Yeah, I'm sure he was thinking about academics." His sarcasm falls from his mouth onto my shoulders, making the weight on me even heavier.

I whirl around on my heel. "You told me this shirt was fine!" My hands clamp my hips, digging my fingers into my jeans to gain a little self-control. "At least I have a shirt on. Unlike your new friend."

Lane blows out a rumbly breath through his nostrils. "Even if Brea was shoving her boobs at me,"— he folds his arms tight across his chest— "what I do or don't do, and with who, is not your concern."

I stumble backward a step. "That's how it is?" I calm my voice and try to gather my shattered pride. "Now that you've graduated, your best friend's opinion means nothing?"

Lane sucks in a quick breath but stops himself before he speaks. His hand runs through his hair. He repeats the action once more before turning away from me, rubbing the back of his neck. Lane whirls back around to face me. "I guarantee he has more than college on his mind."

"Please," I snarl. "What's with *you*?" Not that I expect an answer.

He turns it up again, laughing bitterly. "What's

with you? You don't even know that guy, and you're acting like he's your best friend."

His words slap me across the face.

Cameron yells something at us, but all I hear is a rumble. He runs by Lane and me, stripped to his boxers. Cam's voice bellows through the night air, hollering all the way into the water, leaving a big splash as he sinks below the surface.

I watch silently with my arms dangling, waiting for Cam to pop up, wishing I could sink under the surface with him and wash this night away. When I see him bob in the water, I shift to leave.

Lane latches on to my wrist.

I jerk my arm out of his grasp and continue walking.

CHAPTER TEN

Lane

REGAN SLIPS THROUGH MY FINGERS, AND I WATCH her walk away. Every step she takes, the knife inches further into my chest. This is not the way tonight was supposed to go. I can't help it if Brea won't stop getting up in my business. It's not like I'm into her. Regan's the only person I let in my business, but it's different. She's different.

Grr, I never thought she'd let her guard down and break her own rules, especially for a guy she doesn't even know. I can't believe she's falling for Bobby's moves. He must have laid his "southern charm" on so thick it poisoned her.

All my muscles coil, ready for a fight. Ready to take Bobby on. Even my hands are balled into fists. The wild pounding of my heart against my ribs pumps the energy through my body.

Girls.

I clasp my hands behind my head, pulling at my hair, while Regan slips between the cars and out of my sight. She's the one that came up with her no dating rule. She's the one who came up with the "rules of friendship." No gossip and no backstabbing are good ones, but number three is unfair. No dating within the group? What if I really got close to Haylee or Tobi or... my shoulders fall...her?

A frustrated growl grows behind my clenched teeth, and I whirl around to let it fly out of my mouth over the water.

She's so stubborn. She never gives any guy a chance. At least that's what I thought until Bobby walked into her life tonight. Regan talking to this guy has blown everything out of the water. If she's having such a great time with this stranger, would she agree to go out with Cam? When I leave for college, is someone else going to take my place?

Argh! I haven't been able to stop thinking about her with some other guy all day.

She was sitting on my blanket, on my tailgate, laughing with a guy who was not me. It's a punch to my gut. She betrayed me. But the truth is...I'm not really hers to betray.

I never gave any thought about leaving her to the wolves when I move for college in the fall. When guys ask me if we're dating, I answer no, but make sure everything about me says yes so they'll stay away from her.

Sure, I think about what it would be like to kiss her. That's what guys do—think about girls. A thought like that's flashed across my mind about Tobi and Haylee before, but it's just a thought. I don't actually want to kiss them. But I know the curve of Regan's lips. I've traced them with my eyes for a long time now.

"Dude, did you see that hang time?" Cam sneaks up behind me, shaking the water off his body like a dog.

I shove my hands in my pockets and glance back at him. "Yeah. Nice."

He snickers and takes a few steps to the towel hanging off the bed of his truck. "Where's Regan?" He dries his body and wraps the towel around his waist.

I look back over the water. It's been a long time since I've felt this heaviness caused by a girl. I fill my lungs before I turn around. Her brother made me promise to look out for her. Can I cross that line? Can I let myself go there? Will she?

Joey's voice rings out from behind me. "Nice one, Cam."

Cam chuckles. "Yeah, thanks, man."

I escape and cross the patchy, grass-covered ground to find Bobby and make sure he hasn't followed Regan.

CHAPTER ELEVEN

Regan

LANE'S STUPID WORDS SWIRL INSIDE MY HEAD. *None of my business.*

So what, am I just some silly high school girl now? He's dumping his best friend? Hook/Booker/Bobby—whatever his name is—stands next to Nick, talking to Stacey of all people.

She looks over at me as I pass by and flashes her cruel grin, taking hold of his arm. She continues making her moves on him, angling her dangerous lips to his ear. Probably whispering a hypnotic chant.

Stupid boys.

This is one more good reason to up the ante on my rule. Instead of no boyfriends, maybe it should be a no boys. At all. Cameron and Lane were both over-the-top tonight. Coming from Cameron, yeah, I kind of expect it, but from Lane? His words about Bobby echo in my ears, and it totally ticks me off that he's probably right about him since Bobby's now tangled with Stacey. Bobby's not even her type.

This burning in my throat is more than annoying. If I could tune out all this rattling in my head, maybe the acid will go back to where it came from. I push every last ounce of breath from my lungs as I lay back in the tall chord-grass, pressing the heel of my hands to my stinging eyes.

Crickets, please do your magic and turn this night around.

A squeal echoes from the shoreline. When I sit up to see what's going on, an object flies past me and thuds in the grass. Dead fish. Ugh, the stink is overpowering.

Another fish flies through the air, landing a little closer to me. I can't seem to get away from the drama tonight.

That's it, I'm walking home. It's not that far. Lane has a flashlight in his glove box, but I'm not going anywhere near his truck. I'll see if Cam has one.

I stand and schlep through the grass. Not even one step into my trek, something hits me in the back. "Ouch!"

The same shrill of a voice turns to laughter.

Did they seriously bean me with a dead fish? Why did I agree to come here? I knew this party was bad news, but I didn't know I would end up friendless and getting pelted with rotten fish.

My stinging eyes finally find relief when they flood. Tears spill over my lashes and down my cheeks in a steady stream. I can't believe my Dad listened to Lane and let me come here tonight.

Wiping my cheeks and sniffing, I move as fast as I can out of the grass. I don't stop until I arrive at the passenger door of Cam's truck, a few feet from where he's standing at the hood. "Cam?"

He turns to see who's calling for him. "Hey." The smile in his voice takes a little pressure off my chest, dampening the burn. "How'd you like my cannonball?"

I stay by the door. "Do you have a flashlight I can borrow?"

A loud Stacey cackle fills the cool air and makes me cringe. Hook must be telling her the same line of crap that made me laugh. It sucks the breath right out of my lungs.

Cam makes his way toward me. "Yeah, I should." He's sporting a beach towel around his waist.

I step back from the passenger door so he can rummage through his stuff.

"What do you need the—" Cam halts as soon as he opens the door and the cab light reveals I've been crying. He lowers himself to eye level with me, moving a finger to lift my chin and inspect my face. "What's wrong?"

Tears fill my eyes again. I pull away from his touch and drop my head, trying to will the floodgates to close. My fingers curl into a fist in protest. *Do not cry at this stupid party!*

"Your flashlight? Please." My voice is wobbly.

"What's going on?" He closes the door and waits patiently in front of me.

But I don't want to tell him anything. I just want to go home.

"Where's Lane?"

I've been trying to avoid Lane altogether. I can't watch him get together with another Johanna. And he has the nerve to accuse me of throwing myself at some guy I just met?

"Probably off with some girl." I try to come across as flippant, but I'm not sure it works.

Cam frowns. "Lane?"

I nod, swallow, breathe, repeat. "We had a fight." My voice cracks. "And someone hit me with a dead fish."

"Hit you with a dead fish?" Cam tries not to laugh. He probably thinks I'm joking.

I nod. My shoulders droop even more. I know he's not making fun of me, but his snicker is salt in my wounds.

Cam wraps me in his arms. "I'm sorry."

Any other time, I'd be pushing Cam off me, but I collapse against him and let his warmth and soft shushes calm the crazy ball of emotions exploding inside me.

"I'll take you home if you want. Can I let my shorts dry a little more?" Cam's voice is so soft and sweet.

I nod.

He rubs my back. "You want me to punch Lane for you?"

A tiny smile barely lifts my cheeks, cracking my sadness, and I nod again against his warm chest.

He pulls back and looks at my face. "Serious?"

Cam's silliness cracks my sullen mood even more. "No. I guess not."

His body shakes with quiet laughter, and he brings my head back to his chest, rubbing soothing circles on my back. "Too bad. I haven't been in a fight for awhile. I'm gettin' the itch."

A puny giggle bubbles out of me. Cam would never start a fight with Lane. He talks a big talk, but he's a teddy bear when it comes to his friends.

He leans back to look at me. "You gonna be okay?"

"Yeah." I sound pitiful.

Cam keeps his arm around me and tucks me to his side. He guides our steps to the front of his truck. We watch the idiots in the water and listen to their banter. Cam can be a super nice guy, even if he ticks me off a lot.

"Why'd you want my flashlight? Were you gonna walk home?"

Cam knows me better than I thought. I nod, but don't say anything. All this turmoil is exhausting, and I just want to go home and go to sleep.

Cam rests his head on mine, squeezing my shoulder with his hand. His tenderness lifts the weight I was under. It wasn't that long ago Cam was being an arrogant jerk, pushing my buttons. Right now, he's a gentle giant, exactly what I need. That's a real friend.

"Can I ask you something?" He keeps the quiet tender voice he's been using. "Do you think rule number three is still a good idea?"

My brows pinch together. That came out of left field. "Yeah," I croak, sounding more like an amphibian than a sixteen-year-old girl.

He looks down at me out of the corner of his eye. "We're not freshman anymore. I think we've grown up, don't you?"

How did we go from bad Lane and dead fish to the rules of friendship?

I shrug. Sometimes this guy makes no sense at all.

"Give me a minute to put my clothes on." He laughs. "That sounds naughty." He laughs again. He's so in your face about stuff like that. Not much of a filter, but he held back the teasing at least. "Go tell the girls I'll be back. I'll meet you up at the fire."

I shake my head. "Not the fire." I want to avoid both Lane and Hook.

Cam tightens the towel around his waist. "Okay, where, then?"

I keep my eyes down. "I'll go find them and come back."

Cam gives me another hug, whispering over my head, "I'll be waiting."

CHAPTER TWELVE

Regan

TOBI AND HAYLEE WERE TALKING TO HER BOY-friend and his friend when I told them I was leaving.

I rub my bare arms, hugging myself to stay warm as I trek back to Cam's truck. Of course, I bypass the general direction of the bonfire and keep my eyes down to avoid fueling any gossip about me crying. It's chilly and my body's had all the drama I can take for one day.

A shadowy pair of legs clad in jeans strides out from behind a car ahead of me and takes up my path. I veer to the right. They veer to the right. I veer to the left. They veer to the left. Keeping my head down, I glance up to see who this jerk is.

I sigh and change direction, hoping Lane will just go wherever he was going. I'm too drained to fight again.

"Regan." His voice carries a softer tone than the harsh donkey bray it resembled earlier.

I keep walking. Just because he doesn't sound like a jerk at the moment doesn't mean I want to talk to him.

The plod of his hurried footsteps comes closer. "Regan, wait."

Hurt wells up inside me again. "Go back to your party."

I've almost made it to Cam's truck. I pick up my pace and swallow down the tears and emotions, but they get lodged in my throat.

"Stop running away from me." He grasps my upper arm, turning me to face him.

Running away from him? Oh, he's really got a way with words tonight. "I'm not running from you. I'm going home."

I spin on my heel and continue toward my destination. The burning in my chest makes another show. I press my already balled fist against my sternum, trying and relieve the pressure.

"Please." Lane's soft, pleading voice slices through my cold flesh, straight to my heart.

I freeze to hear what he has to say to me. Cam has turned off the light bars mounted on his cab and brush guard, making it much darker out here by the water, but I see a shadow on the other side of his truck watching Lane and me. It looks like Cam.

The titter of voices from the party hangs in the air, taking up residence with the crickets.

Lane steps so close I think I can feel the heat from his body. "Can we talk?" His voice is barely above a whisper, but it's crystal clear.

My teeth grind together. Part of me wants to tell him, "No, you told me off already, I don't want to hear it again." Another part wants to say, "Took you long enough." I hate it when we fight, but we're like brother and sister. It's bound to happen.

While I'm having my internal debate, Lane's fingers comb my tangles, running down my back. He's been fascinated with my hair since we were kids. Goosebumps prickle all over my arms and down my spine, causing me to shiver.

"You're cold." He hugs me to warm me up. He's trying to bring us back to normal.

I mumble into his bonfire-smoke-drenched

shirt, "Cam's taking me home." I push back against his chest to separate myself and find Cam.

Lane resists my strength and leans his head closer to mine. "I'll take you. You can warm up in my truck while I find Cam. Okay?"

I sigh at Lane's suggestion. "Fine." I nod toward the shadowy figure. "Cam's back here."

Light from a car swipes across Cam's sad face, spiking a surge of guilt inside me. He was really great to me tonight, but I'm sure he'd rather stay here than drive me home anyway.

I wave at him and mouth, "Thanks."

Cam gives me a chin nod, but his expression stays the same.

The light disappears, and I take off toward Lane's pickup, not waiting for Lane to tell Cam what he's probably already figured out.

CHAPTER THIRTEEN

Lane

THE CLOSER WE GET TO REGAN'S HOUSE, THE tighter my muscles become. I'm still not sure exactly what's going on with us—with me.

I pull in her drive and shut off the engine.

Regan's hand pulls on the door handle. "I'll see you at church tomorrow."

"Wait." The security light mounted on the shed casts streams of light that bend through the windshield, highlighting the curve of her lips. I squeeze my eyes shut and rest my head against the back of my seat. "Let's go to the creek for a while."

She sighs. "I'm tired. Come inside."

My head rolls to the side. "Come on."

"Lane," she whines.

I'm not going to talk about tonight around her parents. "Just for a little while."

"Fine," she moans. "I need to tell my parents I'm home."

I grin and wait for her to step out before doing the same. Regan strides across the lawn ahead of me, and I catch myself appreciating her girlish figure. A silent chuckle shakes my chest because it's not the first time I've checked her out.

She stops at the steps to wait for me. I trot up to the door. Her parents won't have a problem with us going to the creek. We usually hang out by the water, fish, watch the moon cross the sky—we've been doing it since we were kids.

After she checks in, Regan grabs a jacket from a hook near the door. We make our way down the path to the creek. Falling in step with each other, I have the urge to slide my fingers between hers. Instead, I shove my hands in my pockets and listen to the critters talk to each other.

I stop before the bank, but Regan continues to the edge of the water. She stares up into the sky, and I go into pacing mode.

I need more time to think about this. I'm not even sure what's going on between us. Does she feel it? Was she jealous of Brea? Did she feel betrayed when she thought I was having fun with another girl? She's going to freak out if I come out and ask her this stuff. How did all this happen?

"Are you going to pace all night?" Regan hasn't moved. The night sky continues to hold her gaze.

I move my feet, swishing through the grass, and come to a stop behind her. "Look, I'm sorry."

She folds her arms in front of her. "What was that all about, Lane?"

A spark ignites inside me, like it did earlier. "You kind of started it." My words come out harsh and not at all like I want. Why can't I say "I didn't like that guy taking my place" instead of crazy, cagey words?

She spins to face me with her mouth gaping open. "What? How?"

I squeeze the back of my neck, grunting at my stupidity. "Do you like that guy?"

"Yeah, he was funny and nice." She shifts her weight from one foot the other while I recover from her words knocking the wind out of me. "He was telling me about this college that might be perfect for me."

Great. He's luring her to his college. "What happened to your no dating rule?"

She rolls her eyes at me and turns back toward the creek. "I'm not dating the guy. Tonight's the first time I've ever seen him in my life. How can I be dating him?" She stretches her arms out wide, swinging back around to me, growing irritated again. "There was never any kind of chance I'd ever be dating him. He's from Alabama, for Pete's sake, and he goes to college in Florida."

I hold my palms up to calm the storm gaining strength inside her. Before I can get any words out, she's at it again.

"Besides, if what you do and who you do it with is none of my concern, then my dating habits are none of yours."

Her words dropkick me. If I could take every word back, I would.

I take a step toward her. "I'm not into Brea." I lift my arms wide wishing she'd walk into them. "She's so not the kind of girl I'm interested in." I scratch my head. "I don't even know why I said those things. I didn't mean it."

Her shoulders relax, and I take another step closer. "I'm sorry. About..." I look down at my thumb rubbing against my open palm. "I thought your no dating rule was a big deal to you, and I didn't want you to break your promise to yourself." *Gah, Lane! That's a total lie.*

"Well, I guess sometimes things aren't what they seem, are they? You and Brea—me and Bobby." She looks down and fiddles with the sleeve of her jacket.

I scoop a strand of her hair, twirling the ends between my fingers. It's always so soft and silky. Even though I've played with her locks like this for as long as I can remember, I realize it's one of the things about us that is more. More than friends, maybe.

She leans her head against my chest, causing a spark when we connect.

"So, you liked him?"

She lifts her gaze to mine, and I hold on with everything I've got. I think maybe she feels it too...the spark between us.

"Stop staring at me." She looks down, breaking our connection.

Maybe she didn't feel it. I've got to recover my sanity. My hand snakes around the back of her neck, and I pull her into a headlock at my side.

"Stop!" She pushes my arms and tries to pull her head out, doing her best not to laugh.

Regan trying to get out of my headlock never gets old.

"It's not funny." She pushes and struggles against me. "We're not ten years old anymore."

Regan pulls as I let go, causing her to stumble back and nearly land on her butt. I can't help my laughter.

She peeks through her messy mop covering her face. "You're such a jerk."

"Aw, come on." I reach for her arm and pull her down with me to lay in the grass.

Our breathing slows while I weave her soft strands around my fingers like a ribbon.

The conversation with Cam from the diner and at the party circulates through my mind. I've got to know what she thinks about it. "I saw you hugging Cameron at the party."

"So?"

"So, what was that about?" I try to keep my voice light and even.

"I was upset." Her irritation is starting to show, but I've got to know what went down.

I coax her the best I can. "And?"

She turns her head toward me. "And he was consoling me because of you. I was ticked off at you, jerk-face."

Maybe I pushed the wrong button. At least I'm

getting some info, which is more than Cam was willing to give me before I left the party. "That's it?"

Her face twitches. "What do you mean, 'that's it?'"

I brush my hand down my face and decide to keep fishing. "Do you have a thing for Cameron?"

She rolls her eyes and laughs at me. "A thing?"

I don't care. I'm pressing the issue. "Do you want to date Cameron?"

Her brows shoot up. "No, I don't want to date Cameron. Rule number three. Hello."

"What if the no-dating-within-the-group rule didn't exist? Would you then?" Maybe I'm pushing too far.

She springs to a sitting position, swinging her arm out to the side. "No! I don't want to go out with Cameron. Geesh! This is ridiculous." Shaking her head, she faces the creek.

I sit too. "You're sure?"

"Are you serious?" She turns back to me. "Oh, my gosh! Yes! I'm sure." She growls, turning away again. "You hug me all the time. It doesn't mean I want to date you. What's with you?"

Nice. Not exactly the ending I was expecting. My breath whistles across my lips as I push it out.

"Okay." I plop back on the ground and keep my mouth shut.

She follows suit.

We need to lighten things between us. I roll to my side, facing her. "Your hair smells like smoke."

"I know it does." She playfully pushes me. "Stop being a jerk."

I chuckle. "Takes one to know one."

Regan falls back into her quietness, and I comb my fingers through her hair against the damp grass. She's probably thinking about that stupid college Bobby was seducing her with. It's no secret she wants to leave this town behind. After today—after feeling this spark between us—there's no way I'm letting her leave me behind too.

Thank you for reading "Spark" by Sally Henson! To connect with Sally and learn more about her books and special offers, visit www.sallyhensonwriter.com.

TELL ME SOMETHING REAL

Kelsie Stelting

CHAPTER ONE

"COME ON, MIDNIGHT!" I STOOD IN MY STIRRUPS and whipped the reins behind me, pushing my horse to go faster over the countryside.

Hot wind slipped through my hair and sent my t-shirt billowing around me. We worked in cadence— my horse, the wind, and me. The thunder of her hooves, the chaos of the breeze, and my panting breath formed a melody sweeter than any song.

We crested the hill, and I pulled back on the reins to slow her down. My own slice of Texas splayed out before me, with black cattle grazing the green grass as far as my eyes could see. I imagined the wispy clouds floating across the sky were painted there just for me and the special scent that filled the air had been designed by God himself, just for this moment.

I never wanted to live anywhere else. Never wanted to be anywhere else.

When Dad said someone needed to check cows that afternoon, I jumped at the chance. Even though it was dry as bones and nearly a hundred degrees outside, I knew I needed to get away from the house. This drama with Rhett and Cheyenne was crushing me.

My brother had cheated on his girlfriend with my best friend, and I didn't know who to be angrier with. Not that I liked Rhett's girlfriend, but she didn't deserve that. And Cheyenne should have known Rhett was off limits. And all the while, my love life was going through an even worse drought than Texas.

Midnight pulled her head down to chomp on some grass, and I leaned forward to pat her neck. Her coat felt moist with lather, but I rubbed anyway. She hadn't gotten me away from my problems, but she'd tried her hardest.

I scanned the pasture, wondering which corner I should take first. Maybe I could start toward the north and loop back to the creek. A short swim would be an awesome way to end this horrible day, and I might even be able to dry off on the ride back home.

I pulled up on the reins, and Midnight

begrudgingly lifted her head. Gently, I tapped my heels to her side and steered her toward the fence. Might as well check that too while I was out.

Usually during the summer, cattle stayed pretty healthy. The main thing was making sure they had water, that the fence stayed strong so they wouldn't get out, and then checking for infections or snakebites. Texas was full of surprises, especially around my house.

Luckily, Midnight was a good horse. She knew to look out for holes and snakes, and if I started her along the fence, she knew to walk it. As we paced through the pasture, my eyes trailed to a spot just over the horizon. I couldn't see it, but I knew Curt lived there.

Curt was older, almost twenty, and worked on the Shilling Ranch as a hired hand for the summer. Ever since we worked cattle together in May, I couldn't get my mind off of him. He was tall and strong—stockier than me, which was rare. I had my dad's muscular build, and having shoulders stronger than most guys wasn't exactly a turn-on.

But Dad always warned me against dating temporary help. He said custom cutters who came to harvest wheat or work on ranches in the summer always had a girl in every town.

Honestly, I'd be happy to be Curt's girl in any

town. But that was about as likely as me forgiving Cheyenne. At least anytime soon.

Off in the distance, I saw a cow separated from the rest of the herd, and my instincts perked. Cattle didn't go out on their own unless something was wrong.

Midnight seemed to notice my interest shift, because her head swung in the same direction. I nudged her side, and we trotted toward the cow, slow enough as not to scare her. I didn't want to cause her any trouble since she'd be calving in just a couple months.

As I got a little closer, I kept a sharp eye on the ground. If she'd been snake-bit, it could be nearby, and the last thing I wanted was to fall off a spooked horse. But I didn't see anything and didn't hear any rattles either.

Midnight and I got a little too close for the cow, and she stumbled away, faltering on a swollen leg.

I swung down off the saddle and put the reins over the saddle horn. Midnight knew to stay.

Slowly, I edged closer to the cow, stopping when she seemed nervous, then moving forward until I stood only a few feet away.

Her knee was swollen to the size of a volleyball. I grimaced. Snake bite.

There wasn't anything I could do at this point

other than to check back on her the next day and make sure it didn't get infected.

I stepped through the buffalo grass back to Midnight and pulled some cake out of the saddle bag. It wasn't really cake but the cows acted like it was. I dropped a handful of the pellets in front of the cow, and she nibbled it up. "Get better, girl."

Midnight was already grazing, ripping up strips of grass and grinding it between her teeth.

"Really? You just ate."

She snorted and flicked an ear back.

I chuckled. "Fine, but it's going straight to your hips."

She kept grazing. Apparently she didn't care.

I walked back to her side and put my foot in the stirrup. Then, I hauled myself up and back into the saddle. We still had half the pasture to go.

CHAPTER TWO

MIDNIGHT WALKED LAZILY TOWARD THE LINE OF trees that marked the creek, and I laid over the saddle, relaxing into her flowing walk. Other than the cow with the snake bite, everything seemed in order.

Sweat prickled its way down my spine and added friction to my underarms and jeans where they rubbed against the leather saddle. The back of my neck burned like I'd regret not wearing sunscreen in a few hours. The stand of the oak trees and their shade couldn't come soon enough. I needed a cooldown, and fast.

Midnight slowed the closer we got to the stream, having to pick her way over old, fallen branches. We drifted under the canopy, and I immediately felt better.

The swishing leaves and cooler breeze felt like a blessing on my skin.

I steered the reins to make Midnight walk alongside the creek. The water flowed slow and was down this year, but I could still get in and cool off.

Once we got close to deeper end, I stopped Midnight and hopped down. She probably needed a drink. I led her to the sandy creek bed, and she immediately dipped her head down. Her soft lips touched the water's surface, and she slurped.

I laughed. Horses drinking never got old.

"Hello?" a voice called.

I jumped. Curt's head and bare shoulders peeked out of the water, only a hundred feet away. Now that I looked around, I saw another horse tied to a tree several yards away.

Midnight seemed totally ambivalent to Curt and his horse, but my heart pounded and my head felt hot. What was he doing here? On our land?

Curt waded closer to me. Fifty feet off. Then twenty. Then ten. I still couldn't find my voice.

The water only came to his knees now, dripping off his boxers.

"Harleigh, right?" he asked.

I swallowed against my dry throat and jerked my head in a nod.

He rubbed his wet hands together. "Sorry, I was checking cattle in that field over there, and Frank said there was a good pond over here, and I..."

"Thought it'd be nice to cool off?" I finished for him.

He nodded, looking toward the ground.

Without his eyes on me, mine felt free to scan his body. Wet, brown hair covered his chest and legs and trailed into his shorts. His shoulders were broad and thick. He didn't look like any guy I'd seen in high school.

Probably because he wasn't in high school, I reminded myself.

"Checking cattle too?" he asked, looking back toward me. He was close enough now for me to see the smattering of freckles on his shoulders.

I nodded. "Yeah."

"Everything clear?"

I grimaced. "No. One got a snakebite. Rattler by the looks of it."

He sucked in a breath through clenched teeth. "Ouch."

I nodded, and for a little bit, the sound of Midnight slurping filled the air.

"You know what I do when I have one with a snakebite?" he asked, walking closer to pet Midnight's neck. "I always give 'em a little cake. I mean, I can't make it better, but it feels like I'm doing something at least."

My lips spread into an easy grin. "No way."

He looked over at me, his hand still on Midnight's mane. "Yeah?"

I flipped open my saddle back and pulled out one of the bigger pellets.

"Great minds think alike." He laughed.

I couldn't get this stupid grin off my face. Curt was standing two feet from me, had the same feeling toward cattle I did, looked amazing shirtless, liked my horse... Gosh, my cheeks were hurting.

"Well, I better get back to the house," I said. I had to get out of there before I branded myself in his mind as a stupid schoolgirl with an even stupider crush.

He eyed me evenly. "You don't wanna swim?"

In the soft, shaded lighting, I could see his eyes were hazel, but not just a mix. They started almost blue around his pupil and faded to soft brown. They looked good with his darker hair.

"I..." My mouth opened and closed with each attempt at an answer. Curt hadn't said he was leaving. And I'd just planned on shimmying down to my sports bra and spandex. Going to the pool in an actual swimsuit made me feel uncomfortable. "I guess so."

Curt jerked his head over his shoulder like he wanted me to follow him and started walking toward the deep spot.

I stood by Midnight, shocked. Was this really happening?

He looked back at me. "You coming?"

My head jerked up and down on its own.

Sunlight filtering through the leaves bounced off his grin. "Good."

With my heart bouncing off the walls of my chest, I led Midnight to a tree and tied her reins to a sturdy branch.

It was now or never.

I started with my t-shirt, feeling self-conscious about my muscular shoulders and flatter chest. Then, I slipped off my boots and wiggled out of my jeans. Adjusting the hem of my spandex, I looked back toward the pond. Curt wasn't anywhere to be found.

He hadn't run off, had he? I looked through the trees, searching for him, then saw a splash out of the corner of my eyes.

He burst through the water and shook his head back and forth, sending a spray of water around him. When his eyes met mine, he smiled.

I glanced back at Midnight. If only I could be as

good at navigating these waters as she was the pasture. "See you soon, girl," I said under my breath.

I chanced a nervous grin back at Curt and stepped carefully over the ground to avoid branches or sharp rocks. I felt his eyes on me, scanning my body, and wrapped my forearms around my waist. Being strong came in handy on the ranch or in sports, but now, in front of a guy, I wished I was a little slimmer, softer, more feminine.

Curt didn't seem to mind, though, because he kept looking at me as I stepped into the water.

"Better?" he asked.

I bent my knees so the cool water rose from my waist to my neck. "It feels like heaven." I waved my arms through the water, feeling it slip through my fingertips and soak through what little clothing I wore.

Curt lifted his chin. "Tell me about yourself."

My cheeks felt hot, even with the water's cooling effect. "Um... What do you want to know?"

"What do I need to know?" His eyes seemed to focus right in on me, and I felt like I was sitting under a magnifying glass.

I dipped my chin down so the tip of it hit the water. "I go to school at Roderdale, I'm really good at volleyball, but I like basketball better, and... I dunno. I mean, what is there to tell?"

"Tell me something real."

I looked at him, studying him now. Something real. "On top of a horse is the only place I feel like me."

CHAPTER THREE

ALMOST AFRAID TO SEE WHAT HE THOUGHT ABOUT that, I tried to gauge his reaction under my lashes. He had his gaze tilted toward the water reflecting the mix of blue and green above, then he gave a sort of half smile half shrug. "Well, alright then."

I stared at him but found myself smiling back. "Alright."

What did two strangers do in a pond? I hated going to the pool because I always felt bored and couldn't just lie around for hours on end like some girls did. But it seemed like this water had become charged with nerves and excitement and every emotion in between, and I didn't know what to do with that either.

He ran both his hands over his short hair. "Wanna see who can hold their breath the longest?"

"What?" I laughed. "Are you serious?"

With a crooked grin, he said, "'Fraid you'll lose?"

I sent a splash his way. "Not a chance."

Chuckling, he said, "You're on. Let's go on three."

"One."

"Two."

A devilish grin flashed across his face, and my breath caught.

At the same time, we said, "Three."

I dropped my feet from under me, pinched my nose, and plunged below the water's surface. The world went silent in my liquid cocoon, but my thoughts ran wild.

Curt rested under the water not two feet from me. He saw me in what equated to a swimsuit and hadn't made up an excuse to leave. And he was intense, not in a creepy way, but in a way that told me he wouldn't shy away from a challenge. From someone like me.

My lungs started burning, but I stayed under, stubborn. I still hadn't heard him splash above the surface.

A few bubbles escaped through my lips. And a few more.

Finally, the sound of him breaking through the water reached me. Music to my ears.

I steadied my feet beneath me and pushed my head into the sweet, warm summer air. I pumped my fist. "Told you I'd win."

His chest heaved, between gasping for air and laughter, and my own mirth blended with his.

A light, tinkling sound I didn't know I had within me filled the air with his deep chuckle and floated past the canopy of leaves and branches. If this ever went anywhere, or if it went nowhere, I'd never forget this moment.

He hung his head, feigning disappointment. "Fine, you got me. But can you do a handstand?"

I scoffed. "Since I was five."

He caught my eyes in a challenging stare. "Prove it."

Raising my eyebrows, I shrugged. I bent at the waist and ducked under the water, pressing my hands into the soft silt and raising my legs until they cleared the surface. Air tickled my legs, and I wiggled my toes, showing off.

I stood back up to see him clapping like I'd won the Olympics. "You missed your calling."

"Yeah, well, I don't exactly have the gymnast build."

"You're right," he said. "I like the cowgirl build better."

My stomach jerked around like I'd swallowed a school of minnows while hand standing. "What about you?" I countered. "Any special tricks?"

He scratched the bottom of his chin. "I can eat a whole ham."

I laughed. "That doesn't count."

"I can do a chin-up."

"You're getting warmer."

He folded his arms over his chest, making his muscles ripple with the water. "Well, we can't all be gorgeous *and* talented."

There were the stomach minnows again. "Come on."

He skimmed his flat hands over the water. "Well, I am pretty good at launching people."

I raised my eyebrows.

"It's true," he said. "I'm pretty popular at pool parties."

"Yeah?"

He grinned. "Let me show you."

Lost in his smile, that wide, happy expression that made my knees sway like the grass in a summer breeze, I nodded.

His expression turned to that intense look, and

he kept his eyes on me as he walked closer. When he stood about six inches from me, he turned around so I had a clear view of his shoulders. Of a black tattoo—a cowboy kneeling in front of a cross decorated his right shoulder blade.

"Grab my hands," he said, lifting them over his shoulders.

I gripped them, and even though my hands were big, his covered them, making me feel secure.

"I'm going to go under," he said. "You put your feet on my shoulders."

My stomach sunk. It would be so embarrassing if he couldn't throw me. "I'm way too heavy."

He turned his head over his shoulder and looked at me, serious. "I've got you."

Still nervous, I nodded.

He plunged below the surface, and just like he said, I put my feet on his shoulders. He rocketed upward, more exhilarating than any roller coaster, and flung me into the air. I hit the water and sank to the bottom, grinning even though I was in the pond.

When I came up, he had a satisfied smile. "Did I tell you, or did I tell you?"

"That was so fun!" A laugh bubbled out my lips. "Definitely a special talent."

He shrugged, and a silence fell between us.

Anywhere else, I would have felt uncomfortable, just looking at him and him looking at me, but here, sheltered by the trees, it seemed like I could do anything, be anyone—even me.

He lifted his hand from the water and rubbed the back of his neck. Holding his fingers in front of his face, he pulled a lip up. "I'm all pruney."

I held my wrinkled fingers out for him to observe. "Same."

"Let's get out?"

Leaving was the last thing I wanted to do. Getting out of the pond meant going back home, back to drama, and back to this life where Curt was the summer help on the next farm over and I was a manly girl no guy could love.

"We can lay out?" he suggested like he was reading my mind. "Dry off?"

"Yeah." My shoulders relaxed. "I'd like that."

CHAPTER FOUR

I TOOK MY PONYTAIL OUT AND DIPPED MY HEAD under the water to calm my hair. It had to look like a rat's nest and a half right about now. Then, I followed him to the bank, almost feeling cold under the breeze. Through the trees, the sun hung closer to the horizon. It had to be half-past five, maybe six.

Curt moved toward his horse, a beautiful bay mare with a wide, white blaze down her face. I didn't walk too close to her since I always wore shoes around horses, especially ones I didn't know, but I would have loved to run my hand over her coat or feel the feather soft fuzz on her nose.

He reached into his saddle bag and pulled out

a worn bath towel. "I brought this for me, but you can have it."

"No, that's okay. I was just gonna lay out on a tree."

"No way." He pushed the towel into my hands. "Mama taught me better than that."

Feeling warmer inside, I walked behind him toward an old oak. I knew that tree—the branch drooped low and wide, perfect for drying off from a swim. The branch had died years ago, and Rhett and I had peeled off all the bark to leave the smooth, white wood exposed.

I draped the towel over my shoulder and rubbed gently since I already felt a burn coming on underneath my tanned skin.

Curt swung up on the branch, and I followed him. There was enough room for both of us. I rested my back against the tree, spread the towel over my lap, and laced my fingers behind my head. He sat with one leg up, staring off at the pasture.

I stayed silent for a moment, listening to the gentle swishing grass and the occasional snort from our horses. It was hard to still my heart when a guy who liked me sat inches away and I knew we'd need to leave soon. Mom or Dad'd come looking for me, and I didn't think they'd buy the whole coincidence story.

"It's so different here than South Dakota," he said.

For the first time, I heard his accent, but I didn't mind. Sometimes that southern drawl girls went crazy over just made guys sound dumb.

"I've only been once," I admitted.

"Mt. Rushmore?"

"When I was ten. I mostly remember being really cold and wanting to go back to that reptile place."

"Reptile Gardens." He laughed. "Sounds about right. We live about half an hour north of there. In the black hills. It's crazy out here without all the trees. You can see forever."

A small smile played over my lips. "I know what you mean." That was why I loved the ranch so much, why I always raced to get up that hill.

"Think you'll stay here?" he asked. "You know, after high school?"

Ugh. After high school. "I have no idea."

I wasn't smart like Rhett. I'd be lucky to keep my grades high enough to graduate, let alone get into college. School didn't make sense like working did. Some of those "smart kids" wouldn't last a second figuring out which animals were sick or learning how to fix up a fence that lasted.

"That's fair. I didn't have a clue either." He

dangled his leg off the branch, slowly swinging it back and forth.

"Yeah?" That made me feel a little better.

"Still don't. That's how I ended up here." He nodded toward his place. "Frank's Dad's uncle. He kind of did a favor to have me out here."

"But it seems like you know what you're doing."

He laughed and nudged my knee with his. "You mean I'm not a city slicker."

Heat found my cheeks. "Well, I just…"

"Nah, I worked on a ranch back home. But my mom wanted me to get out of there, see the world."

"And what do you think of it so far?"

"So far? I like it." His eyes traced a path from my toes peeking off the branch, up my legs, and locked with mine. "A lot."

I tucked a drying strand of hair behind my ear, feeling self-conscious. "You miss anyone from back home?"

Every bit of me hoped Dad wasn't right about guys like Curt having a girl in every town, but I couldn't let my hopes touch the clouds without knowing how far they'd fall.

He shrugged. "My mom, I guess. Dad. I have two younger sisters—a freshman and a seventh-grader. They're alright."

Even though he acted nonchalant, I noticed the way his smooth forehead creased at the mention of his family. But that didn't tell me what I needed to know. "No girlfriend?"

I held my breath like earlier, waiting for the worst.

The crease grew deeper. "Some girls don't get the country."

That made sense. Other girls my age turned their noses up at hard work because it smelled a lot like cow crap and came with early morning alarms. Mom sometimes talked about girls not cut out for the isolation of the country, but I didn't get that part. How could you be alone when you had a horse holding you up and the whole world splayed out before you?

"What about you?" he asked. "No boyfriend?"

I snorted. Not that I meant to—it just came out—but I went with it. "There's not a guy in a hundred-mile radius even remotely interested in dating a girl like me." That feeling right before crying pitched a tent behind my eyes, and I blinked it back. Cowgirls didn't cry—at least not in front of anyone else.

Curt stayed quiet so long I had to look back at him, just to see what he was thinking. I wasn't above jumping out of a tree and making a run for it if I had to.

But his eyes, hard and soft at the same time, held mine. "That's not true."

CHAPTER FIVE

THE AIR GREW THICK, SO VISCOUS I COULDN'T breathe or even begin thinking about what that meant. I jumped down from the tree, hoping the air might thin down there, and looked up at him.

His brows furrowed, and he seemed like he was somewhere between confused and hurt. That look was all wrong on him.

"Let's play truth or dare?" I blurted.

Gosh, I was an idiot. How old was I? Thirteen? And I probably wouldn't have even played back then except Cheyenne made me.

Curt's lips faltered but eventually spread into a grin. "Game on."

He hopped down from the branch, landing

softly for how strong of a guy he was. Coming to stand right in front of me, he said, "Truth or dare?"

I jutted my chin out. "Dare."

His grin came easier now. "I knew it."

Now I felt dumb. "Fine, truth."

"No way." He laughed. "You already said dare."

I rolled my eyes, but couldn't keep the smile off my face. "Fine, what's my dare?"

"I dare you..." He put his fist under his chin. "I dare you to eat a piece of cake."

"Where're we gonna get cake?"

He shook his head, his eyes dancing with mirth. "Cow cake."

My mouth dropped open. "You're kidding."

Grinning wide, he nodded toward my horse. "Come on. Should be a piece o' *cake*. Ha. Get it?"

He started laughing at the pun, and I hated that I joined in too.

"Whatever," I said, turning toward Midnight to hide my smile. "Fine."

He laughed at my back.

I walked a few feet closer to Midnight then looked back over my shoulder. "Really?"

He made a shooing motion with his hands. "Go on."

I groaned and crossed the last several yards

to my horse. She swung her head to look at me, and I patted the soft spot on her nose before moving to my saddle bag and taking out one of the pellets. The greenish-gray piece was about the size of my ring finger, but I broke it off until I had a chunk the size of my thumbnail.

"I gotta see it," Curt said.

Holding the feed in my fist, I walked back to him. "You know what they say. If it looks like a cow and eats like a cow…"

"But talks like a chicken…" He tossed his head back, laughing.

I rolled my eyes and held the little piece out for him to see. Then I popped it in my mouth, crunched a couple of times, and swallowed. "Bleh! That thing tastes like dirt!"

He laughed harder. "I can't believe you ate that!"

"I'm not going back on a dare!"

"I admire that." He wiped at his eyes. "Okay, dare."

"Hey." I gave his shoulder a playful punch. "You're supposed to let me ask."

He hung his head like he felt bad, but grinned at me under his lashes. "Sorry."

I barely found my voice with him looking that

cute. He definitely had an unfair advantage. "Truth or dare?"

"Dare."

Imitating him, I dropped my voice low and said, "I knew it."

He laughed. "Come on, Lane, gimme your worst."

I smiled at him calling me by my last name. "You mean it?"

"A hundred percent."

I looked around the field. Now that I thought about it, truth or dare was a dangerous game in the country, especially since he started us out eating stuff. My mouth still tasted like dirt. "Okay, I've got it."

He cringed. "Let me have it."

"Okay. Go take a cow patty, put it on your head—" At the shocked look in his eyes, I burst out laughing, but held up a finger. "—put it on your head, and walk with it until you get to the water. Then you can jump in and clean off."

"Wait," he said, "are you calling me a shit head?"

I laughed. "If the *poo* fits."

He wagged a finger at me, chuckling. "I think this might be worse than eating cake." He laughed gain. "You proud of yourself?"

I shrugged, smiling sweetly. "At least I let you clean off. I'm going to be tasting this thing all night!"

"Fair point." He put his hands on his hips, drawing my eyes to his muscled torso and the line where his boxers met his skin.

My heart pounded. "Go on, find it."

With his back turned to me, I bit my bottom lip. Curt was so hot! How was this happening?

He bent over and picked up a flat, dried out cow chip and walked toward me, pinching it between two fingers. "I have to put this on my head?"

"Yep."

"And walk to the pond?"

"Uh huh."

"And fling it away."

"You got it."

"And then get wet again?"

I laughed. "I think you got the hang of it."

"Oh." He looked to the side, then sprung forward, grabbing me at the waist and hoisting me over his shoulder.

"Hey!" I screamed, suddenly seeing the ground below me. I twisted to find him holding the chip over his head with his free hand.

"You never said you weren't coming along for the ride!" he gloated.

"Oh my gosh." My heart pounded, giddy. "You're crazy!"

"Yep!"

He flung the cow pie away like a frisbee and crashed into the water, taking me with him.

I plunged under then came back up, gasping, laughing.

His head broke through the water a few feet away from me.

"You're insane!" I smacked my hand on his chest, but he caught it and pulled me closer.

"And?"

My cheeks felt hot, but I couldn't look away from him. His lips were slightly parted, and I wanted to dare him to kiss me, but that would be too cliché.

"Truth or dare?" he asked, the movement of his mouth mesmerizing.

I closed my eyes to clear my head. "Truth."

"What's your idea of a perfect date?"

Anywhere, anything with you, I wanted to say. I opened my eyes again to see his growing darker, intense in the fading evening light.

"My perfect date?" I hedged.

He nodded, his chin dipping into the water.

"Wildflowers. And a movie. And buttery popcorn. And something under the stars."

His lips spread into a smile.

"Truth or dare?" I asked, very aware of his smooth skin and soft chest hair under my hand.

"Truth."

Feeling unsteady, I chanced it. "Earlier, when I said there wasn't a guy within a hundred miles interested in me, you said that wasn't true."

He nodded.

"Yeah, well." I looked down at the water then back to him. "Who's that?"

"You're looking at him."

"You're kidding." No way could this guy—this handsome guy with a smile that could melt the polar ice caps and a frame built from hard work on the farm—no way could he be interested in me.

But he was staring at me with those eyes that said he meant it. "Not even close."

"Really?" It came out as a whisper and blended with the soft colors of sunset.

He nodded and held my hand between both of his. "But that's not how you ask a girl on a date."

My eyes flew open.

"Harleigh." His fingers traced a strand of hair behind my ear. "Will you go out with me?"

So soft I almost missed it, I heard the rumble of an engine. My heart dropped. Dad's truck.

CHAPTER SIX

I PULLED MY HAND OUT OF HIS AND RAN THROUGH the water to shore. "I gotta go!"

Without waiting, I flew over the bank toward Midnight and my pile of clothes. I was still sopping wet, but I yanked on my jeans, fumbling with the button. I didn't even bother with socks or my shirt, stuffing them in my saddle bag instead.

Curt caught my arm. "Harleigh, what's going on?"

I looked toward my hill, forcing my dripping hair back into a ponytail. Dad's pickup crested the hilltop, barely a fuzzy red spot in the distance.

"You want to go out with me?" I asked.

"Of course," he said, emphatically moving his head up and down.

"Want to explain to my dad why we're out here half naked?"

Understanding dawned across his expression, and then he took my arms in both his hands, looking me square in the face. "I'll come by your house at seven tomorrow."

I looked from his hazel eyes to his full lips, reveling in the words he'd said. Before I could talk myself out of it, I touched my lips to his. "I'll see you tomorrow."

His finger brushed his lips, and I grinned at the sight.

Midnight pawed at the ground. She knew we had to go.

I hooked my foot in the stirrup, swung into the saddle, and started Midnight out of the trees, toward Dad's pickup. We reached open pasture, and I started her at a lope. Wind whipped through my hair, cooling my skin, evaporating the water. We worked in cadence—my horse, the wind, and me. The thunder of her hooves, the chaos of the breeze, and my pounding heart formed a melody sweeter than any song.

We met Dad in the middle of the field, along the trail. He had his window rolled down and his arm hanging out the side. He took me in, wet hair, damp jeans, and the grin I couldn't wipe away.

An amused smile turned up the edges of his mustache. "Everything alright?"

"More than alright."

I couldn't wait for the rest of summer.

Thank you for reading "Tell Me Something Real" by Kelsie Stelting! To connect with Kelsie and learn more about her books and special offers, visit www.kelsiestelting.com.

TICKETS ON HIMSELF

Kat Colmer

"have tickets on yourself"

Australian informal: to think highly of yourself, be conceited

CHAPTER ONE

THE MOMENT I OPEN MY BIRTHDAY CARD AND THE tickets fall out, a shocked hush chokes the room.

Nanna Yola beams at me. "It's to see that hottie Sam Stokes. Such a glorious voice. And the way he moves those hips! Now that's what I call talent, Ally." She wiggles her penciled-on eyebrows, and I have to quash the impulse to give her an updated definition of the word talent. "You were such good friends for so many years. I know you must be desperate to see one of his concerts."

I force my lips into something I hope resembles a smile. "You shouldn't have." As in, she shouldn't be using words like "hottie" when talking about Sam

Stokes, and she definitely shouldn't have bought me tickets to his concert.

Everyone knows how I feel about Sam and his artificially sweetened, boy-band vocal chords. The awkward silence and the oh-crap expressions on my parents' and Bea's faces are proof of this. But Nanna's memory has been taking more and more frequent vacations lately. Still, her heart's in the right place. And anyone else would be ecstatic to receive Sam Stokes tickets for their eighteenth birthday.

Anyone but me.

I shove Sam and his swinging hips out of my mind and lean in to hug my well-meaning Nanna. "Thank you. These are... They are..." Stuck for words that aren't of the curse variety, I kiss her papery cheek. She smells of roses and kindness. "I don't know what to say."

I've got to do something, though, because any more of this awkward tension and someone is likely to pass out from holding their breath for too long. Desperate, I throw Bea a "help me" look over Nanna's shoulder.

"Cake!" my best friend booms into the silence. "Isn't it time we did the cake?"

"Yes!" Mom jumps to attention and dashes into

the kitchen. The sudden movement acts like the flick of an "at ease" switch, and everyone relaxes.

I give Bea a grateful smile as we edge over to the table at the far end of the room. "Thanks."

"No problem. Your face looked like it might crack under the weight of all that pretending." Bea plucks two glasses from the table. "So I'm guessing you're not planning on going to the concert?"

"Hell no!" Not even if Sam was the only singer alive and this was my last chance ever to listen to live music.

Bea purses her lips. "Maybe you should go."

My mouth slackens. How can Bea even say such a thing?

She shrugs and unscrews a bottle of lemonade like her suggestion is no big deal. "His music's really changed over the past year. It's not that awful boy band pop. It's...I don't know...different."

"That doesn't mean he's any different." I cross my arms, but Bea holds out my drink and I have to uncross them again.

"And you know this because you actually spoke to him at the last Brinski-Stokes get-together?"

I give the tiny bubbles jostling for space in my glass my full attention. Bea knows I only suffer through those annual meetups because Mom and Sam's mother are such good friends.

"Well?" Bea presses.

I lift my eyes to meet Bea's. "You know full well I can't talk to him without it ending up in a shouting match."

At least, that's how the first Brinski-Stokes get-together ended after he hit the big time. Thankfully, he was on tour for last year's. I don't have high hopes for this year's.

Bea's mouth opens like she's about to comment, but she takes a drink from her glass instead. "What are you going to do with the tickets then?"

Set them on fire. Flush them down the toilet. Cut them up into tiny little pieces the way Sam cut up our friendship three years ago. But as much as flames and scissors and the sewer are an appealing fate for anything relating to Sam Stokes, I probably should give someone else the chance to go to the sold-out concert.

I huff and take a sip of my soda. "Don't know. Give them away, I guess."

Bea's brows almost disappear into the party streamers hanging from the ceiling. "Have you got any idea how much those tickets would've cost? They're A reserves. You can't just"—she waves a hand in front of her face like she's swatting a fly—"give them away like that."

"You have them then."

She's never hidden the fact she listens to Sam's music. At first it hurt, but our friendship is bigger than our differing opinion of Sam Stokes and his fake, out-of-tune pop. Besides, he'd been her friend back then too. It wasn't Bea's fault I'd started to see him as something more.

Eyes gleaming with an idea, Bea looks over the top of her glass at me. "You should sell them. Online. To the highest bidder."

I frown. The idea feels wrong, like I'm making money off Nanna.

"You could buy your nanna something really nice for Christmas," Bea says, as though she's heard my thought. "And you'd probably still have enough left over to go see that singer Pearl something-or-other you like so much. It's a win-win, Ally."

"Pearl Strickland." I rub at the condensation on my glass and consider Bea's argument.

It would be nice to treat Nanna to something special. Almost as nice as it would be to see the very jazz legend Sam and I both worshipped before Australian Idol made a pop idiot of him. The irony is sweet and tastes a little of revenge.

Behind us, a chorus of "Happy Birthday" erupts. I turn to watch Mom carrying a Nutella cake decorated with eighteen candles. Bea bellows out the song, deliberately off key. The image of Sam singing beside her flashes across my mind before I can stop it.

The last time they stood side-by-side at my birthday was three years ago. That afternoon, Sam had given me tickets to see Pearl Strickland along with my very first kiss. Two days later, we'd had the mother of all arguments and then...

No. I wasn't wasting any more time thinking about the stranger Sam had become. I was putting the tickets up for sale online tonight and ridding myself of Sam Stokes for good.

CHAPTER TWO

"YOU'VE GOT TO BE KIDDING ME!" I PUT MY CE-
real bowl on the pile of sheet music next to my laptop
and refresh the TicketBay page with my Sam Stokes
listing. Wow! Looks like Nanna will be getting a nice
little trinket from Tiffany's under the Christmas tree
this year, because some insane person is willing to pay
triple the original price for the tickets.

I shake my head and check the buyer's details.
Jeremy24. Also based in Sydney, Australia. And clearly a
guy with more cash than brains if he's clicked the "buy
it now" button instead of putting in a conservative bid
like any other sane person. I only put that crazy price
up on a whim. I didn't think anyone would actually pay
it.

What is it with Sam Stokes and his stupid music? It's like he's brainwashed everyone on the planet into hero worshipping him. Ugh.

I compose a quick message to Jeremy24 between spoonfuls of soggy Cheerios, telling him he's the lucky (if mentally unstable) buyer of two Sam Stokes tickets, which I'll mail after he's paid. No point organizing anything until I see the color of his money. He might still come to his senses and back out.

But by the time I've showered and dressed, there's a message from Jeremy24 saying he's already paid.

I check my account, and whaddayaknow, the money is there. I type a reply:

Me: Hey there! Thanks for paying so quickly. If you give me your address, I'll post the tickets first thing tomorrow.

I'd post them today—that's how much I'd like to be rid of them—but it's a Sunday, so it'll have to wait. I turn away from the computer and grab my phone. Bea's probably not up yet, but I message her the news that my bank account just had a very healthy deposit.

When I turn back to the computer, Jeremy24 has responded again.

Jeremy24: Actually, I'd rather not risk the mail. My sister would kill me if they got lost in transit! I'm in enough trouble for missing out on the tickets when they first went on sale. She'd be shattered if I somehow messed this up as well. LOL. I'm away for the next two weeks, but will be back in Sydney a couple of nights before the concert. Could I maybe pick them up then?

So the tickets are for his sister. That kind of makes the triple payment sweet. Still stupid, but also sweet. Almost makes me feel bad for taking the guy's money. Almost.

I chew on the inside of my cheek; I don't like the idea of a face-to-face with a stranger I've met on the internet. Then again, he's already paid, so it's not like he's planning to run off with the tickets. If we meet in a public place and I have Bea with me...

I place my fingers on the keyboard.

Me: That should be fine.

Jeremy24: Great! You're a life saver :)

A life saver, eh? His sister must be a huge Sam Stokes fan. No different from most of the female population between the ages of twelve and twenty. I cringe at the thought, not quite sure why it's twisting something in my stomach.

I go to log off the computer, but there's another message.

Jeremy24: Sorry you're not able to make the concert

yourself. Hopefully you can do something fun with the money.

I snort. Better set this guy straight so he doesn't think I'm missing out on anything.

Me: No need to be sorry. I'm able to go, just not a Sam Stokes fan.

Three dots appear in the corner of my screen. He's typing.

Jeremy24: Really? According to my sister, every female between the ages of eight and eighty thinks he's great.

This time I bark a laugh. Eight and eighty. Sam wishes!

Me: You're being way too generous with that age range. And what makes you think I'm female? Maybe I'm a tattooed guy who's into heavy metal and wouldn't be caught dead at a boy band reject Sam Stokes concert.

Jeremy24: Boy band reject. Harsh. But are you? A guy, I mean.

My fingers hover over the keyboard. That's really none of his business. Still, I'll have to give him a description at some point for when he picks up the tickets so...

Me: No. Are you?

Jeremy24: LOL. Yes, I'm a guy. Name's Jeremy, but you've probably guessed that already. No tattoos. I'm eighteen, in case you're wondering.

I may have been wondering, but he doesn't need to know that.

Jeremy24: What about you? Any ink? A lover of heavy metal?

Me: Nope on both fronts. But I'd still not want to be caught dead at a Sam Stokes concert.

Jeremy24: So how'd you end up scalping Sam Stokes concert tickets? ;-)

The wink at the end of his question tugs at the corners of my mouth. The guy might not have any brains when it comes to money, but his sense of humor is intact.

Me: The tickets were a present. Nanna meant well.

Jeremy24: Well, you can tell your nanna they're going to a huge Sam Stokes fan.

Me: So how do you feel about Sam Stokes's music?

Three dots appear in the corner of my screen. Then disappear. It's a good couple of minutes before they show up again.

Jeremy24: His music is better than when he started. It's moved on from boy band pop, but he's still got more to learn.

I frown. He more or less repeated Bea's words from yesterday. Maybe I should listen to a recent Sam Stokes song and see if—I shake my head. What am I even thinking? Then the last part of Jeremy's message catches my attention.

Me: You make it sound like you're some sort of music expert.

Jeremy24: Not an expert, just got a serious interest in it. Am enrolled at the Con for next year.

I jolt up in my seat, almost knocking over the music stand next to my desk. The pages of my latest composition flutter to the ground—a kaleidoscope of black and white butterflies that make up part of my Sydney Conservatorium of Music admission portfolio.

Me: So am I! I'm majoring in jazz. Tenor sax and composition. You?

I tap the side of the keyboard as he types. The dots are taking forever to turn into words.

Jeremy24: Contemporary music. Vocal and composition.

I flop against my seat. What are the chances that this guy's studying at the same music college as me next year? I suck the inside of my cheek then break out in a grin. But contemporary music could mean anything. Even a love for boy band pop. I have to ask...

Me: So if you could see any concert you wanted regardless of cost, who would you see?

Jeremy24: Easy! Sam Stokes for sure!

My bubble of excitement deflates to match the

"Happy Eighteenth" balloons littering my bedroom floor. And here I thought—

Jeremy24: Kidding! Take me to a Pearl Strickland concert and I'll be your friend for life.

My jaw drops into my lap. Again, what are the chances? Finally, someone who understands Pearl Strickland's lyrical genius like I do. Someone who might fill the hole Sam left in my life when he walked out to become a traitorous pop star.

I smile, this time without sucking the inside of my cheek. The chances are looking pretty good.

I hesitate for only a second before I type the next message:

Me: I'm thinking the message function on this site is a bit clunky. How about I give you my number instead?

* * *

When my phone dings for the sixth time in as many minutes, Bea points at it. "Okay, what gives? That thing's been going off all morning."

I tuck the phone into my pocket and clear a plate with remnants of Nutella cake off the coffee table. We've been cleaning up the lounge room for a good hour, and we're still finding food in strange places.

"It's the guy I sold the tickets to," I say.

Bea frowns. "He's come to his senses and is

bombarding you with reasons as to why you should give him his money back?"

"No... Not exactly."

I get a what's-going-on look from my best friend.

"We're talking Pearl Strickland songs. He's trying to convince me 'Heartland Jade' is musically superior to 'The Last Summer,' and I can see what he's getting at because of the complex harmonies in the second half, but..."

Bea's eyes glaze over, and I trail off. Being the loyal friend she is, she's always supported my Pearl Strickland obsession, but she descends into a boredom coma as soon as I start talking about the finer points of music composition. She's a top forty kinda girl.

Bea waves her hand in front of my pocket. "So you've been messaging with this Jeremy guy all morning?"

I go to tell her that, no, it hasn't been all morning, but snap my mouth shut. A glance at the clock reveals it's almost lunchtime, and we've been messaging since just after eight.

I shrug. "Yeah."

My phone dings in my pocket, and I scramble to fish it out.

Jeremy: Okay, tell you what, it's a tie. Heartland

Jade will always be one of my favorites, but those sixteen bars of strings in Last Summer make it a valid contender for equal first place.

His words tip up the corners of my lips the way they have all morning. An overwhelming need to explain myself to Bea straightens my spine. "Turns out he's also going to the Con next year. Then there's the whole Pearl Strickland connection, and yeah, well, we seem to have a heap in common."

"The Con? Interesting."

It's not so much her words, but rather the loaded way she says them that leaves me frowning. I try to read her face, but she ducks to pick up an empty Maltesers packet from under the coffee table. I use the opportunity to quickly type *I can live with a tie* :), then scoop up the trail of Minty wrappers littering the floor between the sofa and TV.

Not two minutes later another ding draws our attention to my pocket. I reach in, itching to look at Jeremy's latest message, but I leave it when I catch Bea's eye. I've been distracted all morning, and it's not fair to her. Besides, if I keep acting all eager she'll read more into it than there really is.

I force myself to push all thoughts of Jeremy aside and take a look around the room. "I think we're pretty much done here," I say with a satisfied nod.

"Great." Bea takes the garbage bag from me. "I'll dump this on my way out."

My brows draw together. "You're leaving? I thought soccer training didn't start till two?"

"The Kraken told us to get there an hour early." Bea heads for the door. "She's getting worse the closer we get to the final."

Bea might moan about Coach Krakenau, but she's as serious about her soccer as I am about my music. Doesn't mean I'm not bummed about her needing to leave early. But it does mean I'll be able to message Jeremy without feeling guilty.

I walk Bea to the door and watch her tear off in her little red Mazda just as another ding chimes in my pocket.

This time I don't hesitate. I pull out my cell, read the message, and break out in a goofy grin.

CHAPTER THREE

FOR THE NEXT TWO WEEKS, NOT A DAY GOES BY that Jeremy and I don't message. We cover a lot of ground.

Movies: he's mainly a thriller fan, but since seeing *The Greatest Showman* he'll watch anything starring Hugh Jackman. (Who can blame him?)

Books: he's read the Harry Potter series. Twice. (Serious points there.) And he's currently into the latest Jay Kristoff trilogy. (Yay! I loved *The Illuminae Files*.)

Food: he'll eat anything, except avocado. (A guacamole gagging incident left him scarred for life.)

Favorite color: teal, like the ocean, which he loves but doesn't get to enjoy enough even though he lives close to the beach and likes to body surf. (Something I wouldn't mind learning!)

Siblings: One younger sister. Gets on okay with her as long as she doesn't make fun of anything to do with his music. (Preaching to the choir here! Can't stand it when Jamie makes fart noises whenever I play my sax. The guy is eleven! He should know better.)

All the messaging has made the time fly, and today's the day we're meeting in person. This afternoon. Only a little over four hours to go. Less than the length of a *Pitch Perfect* movie marathon.

I may be a little excited. Somewhere over two weeks and hundreds of messages it's become more than just a quick meetup to hand over concert tickets. It's now an official coffee date. (Mochaccino for him, double shot cappuccino for me).

But first I need to put up with Sam Stokes at the dreaded Brinski-Stokes family get together. Ugh.

My phone dings. It's exactly the distraction I need.

Jeremy: So is 4 still good for you? I could meet earlier if you want.

Me: Trust me when I say I'd love to, but my mom would kill me if I ditched this lunch any earlier than half past three.

Jeremy: Totally understand. These family friends must be a real drag.

Me: Not all of them. Just the son.

As soon as I send that message, I want to whack my head against my desk. Why did I just mention Sam? I don't want to talk about him, especially not with Jeremy. Sam and Jeremy are at complete opposites of my interest spectrum, and I'd rather not think about the two in the same brainwave.

Jeremy seems to have other ideas.

Jeremy: So what's the story with the son? Does he make fart noises like your little brother when you play your saxophone?

I splutter a laugh at the thought of Sam making fart noises while I play my sax. It'd never happen. Despite everything going sour between us, Sam never belittled my love of music. He understood all about the hours of practice, the grip-you-by-the-throat nervousness during an audition, the underlying passion that beats like a jungle drum beneath all the stress, making it worth it. Which is why his betrayal hurt so much.

My fingers hover over my cell. I still haven't met Jeremy, but I feel like he'd understand.

Me: No fart noises. Just the echo of an old friendship that died when he said some hurtful things a few years ago.

I watch for his reply, but there's nothing for the

longest time. Not even the little dots that tell me he's typing. I suck on the inside of my cheek—maybe I've scared him off with my deep and meaningful comment.

I should head downstairs; the Stokeses are due to arrive at any moment, but then three little dots dance across my screen. I hold my breath and watch them.

Jeremy: You have no idea how much I wish I could take back some of the things I've said to people I care most about. Maybe give the guy another chance?

I clutch the stair railing. He knows nothing about Sam and me. About the words that carved a hole in my heart. I blink back the memory, but it's no use. I still see them in my mind's eye, hear them booming in my head, feel them barreling through me like a stampeding horde of barbed wire-covered rhinos:

You're holding me back.

You're holding me back.

You're holding me back.

The doorbell rings. I swallow, blink again, and type.

Me: Not sure he deserves another chance.

From downstairs, Mom calls, "Ally? Where are you?"

I tell her I'm coming and trudge down the steps. At the bottom of the stairs, my cell dings again.

Jeremy: We all make mistakes. If he's anything like me, he's probably regretting this big time.

I frown at my phone. If Sam truly regretted what he said, then why hasn't he apologized? He's got my number. He could have called. Then I remember: he did. Just after the blowup. But I wouldn't talk to him.

Mom opens the door. I look up, and a mix of emotions hits me. Anger. Regret. Defiance. And a stubborn sense of familiarity and longing that just won't die no matter how much I try to kill it off.

* * *

After the customary hellos and ohs and ahs about how grown up we all are, Sam and I find ourselves trailing behind the others onto the back patio.

Hands shoved deep into the pockets of his designer jeans, his shoulders roll forward like he's trying to fold in on himself. He's sneaking guarded glances at me from beneath a fringe of dark blonde hair. I bet his personal groomer or image coach or whatever he calls the person in charge of his appearance has told him he's not allowed to cut it because all the girls think it looks hot.

And they'd be right, damn it. The too-long hair, the gray-green eyes, the whole boy-next-door-meets-runway-model look he's got going on works annoyingly well. I hate how aware I am of his looks.

We step out onto the patio and...crap! There are only two seats left. Opposite each other at the end of the table.

I throw Mom a pleading look, but she's too busy chatting with Mrs. Stokes to notice my desperation. So I slide into my seat opposite Sam and reach for the water jug to give my hands something to do.

"How've you been?"

His voice startles me, and I nearly spill iced water into my lap. I put down the jug and meet his gaze. It's still cautious but also surprisingly...friendly.

"Good. You?"

"Yeah...me, ah, too."

Well, isn't this riveting. But at least we're not shouting at each other. Yet.

Lunch progresses as it usually does. Jamie drags Sam's little sister in the direction of the pool as soon as he and Eleanor have scoffed down a sausage sandwich each. The Stokeses then ask the requisite questions: How did my final exams go? Am I excited about getting into the Con? What will I be majoring in?

When Mom and Dad ask Sam similar questions, they're careful not to focus too much on the pop star thing. I like to think it's because they know it annoys me, but in truth, it's probably because, surprisingly, he doesn't glam it up. The way he talks about the punishing tour schedule, people wanting to know Sam Stokes the star, not Sam Stokes the guy... I feel sorry for him.

Before long, our parents are back to their own conversation, leaving Sam and me to fend for ourselves.

"So, school," he says. "Weird that we don't have to go anymore after so many years, huh?"

I shrug. What does he know about going to school? He's had private tutors follow him around on tour for the past three years.

He pours himself a drink. "Congrats on getting into the Con."

"Thanks," I say, avoiding his eyes.

It was once our shared dream, one that he pushed aside in the name of fame and fortune. I wonder if he regrets it even just a little?

"I'll be seeing you there."

My head snaps up. "What? How?"

"I got in, too."

That's not possible. "You're barely ever in the country. Last year you spent nine months out of twelve overseas."

Eyes suddenly bright, he angles his head. "Been keeping tabs on me, have you?"

The possible truth of his words slaps me in the face, and my cheeks flame. Have I been keeping tabs on him? Oh man, I have been keeping tabs on him. How else would I know exactly where he was every day of last year? Let's be completely honest, probably the year before that as well.

It takes all my willpower not to drop my face into my hands. I've been keeping tabs on Sam Stokes! What does that mean? No, wait. I don't want to know what that means.

I give myself a mental slap. Focus. "Seriously, how are you going to attend classes when your tour schedule means you'll miss half the course?"

"Distance Ed," Sam says, around a mouthful of salad. "I'll be doing all the theory online."

My mouth drops open. "The Con doesn't offer distance education."

Sam pushes a cherry tomato around his plate. "I'm being given special dispensation."

I cross my arms. "Because you're a rock star?"

His brow pinches like I've hurt him. Good. Why should he get special treatment?

"I've got a solid record as a committed distance education student," he says, still pushing that tomato around his plate.

"How lucky for you." I don't even try to keep the edge from my voice.

He finally looks up. "Ally, can we..." He slides a

hand through his hair, sending that too-long fringe of his falling across his brow.

I smother an eye roll.

"We're doing the same course next year, at the same school," he says. "We should..." He glances down the length of the table at our parents, still engrossed in their own conversation. Eyes somehow equally guarded and pleading, he lowers his voice. "Can we go back? I hate us fighting. I want to go back to the way it was, Al, to being your friend."

I'm stunned. As in, I sit perfectly still in my chair, not even blinking. Finally, the words I've wanted to hear for the past three years hang between us. Inside me, something stirs and opens and— Wait. Something is missing. Something important.

Something that sounds like an actual apology.

I fold my arms tighter across my chest. "A friend doesn't accuse you of holding him back."

Sam cringes. "I shouldn't have said that."

"But you did." And it hurt. Badly.

"I didn't mean—" He leans forward. "Don't you get it? I wanted you of all people to be happy for me."

"Happy?" I scoff. "For selling out?"

"I know that kind of music isn't your thing, but would it have been so hard to support me?" His gaze pins mine. "Because if it'd been me, I would've been there with you every step of the way. Cheering you on, spurring you forward."

"Not holding you back, you mean."

Sam clamps his jaw.

We stare at each other, the words floating jagged and hurtful between us. I'm waiting, I realize, for him to negate them, to say they aren't true. That they were never true, because they were uttered in the heat of an angry moment. But the only sound I hear is something cracking and breaking inside of me. Or maybe that's my phone dinging in my back pocket.

It shocks me up out of my chair. I can't let Mom hear it—no phones allowed at the table—but more importantly, I need to put some space between Sam and myself. I can't believe I thought he'd actually apologize.

I grab an empty bowl of coleslaw and mumble some excuse about going to top it off, then hightail it into the kitchen. My eyes seek out the clock. Twenty-five to three. Mom definitely won't be happy if I leave now, but I can't go back out there. I pull my phone out of my pocket to read the message—and deflate a little. Not Jeremy.

Bea: You surviving?

Me: Barely. Am ready to make a break for it, though. Are you good to meet now?

I'm guaranteed a stern word from Mom tonight,

345

but this is an emergency. I need to get out of here or there's a high likelihood I'll end up on the front page of tomorrow's paper under the headline: *Crazed Teen Knees Pop Star Sam in His Stokes!*

Bea: Sure. Meet at The Thirsty Bean in fifteen.

Good. Now I just need to see if Jeremy is still able to meet me earlier. I send him a quick one liner. He replies straight away, saying he can be there around three.

I grab my purse as well as the concert tickets, and take a quick peek to make sure no one is missing me or the coleslaw. My parents and the Stokeses have taken their conversation across the pool to the cabana lounges, while Sam is still at the table, nose buried in his phone. Probably posting something about the lame BBQ he wishes he'd never gone to. Well, screw him.

I'm heading for the front door when Jeremy messages again.

Jeremy: Everything okay?

Me: No. But it will be in about twenty minutes. Can't wait to meet you :)

I pull the door shut behind me with a smile.

CHAPTER FOUR

BEA'S ALREADY AT THE THIRSTY BEAN WHEN I arrive.

"Let me guess, the annual Brinski-Stokes get-together didn't go so well?"

I huff and pull out a chair next to her. "If it was a paid event, I'd want my money back."

"Sam?"

"Who else?"

She scrunches her nose.

"What?"

She shrugs. "I just thought this time would be different."

The café door opens, and my head snaps up,

taking my heart rate with it. But it's only a group of women in a burst of brightly colored activewear.

"Was there yelling?" Bea asks.

"No." Although part of me wishes there had been.

In some ways, it would've been easier than the tense confirmation that Sam really thinks I held him back. The ridiculousness of it. I mean, really. He's the one who made the decision to throw away everything he'd worked for so he could bop around a stage singing three chord pop tunes instead of making real music. I was being a true friend by telling him he was making a dreadful decision.

Wasn't I?

I toy with the corner of the cafe menu. "Bea?"

"Yeah?"

"Say you decided to ditch your dream of playing soccer for Australia because you were offered a synchronized swimming scholarship. Would you expect me to support your decision?"

Bea screws up her face like she's sucked on a lime, then leans in to sniff me. "Have you been smoking illegal substances?"

I swat at her. "I'm being serious. Would you?"

She's still looking at me all dubious, but she's also got her thinking face on. "Well, yeah. I would."

It's my turn to suck a lime. "But it's the wrong decision!"

She shrugs. "But it's my decision, not yours. So if you're really my friend, you'd take me nose plug shopping no matter how much you hated the idea."

I suck the inside of my cheek so hard I'm pretty sure I've given myself a reverse hickey. Is Sam right? Was I the one who let down our friendship?

The café door opens again. I hold my breath. Then release it on a groan—more women in activewear, followed by some school kids. My phone says it's just past three. I don't know why, but Jeremy strikes me as an on-time kind of guy, so I keep my eyes glued to the door. Sure enough, it opens again and—

"You've got to be kidding me!"

"What? Is he here?" Bea turns.

"If you mean Jeremy, then no. But he is." I point at a guy slinking to the booth seats at the back of the café.

He's wearing a baseball cap pulled low over his face, and a dark pair of sunglasses hides his eyes, but even without the tell-tale too-long blond hair escaping the cap, I'd know the shape of Sam Stokes anywhere.

I push my chair back with a little too much force and stomp across the room toward him. "Are you following me?"

He backs up into the booth. "No."

"So the great Sam Stokes just happens to wander into the same café as me?"

His eyes shoot left, then right, but I don't care if anyone overhears. Let him get mobbed by screaming fans. After all, that's the life he's chosen.

"Ally"—he reaches out a hand, but thinks better of it and tips his head at the booth behind him instead—"can we please talk?"

I cross my arms. "Why? So you can tell me again how much I held you back?"

I can't see Sam's eyes, but the rest of his features tighten, then cave, like they're tired of playing games. "You have no idea how much I wish I could take back some of the things I've said."

My brows furrow together. Those words... Where have I heard them before?

Sam takes off his sunglasses. For a moment I'm distracted by the gray-green plea in his eyes. "Everyone makes mistakes, Al."

My mouth drops open. No. No! It can't be. He can't be—

I whip my cell out and, fingers fumbling, text Jeremy two words: *I'm here.*

And wait.

Three seconds later, there's a chime in Sam's back pocket.

I suck in a breath. Maybe I suck time right along with it, because everything around us slows to a muted crawl while I watch Sam pull out his phone and hold it up for me to see.

I'm here.

Jeremy's here.

Jeremy's Sam.

Sam is Jeremy!

"You lied to me!" It comes out half hiss half whisper. I can't decide what I'm feeling—disbelief or outrage. "Here I thought I'd finally made a real connection with someone, and you...you"—I gasp for air, fighting the rising tears that threaten to tsunami my anger. "And the whole time you were laughing behind my back." I turn for the café door.

"Al, no!" Sam's voice is right behind me. "It was never like that. It's just—Ally, please!" He slips around me, eyes pleading as he walks backwards to avoid me bowling him over. "I wanted to fix things, but you wouldn't talk to me, and the few times we did talk..." He cringes. "You know how that ended, so when I saw an opportunity to be me without you knowing it was actually me, I just..." His face crumbles under the cap that's slipped back to reveal his familiar features. "I

351

shouldn't have pretended to be someone else, but I just wanted... I want us to go back or start over or do whatever it takes, as long as there's an us again, Al. Please, here—" He pulls something out of his jeans pocket and holds it out to me. "This explains it much better."

I frown at the folded square of paper. My pride pins my hands to my sides while the pathetic part of me that still misses Sam urges me to take what he's offering.

But our charged exchange has drawn attention.

"It's Sam Stokes!" some girl yells from the front of the café. That's all it takes. Suddenly, he's surrounded by screaming tweens, thirty-something women in exercise gear as well as The Black Bean's barista staff.

That's my cue to slip out the door where Bea is waiting for me.

CHAPTER FIVE

"SO, THAT WENT WELL," BEA SAYS, OPENING HER front door.

I head straight for her bedroom. What I really want is to go home, bury myself under my pillow, and hide. But since there's a good chance Sam might go back to my place once he's ditched his mob of fans, Bea's pillow will have to do. Actually, Bea's pillow—or rather pillows—will do a much better job anyway, since Bea's bedroom is as girly and pillow-filled as she is mud-streaked and goal-hungry on the soccer field. My best friend is a beautiful study in contradictions.

I clutch her "Don't Annoy My Unicorn" pillow to my chest and collapse onto her bed. "I can't believe I didn't see it. I mean, the whole love of music thing, and

Pearl Strickland, and the fact he was out of town until just before the concert. He played me like one of his stupid pop songs. I'm such an idiot!"

"You're not an idiot." Bea sits next to me. "You've been looking to fill the void Sam left since the day he boarded a plane for his first big gig, and Jeremy fit the bill."

"But Jeremy is Sam!" I say into pink fluff.

"Right. So what does that tell you?"

Confused, I search Bea's face.

"Ally, in the last three years Jeremy is the only person who's managed to put excitement back in your voice when you talk about your music."

"That's because he's Sam!"

"Exactly!"

I frown.

She sighs, like I'm meant to know what the heck she's talking about. "Isn't it about time you admitted to yourself that no one will ever replace Sam and let the guy make amends?"

I scramble backward on my elbows until I'm sitting up. "If he wanted to make amends, he should've talked to me, not pretended to be someone else."

Bea raises a brow. "When's the last time you answered one of his calls?"

I don't need to say it. Bea knows it was a long time ago.

"Right. So there's no way you would've let him show you this." She pulls a piece of paper from under her stack of sports biographies and hands it to me.

I skim the page. Song lyrics. "When did he give you this?" It couldn't have been just now. Bea never went anywhere near Sam at the café.

"Two weeks ago. He wanted me to give it to you on your birthday, but when I saw your reaction to the tickets your nanna gave you, I figured you'd chuck it in the garbage without ever reading it."

She was wrong. I would have set it on fire or flushed it down the toilet. All the things I should have done to the blasted tickets instead of selling them online like Bea suggested I—

"Wait a minute!" I pin her with a narrow-eyed glare. "Exactly how did Sam even know about me selling the tickets?"

She gives me a sheepish look.

My mouth falls open. "Why?"

Bea throws her hands in the air. "Because this has gone on long enough, and I'm sick of watching you love-hate him from a distance. The two of you are meant to be friends! You're like two halves of a freaky Pearl-what's-her-name loving whole. Don't you get it?

You'll be lucky to find someone as good a fit as Sam." She grabs the paper from my hand and shoves it in my face. "And everyone deserves a second chance, Ally."

Lips pursed, I snatch the page back from her and take a proper look at the lyrics. By the third line my throat is thick, and the words start to blur.

And maybe, just maybe, I'm ready to let Sam back into my life.

* * *

The atmosphere in the Sydney Entertainment Center is electric. The place is packed, completely sold out. All six of his shows this month are. The faces that greet me when I look around range from young to old, both male and female, and everyone is infected by Sam's endless energy, dancing in their seats, singing along to their favorite songs. Even I find myself moving to the rhythm next to a hopping Bea. I'm surprisingly disappointed along with the crowd when he announces he's about to play his last number.

"I've got something special for you, Sydney."

The crowd goes off at his announcement like New Year's Eve firecrackers over the Harbor Bridge.

"This last song is my about-to-be-released single called 'Missing Me and You,'" he says over the roar. He looks in our direction even though I know he can't see us with the lights down. "It was written for a very special friend...a friend I owe an apology."

He plucks the opening bars on his guitar. Immediately, everyone pipes down to listen.

"*You were right there from the start,*" he begins. "*And we made music that touched hearts...we wrote songs that opened minds...then I said words that were unkind... it was my words that left you behind...words I wish I could rewind...*"

My throat goes thick like it did when I first read the lyrics, but his voice is a rich, dark dessert of soulful notes, and I can't help but eat it all up.

"*You see, I'm missing you and me...*" The song builds. "*I want us back to the way we used to be...I want us to be more than we used to be...together we can be more, oh so much more, than we used to be.*"

By the end of the chorus, the whole band has come in. Drums and bass and big power chords on the electric guitar turn the ballad into a soulful rock song and the crowd into an adoring, teary mess.

Me included.

He's good. I've always known his voice was good—it had been three years ago, so it's no surprise it's gotten better—but the song itself...it's complex and melodically thoughtful and just...bloody good!

I swipe at my eyes, trying not to be too obvious

about it, but Bea hands me a Kleenex without so much as looking my way. I shrug and take the tissue. She's seen through me for the past three years. It's not like she was going to miss my pathetic blubber fest.

The song ends, and the auditorium explodes in deafening applause. Sam waves his goodbyes before disappearing side stage.

Bea turns to me, face flushed, eyes sparkling with challenge. "You ready for this?"

I fill my lungs with courage. "No," I say, "but I'm going to do it anyway."

***

We're in the line of people with backstage meet-and-greet passes when a lanky guy with an earpiece and clipboard approaches. "Beatrice Hughes and Alison Brinski?"

Bea and I nod.

"Follow me," he says.

We do. Down several narrow passageways until we're ushered into a room with plush couches and a massive TV playing clips from the concert.

"Sam will be with you shortly," clipboard guy says. "Complimentary drinks and a cheese platter are in the fridge." He points and disappears out the door.

Bea doesn't waste time heading for the food.

"Might as well eat something. If that line of people out there is anything to go by, we'll be here for a while."

"I'll just have a bottle of water," I say.

An hour later, the door opens again, and I'm thankful I stuck to water. The sight of Sam, after he sang those words earlier, has my stomach churning with raw emotion. The way his T-shirt molds to his broad chest and shoulders isn't helping my equilibrium either.

"I'm really sorry you've had to wait," he says, stopping in front of the couch. "I have to do the whole photo thing with every VIP, and some of them get real chatty and...yeah." He rubs the back of his neck, his smile apologetic as much as it's shaky. "So, the show... what did you think?"

He's putting the question to both of us, but it's me he's pinning with his eyes, eyes that flicker with uncertainty. He's nervous! Sam Stokes is nervous about my opinion.

The silence stretches a little too long, and Bea jumps in. "It was great! Really good vibe out there. Everyone was feeling it, Sam." When I still don't say anything, she shakes her head and traipses off in the direction of the fridge.

He gives her a smile. "Thanks, Bea." Then he

swings his gaze back to me. "And you Al? What did you think?"

I stand and circle to the back of the couch. "It was...okay."

Sam's eyes never leave me. "Just okay?"

I shrug. "Maybe a little better than okay."

Bea snorts. I throw her a dirty look, but her head is buried in the fridge.

"Your music has...changed," I offer.

He edges around to where I'm standing and reaches for my hand. "Enough for you to come to another one of my concerts?"

I look up and find a completely different question in his eyes, one that's more about us and less about his music.

"You know, I think I might. Although, I'll need to sit somewhere I don't have to see any of those stupid 'Sam Stokes My Fire' fan posters."

His lips fight a smile as he slowly—cautiously— tugs me into a hug. "There are no fans or posters side stage. You can watch the shows from there."

Shows. Plural. As in, several, in the future.

I relax into his embrace, both familiar and new, and tip my head back to search his face. I find what I'm looking for. The same apology he sang about onstage shines a bright gray-green in his eyes.

"Well, in that case I'll brave another concert," I say.

"Yeah?" Sam leans closer, and the end of the word feathers my cheeks.

"Yeah," I want to whisper, but I can't.

Because my lips are busy learning the taste and shape of Sam Stokes.

Thank you for reading "Tickets On Himself" by Kat Colmer! To connect with Kat and learn more about her books and special offers, visit www.katcolmer.com.

UNSTOPPABLE LOVE

LOVE

Michele Mathews

CHAPTER ONE

THE RUSH OF THE MORNING HAD DIED DOWN. I FI-nally had time to wipe off the counter from the remnants of donuts, cinnamon rolls, coffee, and other fancy drinks people used to get their caffeine fix.

The bell hanging over the entrance rang, and a young man about my age walked through the full glass door.

"Hello." I dropped the towel in my hand to a bucket under the counter. "Can I help you?"

"Yes, is the manager around?" He came to stand at the counter in front of me, practically towering over me he was so tall.

"Ava's in the back. I can get her for you."

I had no idea why this guy was asking for her,

but this weird feeling crept into my body. Ava wasn't old enough to have a child his age. She didn't have a younger brother either, so that could only mean one thing—she had hired him to work here. I didn't like the thought of that one bit.

Why me? Why my last summer at home? Why did I have to work with a member of the opposite sex?

I turned to head back to the office and almost collided with Ava. "Sorry. Hey, this guy's asking for you."

"I heard someone mention my name." Ava smiled turned toward him. "Hi, Jace. I'm so glad to see you." She shook hands with him.

"Great to be here. You told me I could start to-day, but I wasn't sure what time I was supposed to be here," Jace said.

Ava paused. "I guess I didn't, did I? I'm sorry about that."

He gave her an easy smile. "No problem."

"It's probably best you came now anyway. Our rush hour is over. Mornings can get a bit crazy around here. Right, Peyton?"

"Oh, yes." My cheeks burned under his gaze.

Why was this guy making me blush? I couldn't stand boys, or young men, or whatever you called them at this age. To me, they really didn't deserve to be called men when they didn't act mature at all. They were just selfish jerks.

Ava waved for him to follow, and I watched as they walked together to the back room. The bell ringing at the front door made me jump, and I swiveled to see who came in.

An older woman approached the counter, and I smiled as I served her, trying not to show how bothered I was by the new employee.

After she left, I continued wiping off the counter and the few tables we had in the bakery's dining area. Just as I finished, Sadie came from the back. She was not only the assistant manager, but best friend Courtney's older sister. She'd helped me get this job.

I jerked my head toward the back room. "What's up with the new guy?"

"Ava hired him to help us with morning prep and some cleanup. Why?" Sadie opened the change drawer and grabbed some of the cash and credit card receipts. Neither Ava nor Sadie liked to keep much money in the drawer once the morning rush was over.

"Just wondering." I put the rag back in the bucket of water to hide my expression.

Sadie shut the drawer. "You had a reason for asking."

I hesitated for a split second. "Well, I thought it would just be us three working here, but I guess not."

"Sorry Peyton." Sadie failed miserably at looking even remotely apologetic. "Ava and I decided we needed some extra help around here, and Jace needed a job... I know Ethan hurt you, but you can't keep avoiding guys forever."

The sound of his name did weird, painful things to my insides, and I trained my gaze on the floor.

Sadie's voice softened. "He's not that bad from what I learned in his interview. You should get to know him. You never know what might happen." She patted my shoulder, and with the cash and receipts in hand, she turned and headed to the back.

I blinked back the burning in my eyes and swallowed at the dry spot in my throat. Sadie could say whatever she wanted, but I wasn't going to play buddy-buddy with Jace. After what happened with Ethan, I didn't want to be around boys. I didn't need any reminders I wasn't good enough. If I wasn't trying to prove my work ethic to my parents, I'd quit right now.

A few sets of footsteps sounded, and I turned to see Ava walking toward the front counter with Jace and Sadie trailing behind.

"Hey, Peyton," Ava said, coming to a stop in front of me, "I want to officially introduce you to our newest team member. This is Jace. He'll be our cleanup guy on the days he's here. Otherwise, we'll be doing what we've always done." Ava flashed a smile at me, looking between Jace and me.

I could tell she thought I'd be happy about the extra help. And, yeah, I'd had to work really hard to keep up with the summer traffic, but still. I fought to keep my expression even. She didn't know about Ethan, even though everyone at my school did.

Jace grinned and extended his hand. "Nice to meet you."

I didn't want to give him the slightest idea I wanted him here, but I couldn't just stare at him, especially in front of Ava and Sadie. So, I reached out and gripped his hand for the briefest of seconds. It felt warm, rough. Not soft like Ethan's had.

"Nice to meet you," I lied.

Sadie watched from behind Jace and Ava, shaking her head.

I swore Jace's smile got bigger, like he was actually happy to be working with me. My stupid imagination was getting in the way again. Sometimes I thought something was happening, but it really wasn't. I freaking hated it when that happened.

Ava's gaze shifted between us, but she finally broke the silence. "Ready to make some dough?"

He snickered at her pun, his eyes lighting up. "Sure." He looked at me one last time before following Ava to the kitchen.

Sadie hung behind, gawking at me. "Could you make it any more obvious?"

"What?" I averted my eyes to the door, thinking I heard it open.

Grinning, Sadie messed with the tablet we used to check customers out. "You think he's cute."

"No, I don't." I gave her a pointed look before staring out the window, hoping a customer would come in and distract her. "Besides, I hate boys right now, remember?" I said it to remind me as much as her.

"Oh, yeah, right." Sadie didn't sound convinced.

I kept my gaze out the window, and finally she finished up whatever she was doing and headed back to the office, leaving me alone.

A couple hours later, Jace returned to the front with a bucket full of clean water and a bright white rag. He started wiping tables off.

"I've already done that," I said over the counter.

His hand paused on the table. "Ava told me to do it."

"Oh, okay." I leaned against the counter and tried not to make it obvious that I was watching him.

He moved from table to table with ease, his

arms flexing and relaxing with each scrub. Now that I looked at him more closely, I could tell he went to the gym quite a bit, and his dark hair... I always told Courtney I wanted to date a guy who resembled Taylor Lautner, and Jace would qualify—

What was I thinking? I was not dating. I repeat. Not. Dating. Not even looking at guys.

He must have felt me watching him because he locked eyes with me and smiled wide.

My heartrate picked up, and I turned my back to him, straightening up some supplies on the shelves.

The bell signaled customers coming in. Over their shoulders, I caught Jace glancing at me. Apparently, I hadn't been the only one staring.

CHAPTER TWO

AS I DROVE TO MY GRANDMA'S HOUSE, ALL I could think about was Jace. One minute I was ready to quit the bakery, and the next minute I couldn't fathom leaving.

Grandma wasn't home when I arrived—probably out with her friends for an afternoon of shopping or something. She'd always been social, even in retirement.

I took my shoes and socks off and laid down on my bed. I lifted up my hips and pulled my phone out of my back pocket to call Courtney. Hopefully she was off work by now.

"Hey, girl, what's up?" a familiar female voice said on the other end.

I closed my eyes against the overhead light and my bad day, but all I could see was Jace's stupid arms and that smile that made my insides dance like a puppet. "I'm ready to quit my job."

"Why would you do that?"

"Ava hired a boy to work there."

"Oh, gosh," Courtney said, hushed. "I'm sorry, Peyton."

The jagged edges of my broken heart burned with each breath, and I swallowed hard. "I never dreamed they'd hire someone else to work at such a small bakery."

Tiger, Grandma's cat, jumped up on the bed, and I ran my hand over his striped fur.

"I mean, Sadie was saying how much business had picked up lately."

"Yeah, but Ava said it would be just us girls when she hired me." I hated the whiney way my voice sounded almost as much as I hated the idea of working with Jace.

"You know Ava. She wears two different colored socks just because she can't choose one." Courtney chuckled.

But I didn't. This wasn't funny in the least.

"Peyton, just because one boy hurt you doesn't mean all boys will. It's not your fault Ethan's a jerk."

Tears stung my eyes, and I wiped them away. "You're just trying to make me feel better."

"Yes, I am, and I hope it worked."

"A little bit." I sniffed. "But it doesn't change the fact Ethan used me for a joke. I dated the guy for months, and I hardly knew him at all. How am I supposed to trust a complete stranger?"

"Maybe you just missed the signs? I mean, maybe all you saw was this cute boy who took an interest in you."

I cringed. Courtney was blunt...and painfully honest. "You might be right."

"I know I'm right. I mean college is going to be a whole new world for you. You'll find that special guy and fall in love someday. Until then—"

"'You'll have to deal with boys. You can't avoid them.' Yeah, yeah." I'd heard the speech before, and I knew Courtney was right. "But I'm only gonna talk to Jace when I have to."

"Maybe you should get to know him. It'd make things at work a little easier," she said, and added, "Of course, it's your decision."

"Yes, it is. I need to go eat a little something. Talk soon."

I didn't give Courtney much of a chance to say anything else before hanging up. I was ready to curl up with a good book and get away from the disaster called today. As bad as I hated to say Courtney was right, she was. I'd have to deal with men for the rest of my life. I couldn't avoid them forever.

The next morning, Jace was already there when I arrived. He stood in the open window of the kitchen, right behind the counter.

He grinned at me and chirped, "Good morning."

How could he be so happy this early?

I kept walking toward the office. "Morning." I was not a morning person, so "good" usually wasn't in my greeting.

In the office, I hung my purse on a hook, grabbed my blue apron, and headed back to the front. I went through the usual routine of setting out pastries, getting the cash register ready, and turning on the "open" sign.

Within a few minutes, people came in, and the steady stream of customers didn't let up for close to an hour. Most had come and gone, but a few remained in the dining area.

I started to grab a wet towel and wipe off the empty tables, but I heard a voice say, "That's my job, remember?"

I turned and found Jace standing behind me, grinning.

"How are you so peppy in the morning?" I asked, handing him the towel.

His eyes caught mine. "It's easy when you work with great people."

That meant me. I shifted my gaze toward the floor and then up to him. He looked like he meant it.

"Besides," he added, "I've learned life is too short. We need to be happy as much as we can. While we can."

"You're right," I said, "but I still can't be this cheery so early. It's just not in me."

"Sure, it is. You just have to choose your attitude first thing."

I rolled my eyes. Right. Like it was that easy. "I basically wake up looking like a zombie coming out of the grave, and I stay that way until ten a.m. At least."

"You don't look anything like a zombie." He leaned against the counter and gazed at me until I had no choice but to look up. His lips quirked into a soft smile. "Zombies don't look anywhere near as beautiful."

My mouth gaped open and closed, unable to form words. What did he just say?

An echo of a smile still on his lips, he walked to a table and began wiping it down.

I stood still, my mouth gaping open and closed with half-formed responses. I couldn't even sort out my own feelings, and this guy was hitting on me? After a day? No. Way.

I followed him and kept my voice low so the customers wouldn't hear us, "For your information, I'm not dating."

Not exactly smooth, but it did the job.

"Don't worry, I'm single too," he whispered and laughed, the corner of his eyes crinkling.

I sputtered for a moment, but finally found my voice and put my hands on my hips. "No, I'm not dating, as in, I'm not interested. At all."

Jace's eyes followed a trail from my eyes to my hands and back up. His lips settled into a soft smile. "That's a shame."

I could feel that stupid swoop in my stomach and the excited grin on my face. I had to stop this. Now. Before it got too far. Before my heart got involved. "Look Jace. You can smile and compliment me all you want, but it's not going to change my mind about not seeing anyone. Nothing can change my mind."

I hoped he bought it, because I was having trouble believing it. Before I could give myself away, I started making my way back to the counter.

"We work together, so it's going to be hard not to see you," Jace said.

My cheeks flamed, and I scanned the room

to make sure no one heard. "Only when absolutely necessary."

I returned to the counter, where I belonged, which was anywhere away from Jace. I had a customer coming in to order anyway. Perfect timing.

I managed to avoid Jace the rest of the day. He stayed in the kitchen, making cinnamon rolls. He even left them on the window between the kitchen and the counter for me without saying anything once they were done.

Ava came into the kitchen a little before three and taught him how to make donuts and pastries for the morning, trying to get a head start. That at least kept Jace occupied so I didn't have to worry about talking to him.

When my shift was over, I put my apron back on its hook, grabbed my purse, and headed to the door.

"Hey, wait a minute!" Jace said behind me.

I pretended I didn't hear him and kept walking. I was almost to my car when I heard, "Hey, Peyton!" Jace's footsteps quickened to a jog.

He caught me before I reached the car. "Hey, I wanted to catch you before you left."

I imagined myself chatting with him, maybe grabbing a cup of coffee somewhere else. Learning about how he came to town or met Ava... None of it ended well.

"I kind of need to get going," I said.

"It'll just take a second." He leaned against the car and ran a hand through his hair. "I was just wondering...Do you have something against me? Did I do something? Am I the stinky kid at work?"

Despite myself, I laughed. "You smell fine. It's just...I can't be around guys right now."

His brows furrowed. "What do you have against men?"

"I'm not telling you that." I pulled on my door handle and got in.

Jace folded his arms on the open window and looked in. "As a representative for the opposite sex, and designated punching bag, I'd like to know."

"All right, fine." I stared at my steering wheel. "I got hurt really bad by a guy a few months ago."

"Really?" He looked incredulous.

"Yes, really," I said and turned the ignition. I didn't need to relive this again.

He didn't move. "I'll tell you what. Let me make it up to you. For the sake of all men, you know." The corners of his lips lifted slightly. "I'll take you out. A real date. Show you how a guy should act."

I looked at him evenly. "Not in your lifetime."

"Come on," he said, dark eyes pleading.

"Why?"

"Because it's me."

I lifted one eyebrow. "What makes you so special?"

"I'm—we—aren't all like that guy who broke your heart. Give me one date to show you."

I didn't know what to say. I bit the inside of my lip as painful and hopeful thoughts rolled around in my head. How could I risk being hurt again?

"Come on, just one chance." He wasn't on his knees, but he might as well have been with the look he was giving me and the begging tone of his voice.

It tugged at my heart. Sure, he worked hard at the bakery and had good manners, but Ethan had looked pretty good at first too. Cute or not, nice or not, how could I go out with him? On the other hand, how could I not?

"It doesn't look like you're giving up anytime soon?"

He shook his head quickly.

I smiled then leveled my lips. "One date. Now, I really need to leave, so..."

"Of course." He moved away from my window. "Do you have a piece of paper so I can write down your number?"

My heart froze in my chest. What had I just done?

Deftly, I reached for the Post-its I kept in my console. Hurriedly, I scribbled down my number address, peeled off the note, and handed it to Jace.

He examined my handwriting. "See you in the morning."

I started my car and pulled away. Glancing in the rearview, I saw Jace walking back inside the bakery. I smiled at his reflection. I hadn't bothered to tell him I didn't work the next day.

CHAPTER THREE

"WHEN WERE YOU GOING TO TELL ME YOU DIDN'T work today?" Jace sounded half amused on the other end of the phone.

A smile tugged at my lips as I sat up in the hammock where I'd lounged for the last half hour. "I wondered when you would figure it out."

Jace snorted. "Cute. But you could have said something."

"You didn't ask if I worked today, so I didn't bother to tell you." I got out of the hammock, walked over to a chair and sat down, watching the ducks swimming along the edge of the lake. Tiger rubbed against my legs, and I scratched behind his ears.

"Touché. I'm surprised you didn't give me a fake number or something."

Now I kind of wished I had given him a fake one. Too bad I hadn't thought of it sooner.

"Well, the real reason I'm calling." The phone sounded like Jace was changing ears. "I wanted to take you out. Tonight."

"I...I don't know."

"It'll be fun. No pressure," Jace said.

And for whatever reason, I believed him. I found myself giving himself my address and telling him he could pick me up at seven. Jace had ended the call before I could come to my senses and cancel.

I sat back in the chair, shocked. but I was freaking out inside too much to move. What. Had. I. Just. Done?

I sent Courtney a text that said *SOS*, and her name immediately lit up on my screen.

"What's going on?" she asked, sounding nervous.

I groaned just a little and put my hand on my forehead to wipe the sweat off. "I have a date with Jace tonight."

"What?"

"You heard me." Besides, I couldn't repeat it again.

"With Jace?"

"Unfortunately."

"Oh, so you changed your mind?" She sounded way too pleased.

"No, he didn't give me a choice."

She sounded concerned now. "What do you mean he wouldn't give you a choice?"

"He was telling me all these things like trying to let him prove not all guys were the same, and he has this stupid smile, and I think he hypnotized me or something!"

Courtney snickered. "He hypnotized you?"

"Yeah, that's exactly what he did." I stood and walked inside toward my bedroom. I couldn't sit still as it was. "No, he caught up with me after work and asked." I paced back and forth at the end of the bed.

"All you had to do was say no, silly."

"Yeah, thanks for sharing that, but now he's picking me up in an hour, and I need help." I stopped pacing and gazed into my closet.

"So why are you calling me? You should be getting ready for your date!"

"I have no idea what to wear. Or what to say. What do people even say on dates?"

Courtney chuckled.

"What's so funny?"

"Nothing. I just want to meet this guy. He sounds like a smart one." She chuckled again on the other end.

"It's not funny, Courtney."

"Yes, it is." She giggled. "You have a date!"

"Alright, fine. I'm hanging up then."

"No, don't. I'll stop," she said, quelling her laughter. "So what do you need from me?"

"I wanted some ideas on what to wear—jeans and nice shirt or a dress? I have my simple black dress one. I hate to dress up too much, but I don't think jeans are enough."

"First of all, does this even matter?"

"Of course, it matters." If I was going on a date, what I wore mattered. Even if I had my doubts about the date. I didn't want to be dressed the wrong way.

"Okay." I could hear her smile through the phone. "Do you know where he's taking you?"

"No. I should have asked." I feel back on the bed. "I'm such an idiot. I should call and cancel."

"Hey, hey, hey. It's okay. Either outfit would work, I think. I mean, we don't have fancy places here in town other than Mel's Steakhouse, and it's a pretty casual place. I've seen people dressed all kinds of ways."

"Thanks, Court." I paused. "I don't know. This feels like a bad idea."

"It's not. But it's already 6:15. You should probably start getting ready."

My heart palpitated. "I really don't want to go, though."

"Peyton, it won't kill you to go on a date. Give him a chance. You never know what might happen."

"That's what I'm afraid of."

"Nothing romantic has to come out of this. You could end up just being good friends," Courtney said. "Relax and have fun."

"Alright. Thanks, Courtney." I hung up and sat on the bed, the one I called mine when I stayed here for the summer, and looked at the clothes I had brought with me.

I stood up and paced again. What in the world was I thinking when I agreed to go out with Jace? I must have had a crazy moment. I wanted to call him back and tell him I changed my mind, but then work would be even more awkward than it already was. I might as well get to know him as Courtney suggested. I could always use another friend—even if he was a guy.

I moved back to my closet and touched my black dress. I had to make up my mind and fast. I tried on the jeans and nice shirt, but the jeans fit a little snug. I didn't remember that when I had worn them last. I yanked them off and tried on the little black dress. It was an A-line so it fit perfectly, as always. Then I put on makeup, taking my time to look my best.

I glanced at the clock. Jace should be here in a few minutes.

A knock sounded on my door. He was early.

My heart raced, and I had to remind myself to breathe. It was just a date, like Courtney said. No big deal.

I smoothed out my dress and stepped the to door, twisted the handle.

Jace stood in front of me in a light blue shirt that contrasted his deep tan and dark eyes. His jeans hung snug against his frame, and My. Heart. Couldn't. Take. It.

"Hey," I said. It came out all breathy. Probably because I'd forgotten to breathe again.

He grinned, and I got lost in his smile, his smooth teeth, the way his eyes crinkled and his nose scrunched ever so slightly.

"You look beautiful," he said.

My stomach swooped, and I folded my arms across myself, not sure how to handle these feelings. "Thanks."

He stuck his arm out for me. "Okay, now. A gentleman always escorts a lady to the vehicle."

My chest lightened just enough for me to laugh,

and I looked my arm through his. This might not be terrible.

Once we were situated in Jace's truck, we were on our way to the little steak house in town. Lake Stevens only had about six thousand people, so fancy restaurants were not in abundance.

For the first few minutes, we rode in charged silence. Finally, Jace said, "You really do look great, by the way."

"Thanks," I said again. "You look great yourself."

He smiled over at me and turned his eyes back on the road. "Have you eaten at this restaurant before?"

"Yes, a few times. My parents know the owners." I fidgeted with my hands in my lap, attempting to calm my nerves.

"So, what do your parents do?"

I stared out the window. My parents. "My dad is a surgeon, and my mom is a doctor."

"Your mom practices here in town?"

"Yes."

"I thought I saw your last name on a sign and wondered if it was any relation to you." He turned into the small parking lot next to the steakhouse and parked two places away from the door. "I'm guessing they met in med school or at a hospital?"

"Med school."

"So why are you staying at your grandma's house?" He peered over at me.

"No reason." Yes, there was a reason, but at this point, I didn't feel like telling him I felt like a complete failure every second I was with my parents or that my grandma was the only one who ever said she was proud of me.

"Boy, you're a woman of little words." Jace turned off the truck, pulled the key out of the ignition, and studied me.

The way he said it—clipped, disappointed—had me feeling defensive. "I told you I'm not dating. I'm not exactly good at this." I stared at my hands in my lap. How could I have been stupid enough to agree to this?

"Do you still want to do this?" Jace asked, his voice soft and low. "I can take you back home if you really don't want to be here."

I looked up at Jace. For a brief couple of seconds, I thought about making him take me home. But I told him I would go on this date, and go on this date I would. I wasn't backing out now. "No, let's go inside." I undid the seatbelt and started to open the door.

"Hold on. I'll come around and get it." He got out and jogged around the front end of the truck.

I hadn't experienced this with Ethan. He

certainly never opened any doors for me. Or walked me to the vehicle. He'd always waited outside and honked.

Inside, the hostess seated us right away. We scanned the two-sided menu—lunch, drinks, and desserts on one side, dinner on the other. I knew what I wanted, but I read every line carefully, wanting any excuse not to talk.

Within a couple of minutes, the waitress took our order, leaving us alone to talk. Goosebumps danced on my bare arms, partially from nerves and partially from the air conditioning. I wished had brought along a little sweater like I usually did. It's what I get for talking to Courtney too long and hurrying to get ready.

Jace rubbed his hands together and gazing at me across the table. "This is a pretty nice place."

I glanced around at the rustic décor and cloth-covered tables. "It's the best restaurant within half an hour of town," I said. "So, you haven't lived here for very long?"

"Oh, so you can say more than a couple of words!" he chuckled.

I smiled a little at him. "As a matter of fact, I can."

"Anyway...no, I moved here a couple weeks ago."

"Why here?"

"It's close to IU. I'll be transferring there in the fall."

Moving to a small town thirty minutes away from school didn't make any sense to me. "Why didn't you move to Bloomington then?"

"My grandfather lives here. I'm using his address so I don't have to pay out-of-state tuition."

"That makes sense." I took a sip of my Coke. If only Courtney could see me now, actually having a conversation with a guy and not totally hating it! "So where are you from?"

"I thought I would be the one doing all the talking and asking all the questions." Jace smirked.

I folded my arms across my chest and fought a smile. "This is a date the last time I checked, so we might as well get to know each other."

"You're right. We should get to know each other. It might make things at work a little more fun." He winked at me and then gave me that big grin of his.

I attempted a smile back, but faltered. Could I really do this?

"I'm from Missouri," Jace said. "I needed a change of scenery, so Grandpa said I could move in. I've stayed with him before over the summers, Christmas break—things like that. I've seen you around, but I'm pretty sure you didn't see me."

For as long as I could remember I'd spent summers at my grandma's. But I was pretty sure I'd remember Jace and his shining dark eyes. How long had he been watching me? How long had I been missing him?

Jace stared into space for a moment, and he gave his head a little shake. "Have you ever lived anywhere else?"

"I've lived here all my life." I fumbled with the silverware wrapped up in the napkin.

Jace shifted his gaze toward the table and watched me. "Have you ever considered leaving town?"

"Maybe someday. I'm going to college in Indy this fall." I finally managed to unwrap my eating utensils.

"Where are you going?"

"U of Indy," I said.

He fidgeted with the straw in his drink. "That's a pricey school."

"Well, yeah, but I got quite a few scholarships to help pay for it. My parents'll cover the rest, even though they're not at all happy about it."

"Why would they be mad? It sounds like money isn't a problem."

"It isn't. They just like to give me a hard time. Said I was a disappointment to them. Actually, their exact words were that I was a 'disappointment to the family tradition of excellence.' That's why I stay with my grandma. She supports me no matter what." I took another drink. "I work at the bakery to save money so I can buy my own stuff and not have to depend on them as much." My cheeks heated. I didn't even know why I shared this stuff with a guy I barely knew. What in the heck was I thinking?

The waitress brought our food, and we ate a few bites in silence.

"So, this boy that broke your heart," Jace began.

My entire body tensed, my heart instantly freezing to ice and my hands turning to claws on my silverware. "I don't want to talk about it." I'd already said more than enough.

"Okay."

We took a few more bites in uncomfortable silence.

"But if I'm going to set the record straight for men everywhere, I probably need to know what I'm up against," he said playfully, but I wasn't in the mood.

I stabbed at my steak so hard my fork hit the plate. "I thought gentlemen weren't supposed to talk about exes on dates? Especially first dates."

"This is different. I'm asking you about it because you seem to think everyone's like your ex."

I still wasn't going to talk about Ethan on this

date, or any date for that matter. It didn't matter what Jace's reasoning was.

I sawed on the steak, cutting easily through the meat. "I can't talk about it. I've put it behind me, and that's it."

He reached across the table and put his hand on my arm. "If you've stopped living your life because of this guy, then you haven't moved on."

His touch set my nerves on fire. I couldn't tell if it was in a good way or a bad way. And the fact that I couldn't tell meant I wasn't ready. Might never be ready. "I want you to take me home."

Jace frowned. "Why? I was just—"

"Because I told you this topic was off limits, and you kept on going." I snatched up my purse and slid to the edge of the booth.

"Wait," Jace said.

I kept going anyway. I'd made it quite a distance from Mel's Steakhouse, even in my heels, when I heard Jace yell my name.

I continued walking and ignored him.

"Peyton, wait!" he yelled again.

I kept walking and texted Courtney to come get me. I couldn't make it the two miles to Grandma's house in heels, and I wasn't going to call her for help. She would play an intrusive version of twenty questions on the way home, and I wasn't in the mood to talk, especially not about this.

I didn't hear Jace again. Good, I'd had enough of him for one night—for a lifetime.

A vehicle pulled up next to me, and I glanced over long enough to see that it was Jace and not Courtney.

"Peyton, please get in the truck. I'll take you home," he said through the open window on the passenger's side.

I never slowed my walking. If anything, I walked faster. But Jace continued driving beside me, and I continued ignoring him.

The sound of his engine died down, and a strange blend of relief and regret coursed through me. Finally. Some time to sort through my thoughts, through this mess.

"Peyton, wait!" Jace called, followed by the sound of his quick footsteps. He caught up and walked along beside me. "Please stop." He caught up and moved in front of me.

I tried to go around him, but no matter which way I tried, he blocked me.

"Get out of my way," I growled, refusing to make eye contact. Anger. That was an emotion I felt comfortable with.

"Why? I thought we were having a nice time."

"I'm done with this date."

"Peyton, let me apologize, please." He gently grabbed my arms.

Frustration and grief and anger at Ethan for ruining this for me met behind my eyes. I fought to hold back the tears until I couldn't any longer. They streamed down my cheeks, and I wiped at them. "I still don't want to talk about Ethan."

Jace rubbed my arm. "I'm so sorry that I upset you," he said. "I had no idea things were that bad between you and that guy."

I sniffed and looked away. "I'm such a mess."

"Why don't we get in my truck, and I'll take you home?" Jace asked.

I wiped at my nose with the back of my arm. "Courtney is on her way to get me."

"Call her back and tell her I'm taking you home."

I looked at him, not sure I wanted to do as he asked. But something deep down told me to give him a chance. After all, he had apologized, something Ethan had never done.

I texted Courtney and told her I was fine.

Once we were in Jace's truck heading back to my grandma's house, I said, "Ethan and I had been dating for months when I saw him kissing someone else."

My throat got thick again, and I swallowed, fighting more tears. "He had no intention of really dating me. It was all a joke his friends put him up to. But I had fallen in love with him, and I thought he felt the same way. Apparently, most of the school knew it was going on, but no one bothered to say anything to me."

"Oh, I'm so sorry, Peyton." Jace grabbed my hand and squeezed it. He pulled over to the side of the road.

"I was so stupid. I was a nerd—good grades, no life. Trying to make my parents happy. He was the captain of the basketball team. Why I ever thought a guy like him would ever be interested in me..." I glanced at him then stared hard at the dash. I couldn't keep crying. I'd already cried enough. "So that's why I don't want to talk about this."

Jace turned toward me so we were facing each other. "You know, I got hurt by a girl back home."

I took in his muscular arms, his angular jaw, his soft eyes, not to mention how he'd only been sweet to me while I'd been a complete jerk. How could a girl ever find it in her to hurt a guy like him? "You did?"

"In fact, it's the reason I moved in with my grandpa this summer. She cheated on me." He pinched the bridge of his nose, blinking hard. "We were opposite of you and Ethan. She was the popular girl. And

I fell in love with her. Hard. I thought we were great together. That she really liked me. We'd been together for *nine months* when she cheated on me...."

My heart wrenched, his pain mingling with my own. "I'm sorry."

"No reason for you to be sorry. It was my own stupid fault."

"Cheating's wrong—no matter what the situation."

"That's true." Jace looked over at me and smiled. "But that's in the past. Here, now, that's what matters." He reached out and cupped my cheek. Stroking the curve of my cheekbone with his thumb, he said, "I'm not like Ethan. Let me prove it to you."

I froze, caught somewhere between his eyes and the fear wracking my chest.

Jace broke the silence. "I would like to get to know you better, if that's okay."

I grasped at straws, reaching for any reason why I shouldn't be dating him, feeling this interested in another guy after what happened. "But we're both going off to college in the fall. We'll be an hour apart."

"We have all summer. Can we just see what happens?" He dropped his hand to cover my own and squeezed.

Part of me wanted to keep this relationship

strictly platonic. Hang out, go swimming, do things as friends, and nothing more. And part of me wanted nothing more than to see what would happen next. Could I really let myself fall for another guy?

"It'll make work more fun," Jace said. "And who knows? We may decide we're not right for each other or we may fall madly in love." He batted his eyes and gave me that big smile of his. "Either way, you have to get over this hatred of men. Don't you want to move on? Experience the summer, college, life?"

More than anything. I'd do anything to get this painful, shameful feeling out of my chest. But fear had me saying, "I don't know, Jace."

"We could have the best summer together, but we won't know unless we try. What do you think?"

This felt vulnerable and crazy and scary, but I wanted all the adventure he was talking about. And I wanted it with him.

A smile tugged at my lips. "I'm willing to give it a try."

He smiled back and gave me a quick peck on the cheek before putting the truck in drive and taking me to my grandma's house. In the driveway, he got out of the truck and walked around to open my door.

He held my hand on the way down the sidewalk and stopped on the porch. Only a couple hours ago I'd wanted nothing more than to never see him—or any other guy—again. Now, I didn't want him to leave.

"So," I said.

He wrapped his arms around my waist and hugged me, and I hugged him back, loving the warmth of his chest and the smell of his cologne.

Still holding me, he said, "I'll see you tomorrow at work?"

My stomach dropped, a freefall into something I couldn't help but be excited about. "See you in the morning."

He pulled back, his hands on my waist, and grinned at me. I matched his smile with my own, then went inside.

With my back pressed against the front door, my smile grew even wider. I had no idea what would happen tomorrow at work or at the end of the summer, but I did know one thing: I was starting to like Jace, and there was nothing I could do to stop it. And why would I even try?

His smile melted my insides every time he looked at me. He treated me with respect in ways that Ethan never had. That spoke to me.

Jace made me realize I needed to move on with my life, and the only way for me to truly know whether

Jace was the right guy for me was to give him a chance. It was time for me to start living my life.

Thank you for reading "Unstoppable Love" by Michele Mathews! To connect with Michele and learn more about her books and special offers, visit www.michelemathews.com.

EDITOR'S NOTE

Thank you so much for taking a chance on this book. In a lot of ways, this anthology came to rest in your hands by a series of chances. I took a chance by editing my first anthology, my fellow authors took a chance by trusting me with their stories, our rock-star foreword writer, Cookie O'Gorman, took a chance by representing nine fellow authors, and you took the biggest chance of all by trusting us with your time. I am so grateful for that.

The authors you've met through their writing embody so much of what *The Art of Taking Chances* is about. They put themselves and their work out there, risking criticism from those they aim to serve. They love hard, as great friends, sisters, daughters, spouses, and mothers. And they work for what they want, oftentimes writing late into the evening or early in the morning, waking before the sun to let their imaginations see the light of day. I've never worked with a group of people so selflessly dedicated to helping each other and leaving a lasting impact on readers. What a privilege it has been.

I hope from these stories, you've glimpsed what taking chances means. To me, it's diving into messiness, falling without seeing where you'll land, and daring to hope, even when the people in your life won't dream with you. It's embracing that terrifying fact that things might not work out, but trusting in yourself enough to know that no matter what, you'll make it through and turn whatever hardship faces you into the biggest springboard imaginable.

Now, it's time to set this beautiful book aside and discover the beautiful, scary, exhilarating chances waiting for you.

Lots of love,
Kelsie Stelting

ABOUT THE AUTHORS

Deborah Balogun, author of "Fangirl"

Like many writers, Deborah discovered her love for the craft when she was a child. Writing everything from songs to poems and short stories—anything to appease the annoying characters constantly chattering inside her head. She now focuses more on longer works of fiction. When she's not writing, Deborah can be found making a beeline toward the kitchen in search of her one true love: guacamole.

Kat Colmer, author of "Tickets on Himself"

Kat Colmer is a Sydney-based author and teacher librarian. She has won several writing awards for her swoon-worthy stories, and written books for audiences across the world. She has a Bachelor of Arts with a Diploma of Education as well as a Master of Education in Teacher Librarianship and loves working with teens and young adults. Having spent a significant portion of her childhood in Germany, Kat speaks fluent German and is looking forward to the day she'll be able to read one of her novels in Deutsch. When not writing or teaching, Kat enjoys spending time with her husband and two children.

Sally Henson, author of "Spark"
Sally Henson is the author of the Regan Stone series. She grew up in rural Midwest wandering through the woods and creeks. That experience has been a tremendous influence on her writing, which lends credibility to the voice of her characters. She combines ingredients of reality with a dreamer's imagination to create sweet and delectable fiction. You can find Sally working and writing in the Heartland with her husband and two children.

Melanie Hooyenga, author of "The Friend Rules"
Melanie is the author of The Rules Series, a YA sports romance series about Colorado girls navigating life and learning to stand up on their own. The "Friend Rules" is a companion story to *The Trail Rules*, the second in the series. Her YA trilogy, the Flicker Effect, follows the life of a teen who uses sunlight to travel back to yesterday. Melanie has lived in Washington DC, Chicago, and Mexico, but has finally settled down in her home state of Michigan. When not at her day job as the communications director of a local nonprofit, you can find her wrangling her Miniature Schnauzer, Owen, and playing every sport imaginable with her husband, Jeremy.

Michele Mathews, author of "Unstoppable Love"
Michele writes women's fiction, nonfiction, and young adult contemporary romance. She works part time as a librarian at an intermediate school and does freelance writing and proofreading. She lives in south central Indiana and is a single mom to two humans and three fur babies. In addition to writing, her passions are photography, reading, traveling (especially the beach!), and Rick Springfield.

Cookie O'Gorman, contributed the foreword of *The Art of Taking Chances*
Cookie O'Gorman writes YA romance to give readers a taste of happily ever after. Small towns, quirky characters, and the awkward yet beautiful moments in life make up her books. Cookie also has a soft spot for nerds and ninjas. Whether it's to talk about her books or just to fan-girl, Cookie loves hearing from readers. Connect with her on her website, www.cookieogorman.com.

Kelsie Stelting, editor of *The Art of Taking Chances* and author of "Tell Me Something Real"
Kelsie Stelting grew up in the middle of nowhere (also known as western Kansas). Her rural upbringing taught her how to get her hands dirty and work hard for what she believes in. Plus, not having neighbors in a 10-mile radius as a child and traveling the world as an adult

made her develop a pretty active imagination. Kelsie loves writing honest fiction that readers can vacation in, as well as traveling, volunteering, ice cream, loving on her family, and soaking up just a little too much sun wherever she can find it.

Seven Steps, author of "Forever And Always"
Seven has been writing for as long as she can remember. Her favorite genres to read are sweet romance, science fiction, dystopian and historical. She is a working wife and mother, as well as a devoted owner of a beautiful cat named Rosie. Seven enjoys hanging out with her friends and family, thrifting, and anything that reminds her of her childhood.

Kayla Tirrell, author of "(Not So) Perfect Chemistry"
Kayla has loved to read as long as she can remember. While she started out reading spooky stories that had her hiding under her covers, she now prefers stories with a bit more kissing. When she gets a chance to watch TV, she enjoys cheesy sci-fi and superhero shows. Most days, you'll catch her burning dinner in an attempt to cook while reading just one more chapter. She currently lives in the sunshine state with her husband and three boys.

Yesenia Vargas, author of "More Than a List"

Yesenia Vargas is the author of several young adult romance books. Her love for writing stories was born from her love of reading and books. She has her third-grade teacher to thank for that. In addition to writing, she spends her time with her family, reading, working out, and binge-watching Netflix. In 2013, she graduated from the University of Georgia, the first in her family to go to college. Yesenia lives in Georgia with her husband and two precious little girls. Check out what she's up to and grab your free book at yeseniavargas.com.

03/24

Printed in Poland
by Amazon Fulfillment
Poland Sp. z o.o., Wrocław

58506340R00249